"Enjoyable—truly worth checking out for fans of fantasy mysteries."
—*Locus*

"The contributors are top players in their own genres, but had no problems placing a foot in the area they normally do not frequent. Each author ensured that the magical elements seemed real, drawing the reader into becoming a believer for the moment, yet did not scrimp on the mystery components . . . The crossing of two genres works on all levels so that the audience of either will appreciate mayhem in a whimsical setting."
—*Midwest Book Review*

"An anthology of mystery stories with an interesting twist . . . For readers of mystery who like paranormal or are looking to get a taste of what's out there in fantasy without diving into a multi-volume set of doorstop novels, this is the perfect pick . . . The perfect blend of mystery and magic."
—*The Romance Reader's Connection*

"Stabenow assembled a stellar group of writers from several genres for this unique anthology . . . every story is worthwhile."
—*Romantic Times*

THE CONTRIBUTORS

DONNA ANDREWS . . . Author of the Agatha Award–winning mysteries *You've Got Murder* and its sequel, *Click Here for Murder* (both featuring artificial intelligence personality Turing Hopper), as well as the multiple award–winning Meg Langslow mystery series

MICHAEL ARMSTRONG . . . Author of the science fiction novels *After the Zap, Agviq,* and *The Hidden War*

ANNE BISHOP . . . Award-winning author of the Black Jewels Trilogy and several other novels of fantasy, as well as a four-story collection set in the Black Jewels world

JAY CASELBERG . . . Author of the science fiction novels *Wyrmhole* and *Metal Sky,* and several short stories

MIKE DOOGAN . . . Winner of the Robert L. Fish Award from the Mystery Writers of America for his first mystery, appearing in *The Mysterious North*

LAURA ANNE GILMAN . . . Author of more than twenty short stories, three media tie-in novels, and *Staying Dead*, the first Retrievers novel, featuring Wren and Sergei

SIMON R. GREEN . . . New York Times bestselling author of twenty-seven novels including the Deathstalker series and the Nightside novels

CHARLAINE HARRIS . . . Author of the Sookie Stackhouse vampire series

ANNE PERRY . . . *New York Times* bestselling author of the Pitt and the Monk detective series, a new series set during World War I, and two fantasy novels, *Tathea* and *Come Armageddon*

SHARON SHINN . . . Winner of the William C. Crawford Award for Outstanding New Fantasy Writer for her first book, *The Shape-Changer's Wife*, and the author of the Samaria novels

DANA STABENOW . . . Author of the Kate Shugak, Liam Campbell, and Star Svensdotter series

JOHN STRALEY . . . Author of the Cecil Younger mystery series

powers of detection

STORIES OF
MYSTERY & FANTASY

edited by
DANA STABENOW

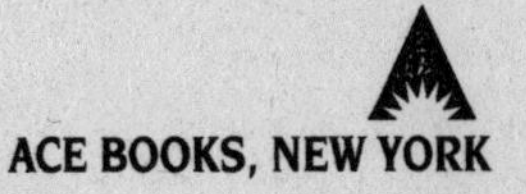

ACE BOOKS, NEW YORK

THE BERKLEY PUBLISHING GROUP
Published by the Penguin Group
Penguin Group (USA) Inc.
375 Hudson Street, New York, New York 10014, USA
Penguin Group (Canada), 90 Eglinton Avenue East, Suite 700, Toronto, Ontario M4P 2Y3, Canada
(a division of Pearson Penguin Canada Inc.)
Penguin Books Ltd., 80 Strand, London WC2R 0RL, England
Penguin Group Ireland, 25 St. Stephen's Green, Dublin 2, Ireland (a division of Penguin Books Ltd.)
Penguin Group (Australia), 250 Camberwell Road, Camberwell, Victoria 3124, Australia
(a division of Pearson Australia Group Pty. Ltd.)
Penguin Books India Pvt. Ltd., 11 Community Centre, Panchsheel Park, New Delhi—110 017, India
Penguin Group (NZ), Cnr. Airborne and Rosedale Roads, Albany, Auckland 1310, New Zealand
(a division of Pearson New Zealand Ltd.)
Penguin Books (South Africa) (Pty.) Ltd., 24 Sturdee Avenue, Rosebank, Johannesburg 2196, South Africa

Penguin Books Ltd., Registered Offices: 80 Strand, London WC2R 0RL, England

POWERS OF DETECTION: STORIES OF MYSTERY & FANTASY

An Ace Book / published by arrangement with the authors

PRINTING HISTORY
Ace trade paperback edition / October 2004
Ace mass-market edition / January 2007

For a complete listing of individual copyrights, please see page 290.
Cover art by Jonathan Barkat. Cover design by Judith Lagerman.
Interior text design by Kristin del Rosario.

For information address: The Berkley Publishing Group,
a division of Penguin Group (USA) Inc.,
375 Hudson Street, New York, New York 10014.

ISBN: 978-0-441-01464-4

ACE
Ace Books are published by The Berkley Publishing Group,
a division of Penguin Group (USA) Inc.,
375 Hudson Street, New York, New York 10014.

PRINTED IN THE UNITED STATES OF AMERICA

10 9 8 7 6 5 4 3 2 1

CONTENTS

INTRODUCTION

This anthology is all Laura Anne Gilman's fault.

A while back Laura Anne forwarded me an e-mail from author Rosemary Edghill, who was putting together a murder-in-a-fantasy-setting anthology. The e-mail came with a message from Laura Anne, which read, "You should do this."

That's Laura Anne, always big with the subtle.

I'd never written fantasy. I don't even read that much of it, because after Middle Earth what is there? I like my speculative fiction hard, nuts-and-bolts, what happens next door. I want to go back to the moon and on to the asteroid belt and Mars and the moons of Jupiter and from there to Beta Centauri. Sword and sorcery is a little too woo-woo for literal-minded me.

But I confess, I'm afraid of Laura Anne, so I doodled around a bit, so I could say "See? I tried!" and she wouldn't hurt me.

And then these two characters showed up between the doodles. Both women. One wore a sword, and the other carried a staff. They had magical powers, some of which appeared at puberty, some of which were acquired. More doodling, and they rode into town, one of them even on a white horse. A young woman was strangled, and by various magical means my duo discovered and brought the murderer to justice.

By the time I stopped doodling I had forty-two pages, and to add insult to injury it was a sword-and-sorcery tale.

It was also twenty pages too long for the anthology. Rosemary asked me to cut it to fit. I refused. I guess I thought my prose was too deathless to be tampered with. Yeah, right.

So after all that, my story didn't even make the anthology.

Fume. So, I thought, I'll put together my own magic-and-mayhem anthology. (Can we spell "hubris"?)

I decided to ask for murder in a fantasy or science fiction setting, to broaden the appeal to both writers and readers. I went downstairs and looked at who was on my bookshelves. Hmm. Here we have Sharon Shinn. Writes the SF Angels-on-Samaria series. Also wrote that most elegiac of fantasy novels, *The Shape Changer's Wife*. Over here is Charlaine Harris, who writes the Sookie

Stackhouse novels, the best vampire series in the bloodsucking genre. And here is Anne Perry, who wrote me a short story for *The Mysterious West*. Could I go to that well a second time? (hyoo'bris, n. excessive pride or self-confidence; arrogance.)

I asked them each to contribute a story, and displaying a touching belief in my ability to get this anthology off the ground, they all did. Sharon has written a lovely little magical boarding school murder, not at all à la Harry Potter, and which she said might evolve into something a bit longer one day. Say a novel? Charlaine has written a story set in that same Sookie universe, and if there was an award for first lines, her name would be on the short list. Anne takes us into the courtroom for a trial by magic, where the verdict isn't what one might expect, and neither is anything else.

I remembered talking to Donna Andrews about writing speculative fiction, and she was also a contributor to *The Mysterious West*, so I asked her for a story, too. She sent me a delightful tale of a mage with a cold, an apprentice with a clue, and a villain with neither.

Then there are the writers who live in Alaska and whom I can personally browbeat into writing for me, Michael Armstrong, John Straley, and Mike Doogan. Michael has written a modern take on an old Aleut legend involving seagulls, and there must be some kind of bird thing going on among the menfolk because John wrote a detective story from the first-person viewpoint of a raven. Mike was the only one of my contributors to weigh in on the science fiction side of murder, although I'm not sure it is murder in the end. You decide. Enjoy his character names while you're at it.

Laura Anne offered a story of her own, based on characters who inhabit a series she had just sold to Harlequin Luna, and recommended I solicit stories from Anne Bishop, Simon R. Green, and Jay Caselberg. Laura Anne's story is a come-hither into a world next to but not quite of our own, seen through the eyes of a cat burglar with, yes, special powers. Anne's story is set in the world of her Blood novels, where a vigilante wearing a jewel of power exacts deserved if harsh justice upon a serial revenge killer. Simon has written a creepy little horror-ish noir story in which Sam Spade would feel quite at home, if Sam Spade was dead. Jay brings back the ancient Egyptian gods to modern-day Cairo, with a last line that will have you all diving under your beds.

I heard Roger Ebert say once that the true test of a good film was how well it sucked you into its world. Same goes for good writing. In this anthology you can smell the coffee on the streets of Cairo, walk on the ceiling with starspawn, and negotiate with extreme care the social intricacies of the world of the Blood. You can run from the raucous call of an Alaskan seagull, and you'd better. You can chow down with an Alaskan raven, and you'd better not. You can belly up to Sookie's bar and order your blood at an appealing 98.6 degrees Fahrenheit. You can meet a gargoyle in a Savile Row suit, go mano a mano with piskies, and sneeze striped bats. You can sweat out the verdict at a trial by magic, conjure a reflecting spell at the Norwitch Academy of Magic and Sorcery, and, I hope, hear the song of the Sword in Daean.

Enjoy your visit to these different worlds, but watch your back.

It's not safe in here.

COLD SPELL

DONNA ANDREWS

"Murder by magic?" Master Radolphus exclaimed.

Gwynn wasn't actually trying to eavesdrop on the headmaster. But how could she help overhearing when his study door hung wide open?

Just then he looked up and saw her.

"You wait here," he said to someone Gwynn couldn't see. "I'll talk to Master Justinian."

What did a murder—even a magical murder—have to do with the Maestro, Gwynn wondered.

But she didn't dare ask. Radolphus strode out of his study, beckoned for Gwynn to follow, and set off in the direction of Justinian's quarters at a half run, his voluminous black robes billowing behind him. When they arrived outside the familiar carved wooden door,

Radolphus stopped. He fished a handkerchief out of his sleeve, pushed up his thick spectacles, and wiped his red and sweating face.

Gwynn bent down to put her ear to the door.

"Is he out?" Radolphus said, panting slightly.

"Oh no, Headmaster; the Maestro doesn't feel well enough to go out," Gwynn said softly. "I just don't want to wake him if he's sleeping."

Radolphus nodded approvingly and patted her head. Gwynn sighed. At twelve, she'd considered it an incredible honor, being apprenticed to Westmarch College's most powerful mage. She still wouldn't trade with any of her fellow students, but after two years, she'd begun to wonder if she owed her assignment to her superior magical talent or her reputation for working harder than any of the other students. Justinian did create a lot more work than the other masters. And needed more looking after than a first-year student.

Suddenly a loud "Achoo!" rang out inside.

"Oh, bother," the Maestro exclaimed.

"He's awake," Gwynn said, pushing open the study door.

The tall diamond-paned windows, normally open wide even in January to let in sunlight, breezes, and any interesting bugs that might be passing by, were closed. The heavy velvet curtains were drawn tight, though a lot of light leaked through the places where the Maestro's cat had shredded them. A mysterious haze drifted through the room from a burning brazier just inside the doorway. Though the healer had assured Gwynn that burning this particular assortment of herbs would ease a stuffy nose, it didn't seem to have had much effect, apart from evicting the goblins who had made a nest under the dining table. To her surprise, Gwynn missed the goblins, if only because they normally kept the place moderately tidy by devouring anything organic that fell on the floor.

The Maestro's great chair stood so close to the hearth that he was in serious danger of setting his slippers on fire again, and he sat, his long frame wrapped in several blankets, frowning at a selection of vials, jars, and flasks arranged on the table beside him. His hair, uncombed for several days, stuck out in random directions, making him look far younger than his thirty years.

And just in case anyone doubted how sick the Maestro was, a small mechanical cigar-cutter in the shape of a gargoyle lay on the table among the medicines, still in one piece. Under normal circumstances, it would take all of fifteen minutes for Justinian to begin disassembling any mechanical object unlucky enough to fall into his hands. The gargoyle had lain on the table untouched for three days.

A teacup teetered in midair in front of Justinian, levitating just beyond his grasp.

"Take care of that, Gwynn, if you don't mind," he said.

Gwynn glanced around to see if the Maestro's latest

sneeze had done any other accidental damage. No, nothing that she could see. No singing andirons, talking cats, invisible furniture, or randomly summoned demons. She sighed with relief. Then she grasped the teacup firmly, removed the levitation spell with a few quick gestures, and set the cup back on its saucer.

"Thank you," the Maestro said. "My head feels twice normal size, with about a tenth of its usual speed."

He sank back into the chair and closed his eyes.

"Oh, dear," Radolphus said. "I was so hoping you only had a slight chill. Because I'm afraid you're needed up at the castle."

"Whatever for?" Justinian muttered.

"There's been a murder," Radolphus said. "It's magical. And also political. The duke asked especially for you to come and deal with it."

"Magical how?" Justinian asked. "Was someone killed by magic? Or did someone kill a mage? Or—achoo!"

A few blue sparks twinkled through the room.

"Bother! What now?" the Maestro asked, appearing to brace himself.

"The bats," Radolphus said, pointing to the archway between the study and the workroom, where the fledgling bats usually slept.

The bats were now brightly colored. Some had stripes.

"Oh, bother." Justinian sighed.

"I think they look very festive," Gwynn said. "I'll change them back later; they're not hurting anyone now."

She was relieved when neither mage objected—she already had the faint beginnings of a headache, the kind you got from doing too many spells in too short a time. Or undoing them, in this case.

"I know you're in no shape to do magic," Radolphus said. "But—"

"We have to at least look as if we're doing something," Justinian said. "Put up a good show for a day or so until my powers are back to normal, and I can actually solve this."

He snagged his glasses from the nearby table and shoved them onto his nose in a determined fashion. Gwynn realized, with dismay, that he'd apparently sat on them again, then mended them with bits of sticking plaster. Ah, well; she'd fix them for real later.

"That's the spirit," Radolphus said. "The duke's manservant's waiting in my study—shall I bring him down? He can tell you more about the problem."

"Might as well," Justinian said. "Just give Gwynn a few minutes to tidy up."

Fortunately, Justinian's definition of tidying only meant throwing an old tablecloth over the cold medicines and helping him into the velvet smoking jacket he liked to wear to impress visitors. Gwynn decided not to mention that at the moment its burgundy color brought out the chapped red condition of his cheeks and nostrils.

"Try not to sneeze while he's here," Radolphus said as he hurried off.

"Mind over matter," Justinian muttered, standing and looking polite as Radolphus escorted in the manservant. Who didn't seem the least bit awed or even curious at being allowed to enter the study of a master magician. He planted himself on the hearth with his back to the fire and stuffed his hands in his pockets—blocking the path to Justinian's favorite chair. The Maestro had to clear the books from one of the other chairs to sit down. Radolphus, long familiar with the condition of Justinian's furniture, chose to stand.

"You Justinian?" the manservant said. "If you are, the duke sent me to fetch you."

"I am," Justinian said. "Welcome to my study."

His dignity was only slightly undermined by the fact that all his m's came out as b's.

"Young for a wizard, aren't you?" the manservant said. "I thought you were all supposed to have long gray beards and warts."

Gwynn glanced at Master Radolphus, who fit the stereotype perfectly.

"Master Justinian is the most gifted mage of his generation," Radolphus said, in his sternest and most dignified headmaster's voice. "Indeed, of our age."

The manservant shrugged.

"And you are?" Justinian asked.

"Name's Reg," the manservant said. "Been working for the duke a month now."

"What seems to be the problem up at the castle?" Justinian said.

"Duke's men caught a pair of anarchists skulking about," Reg said. "Notified the king, and a party of royal guards comes down to take them back to the capital. Duke goes down to oversee the transfer, and one of the prisoners suddenly falls down bleeding and dies. Duke's personal physician checks him over and finds a fresh stab wound in his chest. Only nobody in the room had a sword, or even a large knife, just muskets, and anyway, there's no hole in the bloke's clothes. We figured a magical attack, but the duke's personal magician says he can't detect any magic. So he says for you to come and figure it out."

Gwynn saw Radolphus and Justinian exchange a grave glance. Even she could guess at some of the worries Reg's story stirred up. The possibility that this incident would disrupt the always fragile relationship between their duke and the king. Or worse, that it would cause one or both to become less enthusiastic about protecting mages. The anarchists who'd killed the late king and plagued the current one throughout his reign were as violently opposed to magic as they were to royalty and the hereditary nobility. And so far the king, unlike many of his fellow monarchs, had supported or at least tolerated the mages within his realm. But if the king thought magicians were taking the law into their own hands, his tolerance could vanish overnight. Gwynn shuddered. They'd heard tales of mages hanged or burned at the stake in neighboring kingdoms, and some of the masters had begun to mutter that the college should go underground again.

She saw the Maestro nod to Radolphus. Then he pulled up the collar of his smoking jacket and shivered.

"Of course Master Justinian will come and deal with the problem," Radolphus said.

"Oh, and the duke says while you're at it, you should fix the castle warding spell," Reg added.

"What's wrong with it?" Radolphus asked.

"Stopped working," Reg said, with a shrug. "At least, stopped working reliably. Goes off when there's nothing in range then doesn't do a thing when a bunch of Gypsies wander right through the portcullis. He's pretty worked up about it."

"He could hire some guards," Justinian said.

"He has guards," Reg said. "He wants a warding spell. He's beginning to wonder out loud what good it does him to have a whole college full of mages in the province if he can't get a simple spell done properly when he needs it."

Gwynn wondered if the sudden hint of venom in Reg's voice was an echo of the duke's tone or reflected his own attitude toward magic.

"Of course Master Justinian will investigate the problem with the castle warding spell as well," Master Radolphus said. "Why don't you come with me and take some refreshment while Master Justinian is packing."

Reg pried himself away from the hearth, stuck his hands in his pockets, and ambled out. Justinian reclaimed his chair with an injured air.

"I'm sorry, Jus," Radolphus said, pausing in the doorway. "Pack so you can stay a few days if need be."

Actually, Gwynn did most of the packing, filling a large trunk with the magical supplies the Maestro would require and a small carpet bag with what she might need for an overnight stay. The Maestro packed his medicines in a satchel nearly as large and easily as heavy as the trunk.

It was midnight by the time they set out, and the six-hour trip seemed interminable, despite the relative luxury of the duke's coach. Largely, Gwynn decided, because of Reg. Although he appeared to sleep through most of the journey, his presence prevented any interesting conversation. And even asleep, his sour face and the memory of his brusque, almost rude manner cast a pall over the party. Or perhaps it was that Reg fell asleep so easily despite the jolting of the coach while the Maestro's attempts at much-needed slumber failed miserably. Justinian finally gave up trying and sat, glowering at Reg and muttering under his breath whenever the manservant's snores grew particularly loud.

The Maestro put on his most gracious manner again when they arrived at the castle.

"At least we'll have a good breakfast," he murmured to Gwynn when Reg had deposited them in the duke's entrance hall and gone to announce their arrival. "The duke's personal chef is legendary."

"Finally," the duke said, dashing into the hall. "Let's get straight to work. Reg, go have the kitchen fix a couple of cold plates and bring them down to the dungeons."

Justinian sighed and followed the duke's stout figure down a forebodingly long, steep stairway. Gwynn trailed behind them, glancing nervously from side to side. But apart from being uncomfortably cold and damp, the maze of stone corridors beneath the castle held no particular horrors. From the length of their journey and the number of stairs they descended, the dungeons must be at the other end of the castle from the main gate and at least halfway to the center of the earth.

They finally entered a large, low-ceilinged room with a straw-covered floor. A dozen soldiers stood inside, and even in the flickering torchlight Gwynn could see that they had split into two distinct camps—the black uniforms of the king's guards to her left and the duke's red and gold colors to her right. The two groups eyed each other without liking.

"There's the blighter," the duke said, pointing.

Gwynn, who had never seen a murder victim before,

stared curiously. It—or should that be he?—hung from one of the sets of arm and leg irons bolted to the room's walls at regular intervals. He was slumped so Gwynn couldn't see his face, only the blood that glistened on his body and the surrounding straw. Surely no one could lose that much blood and live.

Wait—the blood was still wet. Should it be, after the half day it had taken for Reg to fetch them?

Justinian stepped over to the body and examined it briefly, glancing once or twice with irritation at the torches. Was he annoyed by the low visibility—or was he, like Gwynn, wondering why the duke wasn't using some form of magic light? Was this a sign that the duke's tolerance for magic was waning?

A figure stepped out of the shadows to the Maestro's side. From his worn black robe, Gwynn deduced he was the duke's personal magician.

"So, what have we here?" Justinian asked.

"Dead prisoner," the magician said. He was a thin, balding man with a look of habitual anxiety etched into his sharp features. "I cast a stasis spell on the body, soon as I could, so you could see it as near as possible to how I found it."

"Stasis spell?" the duke shouted. "I authorized no spells! There's been enough magical skullduggery already!"

"But surely your grace ordered him to preserve the evidence as well as possible for my arrival," Justinian said. "That's what a stasis spell does. It's a lot like what happens when something's frozen. But frozen in time instead of temperature."

"Ah," the duke said. "I see."

He still looked baffled, but apparently decided to let the matter drop.

The stasis spell, Gwynn thought, would account for the still-damp blood.

"So, tell me the features of the case," Justinian said.

As he and the castle mage talked, Gwynn decided that this magical murder was doing the Maestro good. Oh, he'd complained about the cold air and the night journey. But the puzzle before him seemed to keep him from dwelling on his cold. He coughed and sneezed a lot less often, and without any magical side effects.

And she was glad it wasn't her job to figure out what had happened. The evidence was sparse. In fact, apart from the blood-smeared body of the dead anarchist, nonexistent. His live confederate, still chained to the opposite wall, tried to look fierce, and occasionally muttered under his breath about damned unnatural spellcasters. The dozen guards readily demonstrated that their muskets and pistols had not been fired, and the few knives they carried were free of blood, not to mention far too small to have produced the prisoner's wound. And anyway, nothing physical could have produced the wound without piercing the prisoner's shirt and doublet which were, apart from dirt and bloodstains, undamaged.

"Filthy black magic," the surviving anarchist muttered, when Justinian and the castle mage had confirmed this.

"Fascinating," Justinian murmured, as he examined the doublet.

He gestured and murmured a few words. Gwynn recognized the incantation that would strip away the stasis spell. And then another spell, less familiar to her.

Justinian paused as if listening to a sound inaudible to the rest of them, then looked around with unfocused eyes.

"No taint of magic," he murmured, with a puzzled look.

"As I said, my spells couldn't detect anything either," the castle mage said, a little defensively.

"Your spells couldn't detect a turd in your soup tureen," the duke said. "Leave this to a real mage."

But the duke's tone made Gwynn glance in his direction. The duke looked—scared would be an exaggeration, perhaps. But definitely uneasy. It was one thing to see his personal mage baffled. No spellcaster of any real power would settle for a post as a mere castle mage. But to see the powerful Master Justinian baffled—that would make anyone uneasy. Gwynn's own stomach tightened a bit at the thought.

"A fascinating puzzle," Justinian said.

He gestured again, then frowned. Gwynn and the castle mage were probably the only ones who realized that his spell had fizzled. They looked at each other with alarm.

Justinian sighed and rubbed his forehead as if it hurt. Gwynn felt a little reassured. Obviously his stuffed-up head was bothering him. He'd do better when he felt better.

Although he could be in for a miserable few days in the meantime.

"So what are we standing about for?" the duke asked.

"Your grace—" the castle mage began.

"Now that the expert's here, shouldn't you be seeing about the wards?" the duke asked.

The castle mage looked, if possible, even more anxious.

"I've already tried everything I know," he protested. "I was hoping Master Justinian . . ."

"Of course," Justinian said. "My assistant will go and . . . um . . . begin running the tests I've planned to diagnose the problem with the castle warding spell, while I work on the murder."

Me? Gwynn wanted to squeak, but she managed to hold her tongue in front of the duke.

"Ah, there you are, Reg," the duke said, seeing that his manservant had arrived carrying a covered platter. "Show her to the gatehouse."

"Just pretend it's a class exercise and try to find out what's wrong with the wards," Justinian murmured, picking up her small carpet bag and handing it to her as carefully as if it were full of volatile potions. "If the duke's magician hasn't brought down the castle walls trying to fix it, you're not likely to do any harm. If you fix it, marvelous; if not, I'll deal with it when I'm finished with this."

Gwynn nodded and followed Reg back to the gatehouse. It took fifteen minutes—the castle was more like a small city.

"Latest expert on warding spells," Reg said, turning her over to the captain of the guard, who, after quirking one eyebrow, seemed to accept Gwynn's expertise. Or perhaps he was just happy to see Reg leave.

"Not sure what you can do about the damned thing," the captain said. "Works one minute and not the next. Apparently that's a lot harder to fix than if it just flat out didn't work."

Unfortunately, he was right, Gwynn soon realized. Intermittent problems were the worst. She ran tests all morning, and the warding spell worked perfectly. The guards could come and go at will without setting off the alarm bells, but they rang furiously whenever an intruder entered the castle—intruders being represented, for test purposes, by a motley collection of peddlers, minstrels, and Gypsies unfortunate enough to show up at the castle that day.

Gwynn hated to disappoint the Maestro, but she was beginning to think he'd have to solve the problem. Though she'd keep trying for a while, since obviously his own work on the murder wasn't going well. She saw him crossing the courtyard occasionally, always with a slightly more worried look on his face. She didn't want to bother him yet.

Besides, she was a little worried about what would happen when Justinian saw the warding spell's control device: a perfect little miniature of the duke's castle, complete with a working drawbridge and portcullis. Justinian's intense passion for disassembling small mechanical objects was matched only by his complete inability to reassemble them. What if the Maestro decided he needed to take the model apart to repair the spell? Gwynn tried not to think about it.

If she hadn't been so worried, she'd have found the model castle fascinating herself. You could keep track of everything that went on in the castle—outdoors, at any rate—by watching the small, ghostly figures that moved around in it. Gwynn spotted the tiny image of Master Justinian standing on one of the ramparts and paused to watch. From the slumped set of his shoulders, she deduced that things were still going badly. She sighed, turned her back on the model, and tried to think.

"There really doesn't seem to be anything wrong with it," Gwynn muttered.

"Useless things, these magical devices," said Reg, from the doorway. Gwynn jumped; she hadn't heard him come in. And his presence was the last thing she needed. He had a personality like a cold, wet drizzle.

Suddenly the bells began ringing. Gwynn and the captain ran to the front of the miniature castle. They could see a group of small, ghostly figures entering it. A troop of wood trolls, armed with scythes and machetes. And yet, glancing out of the window of the guardhouse, which overhung the real gate, they saw no trolls entering the castle. Nothing was entering the castle, not even a chipmunk.

"It was working fine a minute ago," the captain said.

"If you say so," Reg said, with a shrug. "I've never seen it work right myself."

"Send some of the Gypsies in and out of the gate," Gwynn said.

The captain shouted some orders down into the courtyard. The wards ignored the Gypsies plodding in and out, though they continued to show the purely imaginary trolls wandering about the courtyard.

Or were they imaginary? Gwynn decided to cast a quick illusion-stripping spell on the courtyard. Permanently dispelling illusions was a job for a master mage, of course, but Gwynn thought that if any magically cloaked trolls lurked in the courtyard, she could probably make them visible for a second or two.

"Watch the courtyard and tell me what you see," she told the captain and Reg.

And then she gestured.

"I don't see anything," Reg said. The captain shook his head as well.

Of course they didn't see anything, Gwynn thought. The spell had fizzled. And yet, this morning, when she had cast the same spell on the courtyard as part of her tests, it had worked perfectly. The only illusion she'd dispelled this morning was a passing courtier's toupee spell, but her illusion-stripping incantation had worked, just the same.

What was different now?

"I don't hold with magic," Reg said, lounging in the window. "Useless stuff. Never works the way it's supposed to."

Gwynn suddenly remembered how the Maestro had been able to sneeze without ill effect when Reg had been in his study. And in the coach, all the way from the college to the duke's castle.

"I want you to help with something," she told Reg. She rummaged through her carpet bag and handed him a small crystal. "Here, take this. Go down to the gate, walk out and keep going in as straight a line as you can until I call for you to stop."

"Whatever you like," Reg said, with a sneer. He shoved the crystal in his pocket and sauntered out.

"Keep the Gypsies going in and out," Gwynn told the captain.

Gwynn glanced back and forth between the miniature castle and the outside world as Reg left the castle and ambled toward the edge of the wood. The tiny trolls appeared to be setting the model of the stables afire. The Gypsies were nowhere to be seen in the model, although she could see them well enough in the real world, marching back and forth through the gates with resigned expressions on their faces. When Reg was about a thousand yards from the castle gate, the phantom trolls suddenly vanished from the model and the Gypsies appeared.

"Do you see that?" she asked the captain.

"Now it's working," he said.

"Let him get to the edge of the woods, then call him back."

The captain did so. When the manservant got within about a thousand yards of the castle, the images of the Gypsies winked out in the model, and the phantom trolls reappeared. They seemed to have captured the keep and were throwing tapestries and furniture into the moat.

"I think you may be on to something," the captain said. "What is that crystal?"

"An excuse to get him out of range," Gwynn said.

"I beg your pardon?"

"Could you send someone to fetch Master Justinian?" Gwynn asked.

From the cloud of camphor that arrived with him, Gwynn deduced that the Maestro's cold was no better, and judging from the expression on his face, Gwynn suspected his investigation was still going badly, too. She winced when she saw the duke trailing in his wake, looking like a thundercloud about to spew lightning.

"This better be important," the duke snapped as he entered the room.

"A moment, your grace," Justinian said, and drew Gwynn to one side.

"I'm sorry I've interrupted your work," she began.

"I'm not," Justinian said, rubbing his forehead again. "I'm in no shape to be doing magic. One minute my spells work, the next they fizzle. And even when they work, I'm not finding anything that could account for that poor benighted man's death."

"Perhaps this will help," she said.

She showed him the model castle, where the triumphant miniature trolls were now roasting tiny castle guards on spits and eating them with gusto.

"Fascinating," Justinian said, fingering a model catapult on the castle walls.

"Typical," the duke said, with disgust. "Damned useless piece of junk."

"Patience, your grace," Justinian said, toying with the miniature drawbridge. "Something of great import is afoot."

He looked at Gwynn and nodded.

While the duke and the captain of the guard looked on with puzzled expressions, Gwynn demonstrated how the wards worked again when Reg was out of range.

"Of course," Justinian said. "He's been hovering over me all morning. That explains everything. Follow me!"

He dashed off at a breakneck pace. Gwynn, Reg, and the duke followed him back to the dungeons.

"What are we here for?" the duke asked, when he'd caught his breath.

"I need to question your surviving prisoner," Justinian replied.

The remaining anarchist flinched. Obviously, he was more used to the duke's style of interrogation than the Maestro's.

"You saw the wound in your comrade's chest, did you not?" Justinian asked.

"Filthy magic attack," the anarchist muttered.

"He was wounded before in just the same fashion, wasn't he?" Justinian asked.

"Aye," the anarchist said, looking puzzled. "Stabbed in the chest in a scuffle with the king's guards—must be five years ago. We thought he was a goner, for sure, but we had this mage with us—"

"A mage? With you?" Justinian said.

"A hostage, more than likely," the duke said.

"Something like that," the anarchist said. "Anyway, the mage fixed it. Healed the wound so you couldn't even see it, and we managed to get out of the city that night. Guards were looking for a wounded rebel, not a healthy one."

"Aha!" Justinian said, dramatically. "Most helpful. Now I know how he was killed."

"Some kind of magic," the anarchist muttered.

"No," Justinian said. "He was killed by the complete absence of magic."

"I beg your pardon?" the duke said.

"We already know the castle warding spell has been . . . temperamental," Justinian said. "Have you noticed problems with any other spells? Food preservation spells wearing off prematurely? Healing potions not working as designed? Cosmetic spells not performing reliably?"

The duke nodded and narrowed his eyes. From the murmurs Gwynn could hear from several other people nearby, she suspected that there had, indeed, been many magical malfunctions recently—probably more than the duke ever dreamed.

"The light globes haven't worked for weeks," the castle mage said, glancing up at a flickering torch.

"It's him," Justinian said, pointing at Reg.

"Me?" Reg exclaimed. "I'm no bloody mage."

"We'll see about that," the duke said, gesturing to his guards to seize Reg.

"No, Reg is right, your grace," Justinian said, waving the guards back. "He's no mage. He has no magic whatsoever. Probably born that way. He's what we call a magic null."

"A what?" the duke said.

"A null—he cancels out magic by his very presence. Like water and fire. Pour water on a fire, and it fizzles out. Pour water on gunpowder, and you can't even light it. That's what he does to magic. Snuffs it out like a candle."

"Explains why the warding spell wasn't working, but not how he killed my prisoner," the duke said. "Unless you're trying to tell me that anarchist was a mage. Which doesn't make sense; they hate mages. Besides, you aren't harmed by him."

"It goes back to that wound your prisoner got five years ago," the Maestro said. "The one his confederate here says their captured mage healed. They probably had a knife to his throat, poor man. But he was clever. He didn't perform a healing spell at all."

"That's rot," the remaining anarchist said. "I saw it. One minute he had a great bleeding wound, and the next he looked perfectly fine."

"Precisely," Justinian said. "You said he escaped the city that same night? Healing spells don't work that fast. What I suspect your captive mage did was cast a stasis spell just along the outside of the wound, to stop the bleeding."

"Like the one my spellcaster did before you came?" the duke asked.

"Precisely," Justinian said. "And probably finished it off with an illusion spell, to hide the wound."

"Now I'm not sorry we offed him," the surviving anarchist muttered.

"With a stasis spell, the wound wouldn't bleed or fester," Justinian explained. "It also wouldn't heal. It would stay just as it was the moment that poor captive mage cast his spell. And he probably conjured better than he intended; his stasis spell remained in place these five years until our magic null here walked into his cell and erased it. Reg was there, wasn't he, when the prisoner died?"

"Yes, he was," the duke said.

"So it wasn't really murder after all," Justinian said. "Your prisoner was wounded by the king's guards in the lawful dispatch of their duty. It just took five years for the wound to kill him."

"Of course, we still don't know who sent him to me," the duke said, staring at Reg with narrowed eyes.

"Sent?" Reg said, looking worried. "Nobody sent me. I just needed a job."

"Maybe," the duke said. "Or maybe someone wanted all my magical defenses to fail. We'll see what a little questioning reveals."

"Oh, not much use doing that," Justinian said.

"Why not?" the duke said. "You'd be surprised how well a little close questioning works."

"Yes, but whoever sent him probably bespelled him to make sure he was impervious to torture," Justinian said.

"Torture?" Reg squeaked.

"But Maestro, if he's a magic null," Gwynn began, then stopped herself.

"Then I'll just hang him and be done with it," the duke said.

"Hang him, when he's merely an unwitting tool of something else?" Justinian exclaimed.

"Unwitting? I'll do him one better," the duke said. "Unbreathing—that's more like it."

"And when, with a little effort, the College might discover who sent him . . . and how to turn his abilities to your benefit?" Justinian continued.

"Hmmm . . ." the duke said, looking thoughtfully at Reg, whose earlier smug manner had vanished entirely at the first sign of danger.

It took all of the Maestro's considerable powers of persuasion, but the duke finally agreed to turn Reg over to the college for study.

"We'll waste no time getting him at a safe distance from your wards," Justinian said, beckoning to Gwynn and Reg to follow him as he bowed his way out of the room.

"Thanks," Reg said, when they reached the corridor. "You never know when the old goat will change his mind. Best for my safety if we leave as soon as possible."

"Bother your safety," Justinian replied. "I just want to get home as soon as possible so I can be sick in peace and quiet. I've never seen such a drafty castle."

"A genuine magic null!" Radolphus said, wide-eyed, when Gwynn and Justinian had finished telling the headmaster about their expedition. Although Gwynn did most of the telling while Justinian lay back in his chair, wrapped in three blankets, announcing at random intervals that he'd probably caught his death on the trip back. And, Gwynn noticed with dismay, toying idly with the miniature catapult he'd filched from the duke's model castle.

"I didn't even know there was such a thing," Gwynn said. "But I knew there was something odd about Reg."

"I'm not sure I'd have figured it out all that quickly myself," Justinian said. "It's easy to identify something you know about, and a damned sight harder to deal intelligently with the unknown."

Gwynn glowed at the implied compliment.

"And at least the duke is happy, and can probably keep the king happy," Radolphus said.

"For now," Justinian added.

Gwynn could see that both of their faces looked somber for a moment. Then Radolphus smiled.

"Now's good enough," he said. "And the magic null—they're quite rare! I don't think anyone here has seen the like for a century! Think of the opportunities for research! Of course, we'll have to find him someplace to stay where he'll be harmless. At the very edge of the grounds. But that won't be any trouble, really; not when you consider the benefits."

"Yes," Gwynn said. "To start with, the benefits to Master Justinian."

"To me?" Justinian said, puzzled.

"You've been having such an awful time with this cold," Gwynn explained. "Especially when you sneeze."

"Yes, I'm sorry to be such a burden," Master Justinian said, flourishing his handkerchief dramatically. "It's not fair, asking you to take care of me this way."

"I don't mind, Maestro," Gwynn said, suppressing a smile. "Only the, uh, side effects of the sneezing do seem rather dangerous. But if Reg were around, you could sneeze all you wanted, and nothing at all would happen!"

"I don't know," Justinian said, taken aback. "I'm not sure I'd want him around all the time. It would be like having a dead squid in the room. And besides he—he—he—"

The Maestro sneezed. It was a loud, hearty sneeze, and both Gwynn and Radolphus ducked and covered their heads by instinct.

"Oh, all right," came a squeak.

Gwynn and Radolphus opened their eyes. There, sitting in Master Justinian's chair, almost lost in the pile of blankets and robes, was a tiny blue goblin with watery eyes and a red, chapped nose.

"Change me back, quick!" squeaked the goblin Justinian. "And then bring in Reg. Anything's better than this!"

The Nightside, Needless to Say

SIMON R. GREEN

The Nightside is the secret, sick, magical heart of London. A city within a city, where the night never ends and it's always three o'clock in the morning. Hot neon reflects from rain-slick streets, and dreams go walking in borrowed flesh. You can find pretty much anything in the Nightside, except happy endings. Gods and monsters run confidence tricks, and all desires can be satisfied, if you're willing to pay the price. Which might be money and might be service, but nearly always ends up meaning your soul. The Nightside, where the sun never shows its face because if it did, someone would probably try to steal it. When you've nowhere else to go, the Nightside will take you in. Trust no one, including yourself, and you might get out alive again.

Some of us work there, for our sins. Or absolution, or atonement. It's that kind of place.

Larry! Larry! What's wrong?

The sharp, whispered voice pulled me up out of a bad dream; something about running in the rain, running from something awful. I sat up in bed, looked around, and didn't know where I was. It wasn't my bedroom. Harsh neon light flickered red and green through the slats of the closed shutters, intermittently revealing a dark dusty room with cheap and nasty furniture. There was nobody else there, but the words still rang in my ears. I sat on the edge of the bed, trying to remember my dream, but it was already fading. I was fully dressed, and there were no bedsheets. I still had my shoes on. I had no idea what day it was.

I got up and turned on the bedside light. The room wasn't improved by being seen clearly, but at least I knew where I was. An old safe house, in one of the seedier areas of the Nightside. A refuge I hadn't had to use in years. I still kept up the rent; because you never know when you're going to need a bolt-hole in a hurry. I turned out my pockets. Everything where it should be, and nothing new to explain what I was doing here. I shook my head slowly, then left the room, heading for the adjoining bathroom. Explanations could wait, until I'd taken care of something that couldn't.

The bathroom's bright fluorescent light was harsh and unforgiving as I studied my face in the medicine cabinet mirror. Pale and washed-out, under straw blond hair, good bone structure, and a mouth and eyes that never gave anything away. My hair was a mess, but I didn't need a shave. I shrugged, dropped my trousers and shorts, and sat down on the porcelain throne. There was a vague uneasy feeling in my bowels and then a sudden lurch as something within made a bid for freedom. I tapped my foot impatiently, listening to a series of splashes. Something bad must have happened, even if I couldn't remember it. I needed to get out of here and start asking pointed questions of certain people. Someone would know. Someone always knows.

The splashes finally stopped, but something didn't feel right. I got up, turned around, and looked down into the bowl. It was full of maggots. Curling and twisting and squirming. I made a horrified sound and stumbled backward. My legs tangled in my lowered trousers, and I fell full length on the floor. My head hit the wall hard. It didn't hurt. I scrambled to my feet, pulled up my shorts and trousers, and backed out of the bathroom, still staring at the toilet.

It was the things that weren't happening that scared me most. I should have been hyperventilating. My heart should have been hammering in my chest. My face should have been covered in a cold sweat. But when I checked my wrist, then my throat, there wasn't any pulse. And I wasn't breathing hard because I wasn't breathing at all. I couldn't remember taking a single breath since I woke up. I touched my face with my fingertips, and they both felt cold.

I was dead.

Someone had killed me. I knew that, though I didn't know how. The maggots suggested I'd been dead for some time. So, who killed me, and why hadn't I noticed it till now?

My name's Larry Oblivion, and with a name like that I pretty much had to be a private investigator. Mostly I do corporate work: industrial espionage, checking out backgrounds, helping significant people defect from one organization to another. Big business has always been where the real money is. I don't do divorce cases, or solve mysteries, and I've never even owned a trench-coat. I wear Gucci, I make more money than most people ever dream of, and I pack a wand. Don't snigger. I took the wand in payment for a case involving the Unseelie Court, and I've never regretted it. Two feet long, and carved from the spine of a species that never existed in the waking world, the wand could stop time, for everyone except me. More than enough to give me an edge, or a running start. You take all the advantages you can get when you operate in the Nightside. No one else knew I had the wand.

Unless . . . someone had found out and killed me to try and get their hands on it.

I found the coffeemaker and fixed myself my usual pick-me-up. Black coffee, steaming hot, and strong enough to jump-start a mummy from its sleep. But when it was ready, I didn't want it. Apparently the walking dead don't drink coffee. Damn. I was going to miss that.

Larry! Larry!

I spun round, the words loud in my ear, but still there was no one else in the room. Just a voice, calling my name. For a moment I almost remembered something horrid, then it was gone before I could hold on to it. I scowled, pacing up and down the room to help me think. I was dead, I'd been murdered. So, start with the usual suspects. Who had reason to want me dead? Serious reasons; I had my share of enemies, but that was just the price of doing business. No one murders anyone over business.

No; start with my ex-wife, Donna Tramen. She had reasons to hate me. I fell in love with a client, Margaret Boniface, and left my wife for her. The affair didn't work out, but Maggie and I remained friends. In fact, we worked so well together I made her a partner in my business. My wife hadn't talked to me since I moved out, except through her lawyer, but if she was going to kill me, she would have done it long ago. And the amount of money the divorce judge awarded her gave her a lot of good reasons for wanting me alive. As long as the cheques kept coming.

Next up: angry or disappointed clients, where the case hadn't worked out to everyone's satisfaction. There were any number of organizations in and out of the Nightside that I'd stolen secrets or personnel from. But none of them would take such things personally. Today's target might be tomorrow's client, so everyone stayed polite. I never got involved in the kinds of cases where passions were likely to be raised. No one's ever made movies about the kind of work I do.

I kept feeling I already knew the answer, but it remained stubbornly out of reach. Perhaps because . . . I didn't want to remember. I shuddered suddenly, and it wasn't from the cold. I picked up the phone beside the bed, and called my partner. Maggie picked up on the second ring, as though she'd been waiting for a call.

"Maggie, this is Larry. Listen, you're not going to believe what's happened . . ."

"Larry, you've been missing for three days! Where are you?"

Three days . . . A trail could get real cold in three days . . .

"I'm at the old safe house on Blaiston Street. I think you'd better come and get me."

"What the hell are you doing there? I didn't know we still had that place on the books."

"Just come and get me. I'm in trouble."

Her voice changed immediately. "What kind of trouble, Larry?"

"Let's just say . . . I think I'm going to need some of your old expertise, Mama Bones."

"Don't use that name on an open line! It's been a long time since I was a mover and shaker on the voodoo scene, and hopefully most people have forgotten Margaret Boniface was ever involved. I'm clean now. One day at a time, sweet Jesus."

"You know I wouldn't ask if it wasn't important. I need what you used to know. Get here as fast as you can. And, Maggie, don't tell anyone where you're going. We can't trust anyone but each other."

She laughed briefly. "Business as usual, in the Nightside."

I did a lot more pacing and thinking in the half hour it took Maggie to reach Blaiston Street, but I was no wiser at the end of it. My memories stopped abruptly three days ago, with no warning of what was to come. I kept watch on and off through the slats of the window shutters, and was finally rewarded with the sight of Maggie pulling up to the curb in her cherry-red Jaguar. Protective spells sparked briefly around the car as she got out and looked up at my window. Tall and slender, an ice-cool blonde with a buzz cut and a heavy scarlet mouth. She dressed like a diva and walked like a princess, and carried a silver-plated magnum derringer in her purse, next to her aboriginal pointing bone. She had a sharp, incisive mind, and given a few more years experience and the right contacts, she'd be ten times the operative I was. I never told her that, of course. I didn't want her getting overconfident.

She rapped out our special knock on the door, the one that said yes she had checked, and no, no one had followed her. I let her in, and she checked the room out professionally before turning to kiss my cheek. And then she stopped, and looked at me.

"Larry . . . you look half dead."

I smiled briefly. "You don't know the *half* of it."

I gave her the bad news, and she took it as well as could be expected. She insisted on checking my lack of a pulse or heartbeat for herself, then stepped back from me and hugged herself tightly. I don't think she liked the way my cold flesh felt. I tried to make light of what had happened, complaining that my life must have been really dull if neither Heaven nor Hell were interested in claiming me, but neither of us was fooled. In the end, we sat side by side on the bed, and discussed what we should do next in calm, professional voices.

"You've no memory at all of being killed?" Maggie said finally.

"No. I'm dead, but not yet departed. Murdered, but still walking around. Which puts me very much in your old territory, oh mistress of the mystic arts."

"Oh please! So I used to know a little voodoo . . . Practically everyone in my family does. Where we come from, it's no big thing. And I was never involved in anything like this . . ."

"Can you help me, or not?"

She scowled. "All right. Let me run a few diagnostics on you."

"Are we going to have to send out for a chicken?"

"Be quiet, heathen."

She ran through a series of chants in Old French, lit up some incense, then took off all her clothes and danced around the room for a while. I'd probably have enjoyed it if I hadn't been dead. The room grew darker, and there was a sense of unseen eyes watching. Shadows moved slowly across the walls, deep disturbing shapes, though there was nothing in the room to cast them. And then Maggie stopped dancing, and stood facing me, breathing hard, sweat running down her bare body.

"Did you feel anything then?" she said.

"No. Was I supposed to?"

Maggie shrugged briefly and put her clothes back on in a businesslike way. The shadows and the sense of being watched were gone.

"You've been dead for three days," said Maggie.

"Someone killed you, then held your spirit in your dead body. There's a rider spell attached, to give you the appearance of normality, but inside you're already rotting. Hence the maggots."

"Can you undo the spell?" I said.

"Larry, you're *dead.* The dead can be made to walk, but no one can bring them all the way back, not even in the Nightside. Whatever we decide to do, your story's over, Larry."

I thought about that for a while. I always thought I would have achieved more, before the end. All the things I meant to do, and kept putting off, because I was young and imagined I had all the time in the world. Larry Oblivion, who always dreamed of something better, but never had the guts to go after it. One ex-wife, one ex-lover, no kids, no legacy. No point and no purpose.

"When all else fails," I said finally, "there's always revenge. I need to find out who killed me and why, while I still can. While there's still enough of me left to savor it."

"Any ideas who it might have been?" said Maggie. "Anyone new you might have upset recently?"

I thought hard. "Prometheus Inc. weren't at all happy over my handling of their poltergeist saboteur. Count Entropy didn't like what I found out about his son, even though he paid me to dig it up. Big Max always said he'd put me in the ground someday . . ."

"Max," Maggie said immediately. "Has to be Max.

You've been rivals for years, hurt his business and made him look a fool, more than once. He must have decided to put an end to the competition."

"Why would he want to keep me around after killing me?"

"To gloat! He hated your guts, Larry; it has to be him!"

I thought about it. I'd rubbed Max's nose in it before, and all he ever did was talk. Maybe . . . he'd got tired of talking.

"All right," I said. "Let's go see the big man and ask him a few pointed questions."

"He's got a lot of protection," said Maggie. "Not at all an easy man to get to see."

"Do I look like I care? Are you in or not?"

"Of course I'm in! I'm just pointing out that Big Max is known for surrounding himself with heavy-duty firepower."

I smiled. "Baby, I'm dead. How are they going to stop me?"

We went out into the streets, and walked through the Nightside. The rain had stopped, and the air was sharp with new possibilities. Hot neon blazed on every side, advertising the kinds of love that might not have names, but certainly have prices. Heavy bass lines surged out of open club doors, reverberating in the ground and in my bones. All kinds of people swept past us, intent on their own business. Only some of them were human. Traffic roared constantly up and down the road, and everyone was careful to give it plenty of room. Not everything that looked like a car was a car, and some of them were hungry. In the Nightside, taxis can run on deconsecrated altar wine, and motorcycle messengers snort powdered virgin's blood for that extra kick.

Max's place wasn't far. He holed up in an upmarket cocktail bar called the Spider's Web. Word is he used to work there once. And that he had his old boss killed when he took it over, then had the man stuffed and mounted and put on display. Max never left the place anymore, and held court there from behind more layers of protection than some presidents can boast. The big man had a lot of enemies, and he gloried in it.

Along the way I kept getting quick flashes of déjà vu. Brief glimpses of my dream of running through the rain. Except I was pretty sure by now that it wasn't a dream but a memory. I could feel the desperation as I ran, pursued by something without a face.

The only entrance to the Spider's Web was covered by two large gentlemen with shoulder holsters, and several layers of defensive magics. I knew about the magics because a client had once hired me to find out exactly what Max was using. Come to think of it, no one had seen that client for some time. I murmured to Maggie to hang on to my arm, then drew my wand and activated it.

It shone with a brilliant light, too bright to look at, and all around us the world seemed to slow down, and become flat and unreal. The roar of the traffic shut off, and the neon stopped flickering. Maggie and I were outside Time. We walked between the two bodyguards, and they didn't even see us. I could feel the defensive magics straining, reaching out, unable to touch us.

We walked on through the club, threading our way through the frozen crowds. Deeper and deeper, into the lair of the beast. There were things going on that sickened even me, but I didn't have the time to stop and do anything. I only had one shot at this. Maggie held my arm tightly. It would probably have hurt if I'd still been alive.

"Well," she said, trying for a light tone and not even coming close. "A genuine wand of the Faerie. That explains a lot of things."

"It always helps to have an unsuspected edge."

"You could have told me. I am your partner."

"You can never tell who's listening, in the Nightside." I probably would have told her, if she hadn't ended our affair. "But I think I'm past the point of needing secrets anymore."

We found the big man sitting behind a desk in a surprisingly modest inner office. He was playing solitaire with tarot cards, and cheating. Thick mats of ivy crawled across the walls, and the floor was covered with cabalistic symbols. I closed the door behind us so we wouldn't be interrupted, and shut down the wand. Max looked up sharply as we appeared suddenly in front of him. His right hand reached for something, but Maggie already had her silver magnum derringer out and covering him. Max shrugged, sat back in his chair, and studied us curiously.

Max Maxwell, so big they named him twice. A giant of a man, huge and lowering even behind his oversized mahogany desk. Eight feet tall and impressively broad across the shoulders, with a harsh and craggy face, he looked like he was carved out of stone. A gargoyle in a Savile Row suit. Max traded in secrets, and stayed in business because he knew something about everyone. Or at least, everyone who mattered. Even if he hadn't killed me, there was a damned good chance he knew who had.

"Larry Oblivion," he said, in a voice like grinding stone. "My dearest rival and most despised competitor. To what do I owe the displeasure of this unexpected visit?"

"Like you don't already know," said Maggie, her derringer aimed directly between his eyes.

Max ignored her, his gaze fixed on me. "Provide me with one good reason why I shouldn't have both of you killed for this impertinence?"

"How about, you already killed me? Or haven't you noticed that I only breathe when I talk?"

Max studied me thoughtfully. "Yes. You are dead.

You have no aura. I wish I could claim the credit, but alas, it seems someone else has beaten me to it. And besides, if I wanted you dead, you'd be dead and gone, not hanging around to trouble me."

"He's right," I said to Maggie. "Max is famous for never leaving loose ends."

"You want me to kill him anyway?" said Maggie.

"No," I said. "Tell me, Max. If you didn't kill me, who did?"

"I haven't the faintest idea," said Max, smiling slowly, revealing grey teeth behind the grey lips. "Which means it isn't any of your usual enemies. And if I don't know, no one does."

I felt suddenly tired. Max had been my best bet, my last hope. He could have been lying, but I didn't think so. Not when he knew the truth could hurt me more. My body was decaying, I had no more leads, and I didn't have the time left to go anywhere else. So Maggie and I walked out the way we came in. Maggie would have killed Max, if I'd asked, but I didn't see the point. Feuds and vendettas are for the living; when you're dead you just can't be bothered with the small shit.

Maggie took me back to her place. I needed time out, to sit and think. I was close to despair. I didn't have enough time left to investigate all the enemies I'd made in my personal and professional life. A disturbing and depressing thought, for someone facing eternity. So many enemies, and so few friends . . . I sat on Maggie's couch, and looked fondly at her as she made us some coffee. We'd been so good together, for a while. Why didn't it work out? If I knew the answer to that, we'd still be together. She came in from the kitchen, carrying two steaming mugs. I took one, and held it awkwardly. I wanted to drink the coffee to please her, but I couldn't. She looked at me, puzzled.

"Larry? What's the matter?"

And just like that, I knew. Because I finally recognized the voice I'd been hearing ever since I woke up dead.

I was at Maggie's place, drinking coffee. It tasted funny. Larry? she said. Larry? What's wrong? I felt something burning in my throat, and knew she'd poisoned me. I stopped time with my wand, and ran. It was raining. I didn't dare go home. She'd find me. I didn't know where to go for help, so I went to ground, in my old safe house at Blaiston Street. And I died there, still wondering why my partner and ex-lover had killed me.

"It was you," I said, and something in my voice made her flinch. "You poisoned me. Why?"

"The how is more interesting," Maggie said calmly. She sat down opposite me, entirely composed. "An old voodoo drug in your coffee, to kill you and set you up for the zombie spell. But of course I didn't know about the wand. It interacted with my magic, buying you more time. The wand's magic is probably what's holding you together now."

"Talk to me, Maggie. We were lovers. Friends. Partners."

"That last one is the only one that matters." She blew on her coffee, and sipped it cautiously. "I wanted our business. All of it. I was tired of being the junior partner, especially when I did most of the work. But you had the name, and the reputation, and the contacts. I didn't see why I should have to go on sharing my money with you. I was the brains in our partnership, and you were only the muscle. You can always hire muscle. And . . . I was bored with you. Our affair was fun, and it got me the partnership I wanted; but, Larry darling, while you might have been adequate in bed, you were just so damned dull out of it.

"I couldn't split up the business. I needed the cachet your name brings. And I couldn't simply have you killed, because under the terms of your will, your ex would inherit your half of the business. And I really didn't see why I should have to go to all the trouble and expense of buying her out.

"So I got out my old books and put together a neat little package of poisons and voodoo magics. As a zombie under my control, you would have made and signed a new will, leaving everything to me. Then I'd dispose of your body. But clearly I didn't put enough sugar in your coffee. Or maybe you saw something in my face, at the last. Either way, that damned secret wand of yours let you escape. To a safe house I didn't even know we had anymore. You have no idea how surprised I was when you rang me three days later.

"Why didn't you remember? The poison, the spells, the trauma? Or maybe you just didn't want to believe your old sweetie could have a mind of her own and the guts to go after what she wanted."

"So why point me at Max?" I said numbly.

"To use up what time you've got left. And there was always the chance you'd take each other out and leave the field even more open for me."

"How could you do this? I loved you, Maggie!"

"That's sweet, Larry. But a girl's got to live."

She put aside her coffee, stood up, and looked down at me. Frowning slightly, as though considering a necessary but distasteful task. "But it's not too late to put things right. I made you what you are, and I can unmake you." She pulled a silver dagger out of her sleeve. The leaf-shaped blade was covered with runes and sigils. "Just lie back and accept it, Larry. You don't want to go on as you are, do you? I'll cut the consciousness right out of you, then you won't care anymore. You'll sign the necessary papers like a good little zombie, and I'll put your body to rest. It's been fun, Larry. Don't spoil it."

She came at me with the dagger while she was still talking, expecting to catch me off guard. I activated my wand, and time crashed to a halt. She hung over me, suspended in midair. I studied her for a moment; and then it was the easiest thing in the world to take the dagger away from her and slide it slowly into her heart. I let time start up again. She fell forward into my arms, and I held her while she died, because I had loved her once.

I didn't want to kill her, even after everything she'd done and planned to do. But when a man's partner kills him, he's supposed to do something about it.

So here I am. Dead, but not departed. My body seems to have stabilized. No more maggots. Presumably the wand interacting with the voodoo magics. I never really understood that stuff. I don't know how much longer I've got, but then, who does? Maybe I'll have new business cards made up. Larry Oblivion, deceased detective. The postmortem private eye. I still have my work. And I need to do some good, to balance out all the bad I did while I was alive. The hereafter's a lot closer than it used to be.

Even when you're dead, there's no rest for the wicked.

Lovely

JOHN
STRALEY

It was a piece of good luck. Gunk had been hungry when he came upon the dead thing sprawled under the wharf. It was opened up, with its insides showing to the air, a fine scent rising from the blue-grey bowels, where the last thing it ate would be waiting to be eaten again.

Gunk had spent the morning looking around, singing a soft tune to himself. Humming helped make his eyes sharper, Gunk was convinced of that. In fact, he thought he always heard a little chime each time he found a lovely piece of meat. He had no idea if the sound was actually in the air, like the sound of rocks falling down a slope, or inside himself, like the rumbling of his guts, but he was sure that there was a sound associated with finding a sparkling piece of meat.

At first the insides of any animal seem shiny. This is what had caught Gunk's eye as he had been standing on the lip of a Dumpster back behind the fish plant. It was the sparkling of fat along the red incision. It appeared like a gem back in the darkness under the wharf, and he heard his mysterious little chime. This was a summer kill, no doubt about that. In winter, fresh blood on the snow was an impossible scarlet, not nearly the same as the spilled blood of a grey-green summer. Blood in winter was a hunger red. This summer kill showed more fat, white fat . . . and the blood was more a greasy shadow on the rocks, with hardly any color at all.

The dead thing was tucked back up under the shadow of the dock, where the pearls of water were all drippy and bright, plunking down into the ocean. The dead thing hadn't been there an hour ago, Gunk was certain, because as hungry as he had been he would surely have seen it.

Gunk hadn't heard any loud noises. None of the other real creatures had startled or risen up from their places. Gunk was beginning to worry about the body. He had heard stories of real creatures eating things and getting sick. Sick enough to die. And it was suspected that it was from eating these unlucky dead things. He walked around, looking at it from every angle he could. All big animals looked awkward after death, but humans looked even worse, as if they had fallen down and broken apart on the inside. Finally, Gunk spread his wings a bit and hopped on the top of the human near where its eyeholes were still open.

The eyeholes looked too good, and he started in on them, taking short hard jabs with his beak to get to the tasty juice and the really lovely hard muscle behind. He didn't care if it was unlucky; some opportunities just had to be taken.

A human being came stumbling up the rocks. This one was alive, and very fat. He seemed to be almost as happy as Gunk to find the dead thing.

"Hey! Hey! Get back!" Gunk said to him, but of course this clumsy walker ignored him.

"Goddamn it, Harry," the fat man said to the dead thing. "You are going to get us in a bunch of trouble." This man ran his hands all around the dead thing as if he were looking for something good to eat. He seemed agitated, and for a minute the raven became concerned that he was going to take the tasty dead thing away.

"I know you have it here. Come on, old son, too late to be keeping secrets from me now," the fat one said. Then he jerked his hand out and held something up in front of his flat ugly face. Green leaves, all the same shape and size. The man's eyes opened wide, and for a moment Gunk thought he was going to eat the leaves, which would be very strange.

"Hey! Hey! Hey! Take those things away if you want! Just get the hell away from my dead thing!" Gunk said, but the fat man ignored him.

"Shut up! Shoo!" the ugly one said.

"Hey, hey, hey . . . cut that out!" Gunk yelled back.

Gunk wanted a few minutes alone with the dead thing. He wanted to get some of the fat under the skin and some of the lovely-smelling food cooked down in the intestines before he called the rest of the real creatures over. The only thing worse than not finding food was wasting it by letting it sit too long and letting some other nasty animal get to it. The real creatures would make the best use of the dead thing. It upset him that this human being was trying to get rid of him.

The fat man rolled the dead thing over and kept searching it. He stuffed the leaves in his own pocket, then rolled the dead thing down the slope toward the water. The ugly one stuffed rocks into the outer folds of the outside skin where he had gotten the leaves.

"Hey! Hey! Hey!" Gunk yelled.

"So long, buddy boy," the fat one said. Then he rolled the dead thing into the deep water.

"Doo doo!" Gunk screamed. "You big basket butt! What the hell are you doing!" The raven was livid. He hopped up and down, then walked straight up into the air by the man's face. "Hey! Hey! Waste! Waste! Waste!"

Gunk was so mad he decided to follow the ugly one until the ugly one killed something else. He hadn't taken any food at all, and this fat man must certainly eat a lot, so it seemed clear to Gunk the fat man would have to kill something again soon. Gunk would be ready. He would rush right in and not wait for this stupid basket butt to waste another beautiful dead thing by giving it to the skittery little sand fleas and the sad swimmers who flew on the surface of that other world.

The fat man waved him off. "Gawh! Get the hell away from me!"

Gunk hopped on the wires above the street, following the fat man as he lurched along on his strange round legs.

"You can't lose me, fat boy!" Gunk yelled. "Don't even try! Go and kill something else and hurry up about it."

The day carried a slurry of scents from the fish plant and the dump up the hill. Gunk liked this section of the waterfront even if he had to compete with the dim-witted eagles and the bothersome crows. There were black mushrooms of garbage in the backs of buildings, and now and then he was lucky enough to find a dead dog in the ditch. Once he had even found a hapless eagle who had gotten too close to the transformers on the buzzing power poles and had cooked himself up and fallen onto the street for Gunk to find.

Gunk's world was a gorgeous curve and tumble of rock and waterways, lumps and swales, places of shade and sunlight, updrafts and calm. The world glittered and curved from Gunk's perspective, and everything human beings did transformed into hard angles and bossy lines that cut across anything in their way. Maybe that was why the fat one was so stupid and wasteful.

Gunk stopped yelling at him, thinking that it might ruin the human's hunting luck. Gunk had learned this by following brown bears. If one of the real creatures spoke too loudly, whatever it was the bear was hunting would overhear and go to ground or disappear up into the mountain. It was bad for the bear and for Gunk, so he shut up and flew down the street to the wire high up on the intersection. He'd wait for the man. Humans were easy to follow because of their love of straight lines and hard edges. They always stayed on their paths, and you could always hop up ahead to the next intersection. It was sad in a way. Humans were even more predictable than the bears.

"Gunk! What? What? What?" Tawk called out to him from a low alder tree above his favorite garbage can.

Gunk said nothing. He tried to be invisible because he didn't really want to have to deal with Tawk while he was waiting for the fat human to kill something else.

"Hey Gunk! Hey Gunk! Hey Gunk!" Tawk came and settled next to him, causing the wire they were both on now to sway.

"Gunk! Gunk! Hey! Hey! Hey!" Tawk said. Tawk was one of the real creatures, but he was not exceptionally bright. "I heard there was a big dead thing somewhere down by the water shadows. Did you see it?"

"No," Gunk said, not taking his eyes off the fat man.

"I thought I could smell it, but I wasn't sure," Tawk

said, then he followed Gunk's gaze, knowing that he was watching something important.

"Does that fat man have something . . ."

"Listen, Tawk," Gunk cut him off quickly and pointed with his beak back toward town, "there is music in the big building. Someone playing piano. It's really quite lovely. I just heard it. You should go and listen."

"Really?" Tawk said, standing alert as if the music was happening right then, right now. "Big building, you say?" And before Gunk gave him an answer Tawk was away.

Real creatures love nothing so much as music. Tones rising and falling tickled a real creature as if those sounds contained the voices of all their relatives. When real creatures heard music they could barely think straight, so caught up were they in the flying tones. They loved music almost as if it were invisible food. In the summer the real creatures gathered near the back of the big building when the Dumpsters were full from the tourist lunches, and human beings played music inside with the doors open. Gunk didn't want to tell poor Tawk that it was only a school group listening to a recording of Glenn Gould playing the Goldberg variations. Tawk couldn't tell the difference between the Goldberg variations and a piece of cherry pie, but at least he wasn't distracting Gunk any longer.

Yes, real creatures love nothing so much as music . . .

unless it is some tasty dead thing ripening in the sun. When Gunk turned his attention back to the street, the fat man was gone. "Awww," said Gunk. Then he flew down into the street, to the stop sign where the streets crossed. There was no fat man. He flew to the top of the dead spruce behind the ball field. No luck. Then he flew to the buzzing electric pole near the hospital. Nothing.

Deer can disappear up inside a mountain, and river otters can turn themselves into water, but everybody knows human beings cannot disappear. They can walk into buildings or crawl inside noisy machines, but they never leave without a trace. So the fat man must be in one of the buildings back on the street where Gunk had been distracted by that stupid Tawk.

As he began gliding through the air, Gunk was feeling guilty about how he had treated Tawk. Tawk was kind of slow, and Gunk certainly didn't want to share the first few minutes of his dead thing with him, but Tawk was a real creature, after all, a real creature and a loyal friend. He would be sure to let Tawk know when he found the new dead thing. He would let him know after he had had a few minutes alone with it.

Gunk found the place he had last seen the fat man, and he landed in the middle of the sidewalk and began waddling down the street. Sometimes you had to get close to the ground and look carefully. "Hey!" he said softly, not wanting to be heard by any other real creature. "I'm looking for a fat man who smells like a dead thing. Anybody seen anything?"

The dog tied up in the muddy yard lifted his tired head and looked over. "Nope. Wasn't paying attention. Sorry." And he put his head back on top of his dirty paws.

"Me. I might have seen him," a skinny brown cat with scars running across her face said from under the sagging wooden stairs. "What's in it for me?" She watched Gunk with a steady gaze. Cats cannot be trusted unless you are certain you are out of their jumping range, or offering them something well within the realm of their own self-interest.

Gunk took two short hops backward. "He killed a human being just a bit ago, but he wasted it. I'm assuming he's a decent hunter and must be going to kill something again soon."

"And this means what to me?" The cat hunched low on all fours.

Gunk hopped up on the handrail of the porch. "When I find the new dead thing, I will tell you about it first. I'll tell you where to find it, and I'll give you five minutes before I tell the other real creatures."

"Ten minutes."

"Seven," Gunk said immediately, in a tone that betrayed just enough impatience. "And only if what you tell me turns out to be accurate."

The cat stretched and licked her front paw. "Fine," she said, "he went in the door across the street. Just a few minutes ago."

"Thank you," Gunk said, and he stood up straight to glide over.

"And . . ." the cat added, "someone else followed him in there." And she motioned with her flat nose to the automobile left running in the street.

Why hadn't he noticed it before? There was that weird hissing of voices coming from inside, and no one was sitting in it. The car had lights on top, and they were alternating blue and white. "Awww," Gunk said. He hoped he wasn't too late.

The doors, of course, were shut tight, and the windows were down. He could hear human beings talking through the windows. He walked straight over to the glass and knocked once. "Hey, Hey, Hey. Any dead thing in there is mine!" He couldn't believe that another human being was going to get to his prize first. The fat man was in there, he was sure. He walked stiffly to the window and craned his head as far as he could around the corner of the window frame. There was another man in the house. This man had a big leather belt and a bunch of jangly things hanging from it.

He had to get inside. Gunk looked around, and the very top window was open just a crack. Now, usually real creatures will not go anywhere there is not lots of sky, but this was an emergency, so he pushed through the crack and walked down to the edge of the stairs. He looked down and saw no one, so he risked flying down to the next stair landing. There he saw the fat man slumped in a chair and the other man with the creaky leather belt standing over him. The standing man was angry. The fat man had both hands on his lap. He had taken off his coat and it was resting just under his hands. It didn't look or smell like there was fresh blood anywhere. Gunk could make out the faint smell of the old dead thing this stupid, wasteful man had rolled into the ocean back under the wharf. It gave Gunk hope that there wasn't a new, lovely dead thing yet.

"Come on, Stan. It's a little hard for me to believe that you just found the money on the sidewalk," the standing man said.

"I don't care what you find hard to believe. It's the God's truth."

"Stan, you know you're not under arrest. I'm here in your own house to ask you to tell me the truth. It will go a lot easier for you if you do. It will go a lot easier for his family if we recover his body. Where did you put him, Stan. Please tell me."

"I have no idea what you're talking about, Officer."

"So that's your story then? You found the five hundred dollars you say he owed you lying on the sidewalk in front of his business?"

"It's not my story. It's the truth. Now I'm asking you again, either put me under arrest or leave."

"Well, Stan, I'm going to leave for a minute anyway. But I have to tell you I'm going to have a lot more questions."

"I ain't afraid of questions," the fat man said, still sitting in his chair, but with one of his hands now under the coat that was lying across his lap.

"Okay then, I'll be going," the standing man said, and he turned his back on the fat man with his one hand under the coat on his lap. Gunk noticed that the sitting man seemed a bit more relaxed, and that worried the hungry bird.

The standing man was almost out the door and Gunk could stand it no longer.

"Hey! Hey! Hey! Kill him. Kill him. Kill him," Gunk screamed from the top of the staircase.

The sound scared the fat man, and he jumped out of his chair with a gun in his hand.

"Drop it . . . NOW," someone yelled, and Stan looked for a long moment at Gunk on the stairs. He looked at him as if he recognized both him and what was coming next.

"Well somebody shoot, for crying out loud!" Gunk screamed, while the fat man turned with the gun still in his hand and two loud blasts came from the doorway. Blood spatter as lovely as summer-ripened raspberries sprayed across the room.

It wasn't until the smoke had cleared and the chiming in his head had stopped that Gunk realized that there was music playing. The police officer pressed his hand down into the fat man's throat and shook his head slowly back and forth. All Gunk could hear was the sound of a cello. The great fat man had been listening to Pablo Casals playing one of the Gamba Sonatas, and when the police officer left the room Gunk found himself quite alone with the corpse of this wonderfully abundant human being. It was nearly perfect. He was dimly aware of the sirens and footsteps outside, but Gunk didn't care, even if he couldn't see the sky or hear the treacherous cat padding down the stairs for her payoff.

"Lovely, lovely," he said to himself, and as the sonata came to rest he waddled over to the dead man's open eye and just before plucking it out he added one more time: "lovely."

the PRICE

ANNE BISHOP

"Well, shit, sugar. Someone had a party and didn't invite me." And it was the kind of party I used to like. Nasty.

And yet, as I stood in the doorway, looking at what had been a nicely decorated sitting room, I felt edgy, uneasy. There's no law against murder among the Blood, and if I'd come upon a room like this when I lived in the Realm of Terreille, I wouldn't have thought twice about it. But in the Realm of Kaeleer, the Blood still live by the Old Ways, and the whole dance of Protocol and power usually works to keep confrontations from becoming fatal.

So what happened last night that ended with three men being hacked to pieces, resulting in a room now redecorated in a blood-and-gore motif?

And why did I think *hacked?* Using Craft and the

power that makes the Blood who and what we are, a person could do just as much damage to a human body. But something in the room whispered to me that this was . . . not personal, exactly, but definitely a hands-on killing. There was a lingering sense of fury and hatred here.

I know those feelings well, and my past contained rooms just as messy. But there was something else here that I almost recognized but couldn't quite name.

Of course, that could have been nothing more than annoyance with myself for being at the scene. If I'd stayed home this morning, I would have been tucking into breakfast right now. But I'd gone for a walk and ended up at this establishment because they serve a fine breakfast—and because this place was the closest thing to a Red Moon house in Kaeleer. So I'd come here to take a look at my past, which had contributed to my recently failed romance.

The Blood have a saying: Everything has a price. The price for my first attempt at a physical relationship with a man where money didn't change hands was a bruised heart. Funny how the heart gets bruised when someone tells you you're not what he wants—even when you already know he's not what you want either.

But there's nothing like a bit of slaughter to take a person's mind off her own problems.

Using Craft, I stepped up on air so that I was standing a handspan above the carpet. I walked into the room. Three male bodies were splattered over the carpet, the walls, the furniture, and the painted screen that turned one corner of the room into a private area. I assumed there were only three because I found three left hands—and I found other body parts in triplicate.

"Lady Surreal?"

As I turned toward the doorway, I lowered my right hand and called in my favorite stiletto, using Craft to keep it sight shielded so it wouldn't be obvious I had a weapon ready. A moment later, when I recognized the man in the doorway, I vanished the stiletto.

"Prince Rainier."

Rainier was an Opal-Jeweled Warlord Prince from Dharo, another Territory in Kaeleer. I'd seen him a few weeks ago at a party here in Amdarh and, more recently, enjoyed dancing with him at a family wedding. I'd also noticed him in the dining room this morning, reading a book while he ate breakfast. A fine-looking man with a dancer's build, fair skin, dreamy green eyes, and a mane of brown hair, he stood out in Dhemlan's capital city, where the residents had the common coloring of light-brown skin, black hair, and gold eyes. Which was, actually, the common coloring of all three of the long-lived races.

Being half-Hayllian, I had the black hair and light-brown skin, but my eyes were gold-green and my ears came to delicate points—the legacy of my mother's people. I was also a Gray-Jeweled witch, so my power was darker and deeper than his. That didn't mean I could afford to be careless. Warlord Princes were natural predators and also very protective. That should have been a contradiction, but it wasn't; it just made them extremely lethal.

"Why did they ask you to see this?" Rainier said as he looked behind the painted screen. He paled, and I didn't imagine his breakfast was sitting well, but when he moved away from the screen, he studied the room with a hunter's eyes.

"Maybe because I wear the Gray," I replied, shrugging. Or maybe because the owners of this place had heard a few things about me and wanted my professional opinion. "And you?"

Grief tightened his face. "I had an appointment here after breakfast."

Here. Not just in this establishment, but *here*. "You knew them."

"If these are the same young men who reserved this room, then, yes, I knew them."

"What were they doing?"

"A weekly lesson. I was hired as a secondary instructor."

It was better not to ask about that while I was still in this room.

"They didn't deserve this," Rainier said quietly.

"Are you sure?"

"Yes, I'm sure." His voice sharpened. Everything about him sharpened.

I nodded and looked around again. He knew these men; I didn't. "So. Three men were killed for no apparent reason. If there wasn't a reason, there wasn't a payment. Which means no one hired a professional to get rid of them."

"A professional? You mean an assassin? How do you know it wasn't?"

"Because I am a professional. Was a professional." I shrugged. "There's not much call for assassins in Kaeleer."

"I'd heard—" He fumbled, belatedly remembering that I was related to the most powerful Warlord Princes in the Realm of Kaeleer.

"That I was a whore? I was that, too. You could say one career led to the other."

Wariness in his eyes now.

"I didn't kill them," I said. "If I had, I would have done a better job of it. Let's go. There's nothing more to do here."

He was under no obligation to go with me, but he followed me out of the room, stayed with me while I talked to the owners, and made suggestions about who they should talk to in the Queen of Amdarh's court to report this incident.

When I left the building, he went with me, walking on my left—a signal to everyone who saw us that I was the dominant party. As a Warlord Prince, he belonged to a higher caste than I, a mere witch, did. But my Gray Jewels outranked his Opal. In the knife-edged game of power the Blood play on a daily basis, which of us held the high card in terms of authority could change in the blink of an eye.

I turned a corner, heading away from the theater district with its playhouses and music halls. Those streets would be quiet at this time of day. I wanted the bustle of people and the distraction of shops.

Even this early in the morning, there were plenty of people in the shop district, plenty of faces . . .

"We didn't find their heads."

"They were behind the screen," Rainier replied grimly.

"Damn. It might have helped to see what they'd looked like." Might have given me a clue about why the murder had happened. Of course, I could have used a clue about why I was still chewing over this. I'd made a good living killing men. I should have been able to shrug these deaths off. I couldn't—because something just wasn't right about the kills.

"It wouldn't have helped," Rainier said. "Their faces were burned past recognition." He paused, then added, "Witchfire."

Knowing how fiercely witchfire can burn, I swallowed hard, glad I hadn't managed to get breakfast. Did make me reassess my companion's nerves, though. He'd looked at those faces and had kept *his* breakfast down.

"So, what kind of lessons were they getting?" Maybe knowing why the men had been in that room would help me figure out why they died.

"Sex," Rainier replied.

I stopped walking. People flowed around us. "How many women?" I could feel my blood chilling, feel the old rage rising.

He looked puzzled. "One."

Some of those messy rooms in my past had occurred when the males had thought the odds were in their favor for rough sex without the female's consent. They learned how deep and pure female rage can be. Of course, they died learning it, so the lesson didn't do them much good.

Rainier shook his head. "It's instruction, Surreal. Frank discussion about what a woman wants from a lover. Some demonstration."

"Demonstration." Maybe the little bastards had gotten exactly what they deserved.

Rainier took my left hand in his right and lifted it, his eyes never leaving mine. His lips, warm and soft, surrounded one knuckle. The tip of his tongue stroked my skin.

A sweet, unexpected feeling flowed through me, banishing anger.

He released my hand, and said quietly, "Demonstration."

Hell's fire, Mother Night, and may the Darkness be merciful. He must have been a dedicated student when he'd been learning those lessons. I had to clear my throat in order to get my voice back. "So." I couldn't think of anything else to say.

His smile was pure male as he took my arm and started walking again.

"Understanding what pleases is just as important in a man's personal life as it is if he serves in a court," Rainier said.

Hard to argue, since that little demonstration made me feel deliciously female and desirable. But it also plucked at the edgy, uneasy feeling I'd had in the room, so I looked for something else to talk about—and stopped walking half a block from a corner.

"What's he doing?" The boy was shepherding females from one side of the street to the other. That was obvious. Why he was doing it wasn't.

"Who?" Rainier looked around, then grinned. "Oh. He's training. Since there are two boys about the same age at the other corners, their instructor is probably sitting in that coffee shop across the street, keeping an eye on them."

Things were different in Kaeleer, but . . . "You *train* males to be a pain in the ass?"

"We train them to serve."

"That's what I said." My comment annoyed him. I didn't care. If he spent one day on the receiving end of that kind of stubborn attention, he'd have a totally different opinion about a male's right to serve.

Then my stomach growled.

Rainier studied me. "Would you like to go to the coffee shop? They don't serve meals there, but they do have baked goods."

"Fine." I stepped away from him. "I'll meet you there."

"Surreal."

I heard the warning in his voice, but I ignored it and walked to the corner. I'd noticed the boy stepped aside if a woman already had a male escort, and I was curious.

A cute puppy, all bright-eyed and eager. A little Yellow-Jeweled Warlord. A miniature man. His eyes widened when he saw my Gray Jewel, but he took a deep breath and smiled.

"May I be of service, Lady?" he asked.

Protocol. Specific phrases that had specific answers. Protocol balanced power, giving the weaker among the Blood a safe way to deal with the stronger.

"I'm going to the coffee shop across the street," I replied.

"Then I will escort you, if it pleases you."

I held out my left hand. He slipped his right hand beneath it, checked the street to make sure no horse-drawn carriages or Craft-driven coaches were approaching the crossing, then led me across the street.

"Thank you, Warlord," I said when I had been safely delivered to the door of the coffee shop.

"It was my pleasure, Lady."

And it was. I could see it in his eyes. There would be bitches who would bruise his ego, dim the pleasure in those eyes. There would be many, many more witches who would gently reinforce his training, confirming his place in the world as a man worthy of courtesy and consideration, a man valued for who and what he was.

While I waited for Rainier to join me, I watched the boy escort two young witches across the side street. He continued up the street with them past three shops before one of the women murmured something—obviously a reminder that his duty was completed, since he stopped and turned back. As he passed the alley between two of the buildings, he hesitated, took a step closer toward that shadowy place that would put him out of sight.

Edgy. Uneasy.

He was almost at the mouth of the alley.

Something wrong.

Using Craft to enhance my voice, I bellowed, "Warlord! Here! *Now!*"

As I ran across the street, I began to appreciate the value of training. The boy didn't hesitate. He spun at the sound of my voice and ran away from the alley just as *something* reached out to grab him. Something sight shielded. I couldn't *see* it, and yet I *could* see it, like an afterimage that remains on your eyelids after you close your eyes. A robed arm. A gloved hand. Reaching for the boy.

As he ran past me, I grabbed a fistful of his shirt and

swung him behind me, throwing a Gray shield around both of us at the same time I called in a hunting knife—a big knife with a wickedly honed blade. I probed the alley with my psychic senses. No one there anymore, but I picked up a hint of the same fury and hatred that I'd sensed in that room.

"Stay here." I released the boy but kept a Gray shield around him as I moved toward the alley. Into the alley.

Female. I was certain of that now. Definitely a witch skilled in her Craft.

"Everything has a price, bitch," I said softly, even though I knew she was gone. "Maybe you had a reason to go after the men—or thought you did. But not the boy. Not a child. Everything has a price—and when I catch up to you, and I will, I'll show you how to paint the walls in blood."

"Surreal?"

A light psychic touch, full of strength and temper. Rainier at the mouth of the alley, guarding my back.

I backed out of the alley, staying alert in case the bitch was skilled enough to hide her presence. I didn't turn away until Rainier's fingers brushed my shoulder. As I turned to face the street, I got my next lesson in how well Blood males are trained in Kaeleer.

There were hard-eyed, grim-faced men everywhere. A female had yelled on a public street. It didn't matter that it had been a command and not a cry of fear or distress. A female had yelled—and they'd responded.

They'd poured out of the shops, out of the carriages and coaches. Whatever had upset the female was going to be fixed. *Now.*

Which explained why assassins weren't needed in Kaeleer.

Protocol was the only tool I had—especially since the Warlord Prince standing beside me had risen to the killing edge to become a living weapon.

Using Craft again to enhance my voice, I said, "Thank you for your attention, gentlemen. There is nothing more to be done here." I raised the hunting knife, so the men who could see me couldn't fail to notice it. Then I vanished it and lowered my hand.

I waited, hardly daring to breathe until I saw the men in front of me relax. Communication on psychic threads rippled over the street. Men returned to their carriages and coaches, to the shops or interrupted meals.

I heard Rainier release a slow breath as he worked to step back from the killing edge.

When the boy's instructor joined us, I released the Gray shield I had put around the little Warlord. The puppy couldn't tell us more than a lady had called to him, asking for help. He'd hesitated because he couldn't see her, and she'd sounded . . . strange.

She hadn't been able to mask her hatred. It must have bled into her voice. And it was going to piss her off that her prey had escaped. Which meant another man was going to die.

After the instructor bundled his students into a carriage and drove away, Rainier wrapped a hand around my arm.

"You need something to eat," he growled.

I did, but I heard "I'm going to fuss over you" in that growl, and I really didn't want to be fussed over. "Don't worry about it, sugar. I can—"

His fingers tightened. "Lady, let me serve or point me toward something I can kill."

Shit shit shit. Warlord Princes rose to the killing edge in a heartbeat, but they couldn't always come back from it on their own. You either pointed them to a killing field or gave them something else to focus on—which usually meant a female they could fuss over and look after for a while.

"I could use a meal." I shook off his hand, saw the temper in his eyes chill, and immediately linked my arm through his to give him the contact he needed. We walked for several minutes before he chose a dining house that had a small courtyard in the back for guests who wanted to eat outdoors.

I don't know what passed between Rainier and the Warlord waiting on the tables in the courtyard. We weren't asked what we wanted to eat—I wasn't, anyway—but I'd barely settled in my chair when coffee, glasses of red wine, and a basket of bread appeared on the table. That was swiftly followed by bowls of greens that were delicately dressed, thick steaks, vegetables, and some kind of casserole made of potatoes, onions, and sausage. The meal lasted long enough for the wild look to fade in Rainier's eyes—and for me to reach a few conclusions.

I leaned back in my chair. "There's a killer out there." Which pretty much described anyone who was Blood, but I was making a distinction between the potential in all of us and someone using that potential.

Temper flared in Rainier's eyes. "There was no reason to go for that boy."

"Sugar, I don't think reason has much to do with this."

He frowned. "You think this killer is a witch who has slipped into the Twisted Kingdom?"

I didn't think she was insane in the way he meant, but hate can be its own kind of madness.

He sighed. "Then we have to find her and give her what help we can."

"No, we have to find her and kill her."

"But—"

"No." I studied him. "You didn't sense anything in that room or in the alley, did you?"

He shook his head.

"I did. Maybe it's because I'm . . . familiar . . . with what I felt that I was able to sense it at all."

Rainier swirled the wine left in his glass. "What kind of men did you kill, Surreal?"

"The ones who broke witches, killed witches, tortured

witches, shattered their lives." I drained my glass. "The ones who preyed on children."

"You became an assassin to pay them back for . . . ?"

"My mother. And for me." I set my glass on the table. "Are you coming with me, Rainier?"

"Where are you going?"

"Hunting."

He studied me for a long moment before he nodded. "I'm with you."

I collapsed on a bench in one of the little parks that were sprinkled throughout Amdarh. Even in the city's busy shop district, you couldn't go more than two blocks without finding a plot of green that provided shade or a dazzle of color from flowers or the soothing trickle of a fountain.

"The bitch is good, I'll give her that," I said, when Rainier joined me on the bench. We'd been hunting for two days—and two more men had died. One was an old man tending a shop for a friend who was ill. The other was a young Warlord who had shielded himself long enough to send a warning on a psychic thread. Despite men converging on the spot from all directions, the witch had still managed to slip past them.

"Here." Rainier gave me a glass bowl and a spoon he'd gotten from a food stand nestled in one corner of the park.

"What is it?" I poked the spoon into the shaved ice in my bowl.

"Flavored ice," he said as he dug into his own bowl.

I tried some. The ice, flavored with berry juice, was just the refreshment I needed after hours of prowling the streets. Halfway through, I started poking at the treat, my pleasure in it gone. Edgy. Uneasy. Worried about something I didn't want to put into words.

I sighed. "We've been hunting for two days, and we don't know any more than we did when this started."

"You know more than you think," said a deep voice—heavy silk with a husky undertone of sex.

Rainier tensed, instantly wary. I looked over at the black-haired, golden-eyed man standing near the bench. I hadn't seen him approach, hadn't heard him, hadn't sensed his presence until he wanted it felt.

If you wanted to look at a prime example of a beautiful predator, Daemon Sadi was it. If you wanted to survive the encounter, looking was all you did.

Daemon settled on the bench with the feline grace that, combined with that body and face, made a woman's pulse spike—even when the woman knew what could happen to her if the Sadist became annoyed. He was a Black-Jeweled Warlord Prince, the most powerful male in Kaeleer. He was also, may the Darkness help me, family.

"You're supposed to be on your honeymoon," I said.

"We are. Jaenelle and I came back to Amdarh for a

day to visit the bookshops and pick up a few supplies before going to the cottage in Ebon Rih." He paused, and his eyes got that sleepy look that always scared the shit out of me. "That was the intention anyway." He looked at Rainier. "Surreal and I have a few things to discuss. Why don't you take a walk?"

"Lady Surreal and I are working together," Rainier replied.

I could have smacked Rainier for the subtle challenge in his voice. He knew better than that.

"Fine," Daemon said—and he smiled.

Rainier paled. He excused himself and retreated. Not far. That Warlord Prince temperament wouldn't let him back down all the way. So he settled on another bench where he could keep me in sight.

"Are you going to share that?" Daemon asked.

I handed over the bowl and spoon. "I thought you liked Rainier."

"I do. What does that have to do with anything?" Daemon took a spoonful of flavored ice before handing it back to me. "Mm. That is good."

"We *are* working together."

"Whatever you tell him is your business." He studied the park and waited.

"All right," I finally said. "What do we know? There's no reason for the killings."

"Just because you don't know what it is doesn't mean

there isn't one," Daemon said, his tone a mild scold. "Consider the predator instead of the prey. She's an opportunistic killer. She's not hunting for a particular man or a particular kind of man. She strikes when she can, where she can. She attacks males who wear lighter Jewels, so the odds are she wears at least the Opal Jewel."

"But not a Jewel that's close in strength to the Gray," I murmured. "Her sight shield couldn't hide her from me completely the one time I spotted her."

Daemon nodded. "So you know you can take her without getting hurt unless you're careless. She also chooses males who aren't prepared to defend themselves, which indicates she wants the thrill of spilling blood without the risk of their fighting back."

I huffed in frustration. "You arrived in Amdarh today. How did you figure all this out so fast?"

He laughed softly. "I've been playing this game a lot longer than you have. Besides, Lady Zhara and I had a chat this morning before I came looking for you, and she gave me all the information she had about the killings."

A few weeks ago, the witches in Amdarh got their first taste of what it's like to dance with the Sadist. After that unfortunate incident, I bet Zhara, the Queen of Amdarh, was thrilled to have a chat with Daemon.

Then he looked at me. "Are you worried that you'll find a mirror when you find her?"

Damn him. He knew.

"She's not a mirror, Surreal. You never made a kill that wasn't deserved. You took pleasure from the killing, but you never killed for pleasure. There's a difference."

"You don't know all the kills were deserved."

He just looked at me.

We've known each other for centuries. I was a child when I met him, when he helped my mother and me. I'll never know how closely he kept track of me after I began my career with a knife, but now I had no doubt, none at all, that if I'd become a killer in the same way the witch we hunted was, I wouldn't be sitting here. He would have destroyed me long ago. I shouldn't have felt relieved knowing that, but I did.

"How do we find this bitch, Sadi?"

"If you can't find the predator, give the predator a reason to find you. Provide irresistible bait." His smile was gentle and vicious. "The prey that seems the sweetest is always the one that got away."

I crouched in front of the little Yellow-Jeweled Warlord. The miniature man. My irresistible bait. "You know what to do?"

"Yes, Lady," he said, his voice so subdued I could barely hear him.

"I'll be close by."

He nodded. "If she cuts me, will it hurt?"

I looked toward the table tucked in the back corner of

the coffee shop. Jaenelle Angelline looked back at me, her sapphire eyes full of something feral and dark.

"Yes," Jaenelle said gently, "it will hurt." She pointed to the wooden frame that held the web of illusions she'd created to play out this game. "By itself, the illusion I've made of you will fool the eye, but in order to fool the hand when someone touches it, it has to be linked to you. While nothing will actually happen to *you,* you will feel whatever happens to it."

The little Warlord looked into those sapphire eyes. Whatever he found there gave him what he needed. "I will serve to the best of my ability."

Jaenelle smiled. "I know."

I gave the little Warlord one last, long look. He had a loose button on his jacket. It hadn't been loose yesterday evening when the boy and his instructor came to the family town house so that Jaenelle could build the web of illusions.

Some of the tension inside me eased. It was such a little detail, but I'd be able to use it to tell when the switch was made and the illusion took the boy's place out on the street.

We took our positions. Daemon stayed in the coffee shop with Jaenelle. The boy's instructor took his usual place at a window table. Rainier and I sight shielded before leaving the shop. He crossed the main street to tuck into a doorway near that corner. I crossed the side street, settling into a doorway just beyond the alley. The boy went to the corner to perform escort duties, leading ladies across the street.

We watched, waited. So far, all the killings had taken place in this part of the city, but there was no guarantee the bitch wouldn't start hunting somewhere else, no guarantee she'd come close enough to spot the bait.

An hour passed. We watched. Waited. I tensed every time a lone female approached the corner, every time the boy offered his hand as an escort—and breathed a sigh of relief every time he stepped into the coffee shop to receive advice from his instructor. But every time the small figure left the coffee shop, it was still wearing a jacket with a loose button.

I gritted my teeth. I trusted Jaenelle, and I could understand her delaying as long as possible before making the switch in case someone *could* recognize the illusion for what it was. But, Hell's fire, why was she waiting so long?

We were coming up on the two-hour mark, which would end the training session, when something drifted toward me on the air. Something that made me edgy, uneasy. I scanned the people going about their business, cursing when I lost sight of the boy as a carriage passed by. Then I saw him again. And I saw her. She came from Dhemlan, so there was nothing about her looks that would attract attention, but I knew it was she.

They crossed the side street on the opposite side from me. I held my breath and hoped Jaenelle could still make the switch from boy to illusion before the rest of this game was played out.

The witch said something to him that made him smile, brought out that bright-eyed puppy eagerness to please.

They crossed the main street. He stayed at the corner. She continued up the street, toward the alley. Toward me.

She glanced at the alley, then stopped and cried out, "He's hurt! Mother Night, he's hurt!" She looked around frantically. "Help me, Warlord. Help me. He's hurt!" She darted into the alley.

The boy stayed true to his training. A female had cried for help. He ran into the alley after her.

And I saw the loose button on his jacket.

I heard his panicked cry as I rushed into the alley.

"Let him go, bitch," I snarled, calling in the hunting knife.

She whirled to face me, the boy held against her, a knife as mean as mine pressed against his neck.

Her eyes danced with the glee of the kill. The smile she gave me was malignant.

"Let him go," I said again. I saw terror in the boy's gold eyes, but I had to play out the game—and hope.

"There's no law against murder." She pressed the blade against the boy's neck hard enough to cut the skin. Blood trickled from the wound.

"True. But it's also not condoned when there's no reason."

"He's male. That's reason enough." She pouted. "You're female. You should be on my side."

When the sun shines in Hell, bitch. "Let him go."

"All right."

She ripped the knife across the boy's neck and throat. Blood sprayed the alley walls. Sprayed her. Sprayed me.

I just stood there, frozen by the feel of warm blood on my face. *We failed.*

"Why?" Before I finished with her, I was going to get an answer. "Tell me why you killed those men, killed this boy."

The alley was suddenly filled with hatred, with fury . . . and bitter hurt. *That* was the other thing I'd sensed in that first room but couldn't quite recognize.

I knew that feeling, too. Didn't matter. Not with that boy's blood on me. "What happened, sugar? Did your lover walk away after taking all he could stomach from you?"

Her fury drowned out the bitter hurt. "He didn't walk far." She pouted. "But the males in the village were so angry about him dying like that my aunt commanded that I stay in Amdarh for a while. They exiled me, a Queen's niece, from my own village because of that bastard."

"That doesn't explain killing the men here." Something wasn't right. Broken heart or not, something wasn't right.

"They're all the same!" she shouted. "They make you feel special until the contract ends, then they walk away."

"The man you killed was a consort under contract?" No wonder the men in the village were pissed off. If he'd fulfilled his contract, a consort had the right to walk away without repercussions.

"He was better than the other ones I've had, and I wanted to renew the contract. But he refused. The bastard started packing his things the minute after the contract ended."

"Guess he just didn't want to spend another year in bed with a snotty little bitch." I studied her. She wasn't nursing a bruised heart. A bruised ego, maybe, but not a bruised heart.

That malicious gleam filled her eyes again. At that moment, I hated her with everything in me.

"I can do anything I want with a male," she said. "No male is going to make me feel special, then walk away. Never again. And there's nothing you can do about it."

"Now that's where you're wrong." I smiled. "As you pointed out, there's no law against murder."

Before she even thought to run, I created a Gray shield bubble around her, trapping her.

"Everything has a price," I said softly. "I'm calling in the debt for the men you killed here in Amdarh—and the boy." Especially the boy. "You like splattering the walls with blood and gore, sugar? Well, now's your chance."

I gave her one moment to realize what was going to happen. Then I fed all of my own fury into my Gray Jewels as I unleashed their stored power and slammed it into her. Her body exploded, a storm of red mist and white bits of bone swirling in a Gray bubble. I thrust a rapier of Gray into the mind I could still sense in that mist, breaking her power, finishing the kill. There would be no ghost or demon-dead to haunt this alley.

Then it was done. Debt paid. But the price for stopping that bitch was much, much too high.

"Surreal."

Grief tightened my throat, but I obeyed the command in that deep voice and walked to the mouth of the alley . . . where Daemon waited.

"You played the game well," he said. "Why didn't you splatter her over the walls? You wanted to."

"After what she'd done, it didn't seem fair to have men spend a couple of days scrubbing her off the bricks."

He looked into the alley. "Leave the bubble. I'll take care of it later."

I nodded, feeling heartsick. "All of this because males are trained to serve, to please."

"Hardly," Daemon replied dryly. "That was her excuse. I've seen her kind too many times over the years. She liked inflicting pain, and she liked having control over the person while she did it. She didn't kill any of those men because they were trained to serve; she killed them because they had the right to walk away from someone who wanted to hurt them."

He was right. I knew he was right, but . . . "I guess I should—" I looked down at my clothes.

No blood.

I turned and looked into the alley. No blood sprayed on the walls. No small body.

"No one can create an illusion the way Jaenelle can," Daemon said softly.

No small body in the alley. "When . . . ?"

"She made the switch the first time the boy came back into the coffee shop for instructions. She needed him on the street just long enough to hone the details in the illusion."

Jaenelle would pay attention to the details—right down to a loose button on a jacket. Which meant I'd watched an illusion for most of those two hours and never known the difference.

Relief made me dizzy, weak. Daemon put his arm around my shoulders and led me to the coffee shop. Rainier entered the shop just behind us.

The little Warlord sat on a chair at the back of the shop. He looked shaken, but he was safe. Whole. Alive.

"Hmm," Jaenelle said as she gently probed the boy's neck. "Swallow now. Does that feel sore?"

"A little," the boy replied.

Caught by those sapphire eyes, he didn't look shaken anymore. A bit dazzled, but not shaken. Jaenelle had that effect on males.

"Hmm," Jaenelle said again. "There's no damage, no injury. But I think a bit of medicinal care is still required."

The boy's eyes widened. "Medicine?"

I guess bravery only goes so far.

"Mm. A dish of flavored ice twice a day for the next three days will take care of the soreness." Jaenelle's eyes sparkled with laughter. "Can you handle that?"

The boy grinned. "Yes, Lady." He bounced off the chair and came over to stand next to Rainier and me.

"Now," Daemon said, slipping a hand around Jaenelle's arm to coax her to her feet. "Since everything is settled, my Lady and I will take care of our shopping and resume our honeymoon."

"Daemon is going to teach me how to cook," Jaenelle said, smiling at him.

"Oh, how"—*brave of Daemon*—"nice," I replied.

Everything has a price. I wasn't sure who was paying whom with the kiss that followed, but it was certainly a demonstration.

After watching for a few seconds, the boy tugged on Rainier's sleeve. "Am I going to learn how to do that?"

Rainier grinned. I closed my eyes.

Daemon broke the kiss and chuckled as he led his Lady out of the coffee shop.

Within a few minutes, the boy and his instructor were gone as well.

"Well," Rainier said. "It's been interesting, Lady Surreal."

"That it has, Prince Rainier."

He hesitated. "What are you doing this evening?"

Soaking in a deep tub of hot water. Sleeping. "Why?"

"Would you like to go dancing?"

We would never be lovers. Just then, that was a point in his favor since I wasn't ready to spend time with a man who wanted to be a lover. But maybe we could have some fun together as friends.

I smiled at him. "Yes," I said, "I'd love to go dancing."

fairy dust

CHARLAINE HARRIS

I hate it when fairies come into the bar. They don't tip you worth a toot—not because they're stingy, but because they just forget. Take Claudine, the fairy who was walking in the door. Six feet tall, long black hair, gorgeous; Claudine seemed to have no shortage of cash or clothing (and she entranced men the way a watermelon draws flies). But Claudine hardly ever remembered to leave you even a dollar. And if it's lunchtime, you have to take the bowl of lemon slices off the table. Fairies are allergic to lemons and limes, like vamps are allergic to silver and garlic.

That spring night when Claudine came in I was in a bad mood already. I was angry with my ex-boyfriend, Bill Compton, a.k.a. Vampire Bill; my brother Jason had once again postponed helping me shift an armoire; and I'd gotten my property tax notice in the mail.

So when Claudine sat at one of my tables, I stalked over to her with no very happy feelings.

"No vamps around?" she asked straight away. "Even Bill?"

Vamps like fairies the way dogs like bones: great toys, good food. "Not tonight," I said. "Bill's down in New Orleans. I'm picking up his mail for him." Just call me sucker.

Claudine relaxed. "Dearest Sookie," she said.

"You want what?"

"Oh, one of those nasty beers, I guess," she said, making a face. Claudine didn't really like to drink, though she did like bars. Like most fairies, she loved attention and admiration: My boss Sam said that was a fairy characteristic.

I brought her the beer. "You got a minute?" she asked. I frowned. Claudine didn't look as cheerful as usual.

"Just." The table by the door was hooting and hollering at me.

"I have a job for you."

Though it called for dealing with Claudine, whom I liked but didn't trust, I was interested. I sure needed some cash. "What do you need me to do?"

"I need you to come listen to some humans."

"Are these humans willing?"

Claudine gave me innocent eyes. "What do you mean, Precious?"

I hated this song and dance. "Do they want to be, ah, listened to?"

"They're guests of my brother, Claude."

I hadn't known Claudine had a brother. I don't know much about fairies; Claudine was the only one I'd met. If she was typical, I wasn't sure how the race had survived eradication. I wouldn't have thought northern Louisiana was very hospitable toward beings of the fairy persuasion, anyway. This part of the state is largely rural, very Bible Belt. My small town of Bon Temps, barely big enough to have its own Wal-Mart, didn't even see a vampire for two years after they'd announced their existence and their intention to live peaceably amongst us. Maybe that delay was good, since local folks had had a chance to get used to the idea by the time Bill showed up.

But I had a feeling that this PC vamp tolerance would vanish if my fellow townsfolk knew about Weres, and shifters, and fairies. And who knows what all else.

"Okay, Claudine, when?" The rowdy table was hooting, "Crazy Sookie! Crazy Sookie!" People only did that when they'd had too much to drink. I was used to it, but it still hurt.

"When do you get off tonight?"

We fixed it that Claudine would pick me up at my house fifteen minutes after I got off work. She left without finishing her beer. Or tipping.

My boss, Sam Merlotte, nodded a head toward the door she'd just exited. "What'd the fairy want?" Sam's a shifter, himself.

"She needs me to do a job for her."

"Where?"

"Wherever she lives, I guess. She has a brother, did you know?"

"Want me to come with you?" Sam is a friend, the kind of friend you sometimes have fantasies about. X-rated.

"Thanks, but I think I can handle Claudine."

"You haven't met the brother."

"I'll be okay."

I'm used to being up at night, not only because I'm a barmaid, but also because I had dated Bill for a long time. When Claudine picked me up at my old house in the woods, I'd had time to change from my Merlotte's outfit into some black jeans and a sage green twin set (JC Penney's on sale), since the night was chilly. I'd let my hair down from its ponytail.

"You should wear blue instead of green," Claudine said, "to go with your eyes."

"Thanks for the fashion tip."

"You're welcome." Claudine sounded happy to share her style sense with me. But her smile, usually so radiant, seemed tinged with sadness.

"What do you want me to find out from these people?" I asked.

"We'll talk about it when we get there," she said, and after that she wouldn't tell me anything else as we drove east. Ordinarily Claudine babbles. I was beginning to feel it wasn't smart of me to have accepted this job.

Claudine and her brother lived in a big ranch-style house in suburban Monroe, a town that not only had a Wal-Mart, but a whole mall. She knocked on the front door in a pattern. After a minute, the door opened. My eyes widened. Claudine hadn't mentioned that her brother was her twin.

If Claude had put on his sister's clothes, he could have passed for her; it was eerie. His hair was shorter, but not by a lot; he had it pulled back to the nape of his neck, but his ears were covered. His shoulders were broader, but I couldn't see a trace of a beard, even this late at night. Maybe male fairies don't have body hair? Claude looked like a Calvin Klein underwear model; in fact, if the designer had been there, he'd have signed the twins on the spot, and there'd have been drool all over the contract.

He stepped back to let us enter. "This is the one?" he said to Claudine.

She nodded. "Sookie, my brother Claude."

"A pleasure," I said. I extended my hand. With some surprise, he took it and shook. He looked at his sister. "She's a trusting one."

"Humans," Claudine said, and shrugged.

Claude led me through a very conventional living

room, down a paneled hall to the family room. A man was sitting in a chair, because he had no choice. He was tied to it with what looked like nylon cord. He was a small man, buff, blond, and brown-eyed. He looked about my age, twenty-six.

"Hey," I said, not liking the squeak in my voice, "why is that man tied?"

"Otherwise, he'd run away," Claude said, surprised.

I covered my face with my hands for a second. "Listen, you two, I don't mind looking at this guy if he's done something wrong, or if you want to eliminate him as a suspect in a crime committed against you. But if you just want to find out if he really loves you, or something silly like that. . . . What's your purpose?"

"We think he killed our triplet, Claudia."

I almost said, "There were three of you?" then realized that wasn't the most important part of the sentence.

"You think he murdered your sister."

Claudine and Claude nodded in unison. "Tonight," Claude said.

"Okey-dokey," I muttered, and bent over the blond. "I'm taking the gag off."

They looked unhappy, but I slid the handkerchief down to his neck. The young man said, "I didn't do it."

"Good. Do you know what I am?"

"No. You're not a thing like them, are you?"

I don't know what he thought Claude and Claudine were, what little otherworldly attribute they'd sprung on him. I lifted my hair to show him that my ears were round, not pointed, but he still looked dissatisfied.

"Not a vamp?" he asked.

Showed him my teeth. The canines only extend when vamps are excited by blood, battle, or sex, but they're noticeably sharp even when they're retracted. My canines are quite normal.

"I'm just a regular human," I said. "Well, that's not quite true. I can read your thoughts."

He looked terrified.

"What are you scared for? If you didn't kill anybody, you have nothing to fear." I made my voice warm, like butter melting on corn on the cob.

"What will they do to me? What if you make a mistake and tell them I did it, what are they gonna do?"

Good question. I looked up at the two.

"We'll kill him and eat him," Claudine said, with a ravishing smile. When the blond man looked from her to Claude, his eyes wide with terror, she winked at me.

For all I knew, Claudine might be serious. I couldn't remember if I'd ever seen her eat or not. We were treading on dangerous ground. I try to support my own race when I can. Or at least get 'em out of situations alive.

I should have accepted Sam's offer.

"Is this man the only suspect?" I asked the twins. (Should I call them twins? I wondered. It was more accurate to think of them as two-thirds of triplets. Nah. Too complicated.)

"No, we have another man in the kitchen," Claude said. "And a woman in the pantry."

Under other circumstances, I would've smiled. "Why are you sure Claudia is dead?"

"She came to us in spirit form and told us so." Claude looked surprised. "This is a death ritual for our race."

I sat back on my heels, trying to think of intelligent questions. "When this happens, does the spirit let you know any of the circumstances of the death?"

"No," Claudine said, shaking her head so her long black hair switched. "It's more like a final farewell."

"Have you found the body?"

They looked disgusted. "We fade," Claude explained, in a haughty way.

So much for examining the corpse.

"Can you tell me where Claudia was when she, ah, faded?" I asked. "The more I know, the better questions I can ask." Mind reading is not so simple. Asking the right questions is the key to eliciting the correct thought. The mouth can say anything. The head never lies. But if you don't ask the right question, the right thought won't pop up.

"Claudia and Claude are exotic dancers at Hooligans," Claudine said proudly, as if she was announcing they were on an Olympic team.

I'd never met strippers before, male or female. I found myself more than a little interested in seeing Claude strip, but I made myself focus on the deceased Claudia.

"So, Claudia worked last night?"

"She was scheduled to take the money at the door. It was ladies' night at Hooligans."

"Oh. Okay. So you were, ah, performing," I said to Claude.

"Yes. We do two shows on ladies' night. I was the Pirate."

I tried to suppress that mental image.

"And this man?" I tilted my head toward the blond, who was being very good about not pleading and begging.

"I'm a stripper, too," he said. "I was the Cop."

Okay. Just stuff that imagination in a box and sit on it.

"Your name is?"

"Barry Barber is my stage name. My real name is Ben Simpson."

"Barry Barber?" I was puzzled.

"I like to shave people."

I had a blank moment, then felt a red flush creep across my cheeks as I realized he didn't mean whiskery cheeks. Well, not facial cheeks. "And the other two people are?" I asked the twins.

"The woman in the pantry is Rita Child. She owns Hooligans," Claudine said. "And the man in the kitchen is Jeff Puckett. He's the bouncer."

"Why did you pick these three out of all the employees at Hooligans?"

"Because they had arguments with Claudia. She was a dynamic woman," Claude said seriously.

"Dynamic my ass," said Barry the Barber, proving that tact isn't a prerequisite for a stripping job. "That woman was hell on wheels."

"Her character isn't really important in determining who killed her," I pointed out, which shut him right up. "It just indicates why. Please go on," I said to Claude. "Where were the three of you? And where were the people you've held here?"

"Claudine was here, cooking supper for us. She works at Dillard's in Customer Service." She'd be great at that; her unrelenting cheer could pacify anyone. "As I said, Claudia was scheduled to take the cover charge at the door," Claude continued. "Barry and I were in both shows. Rita always puts the first show's take in the safe, so Claudia won't be sitting up there with a lot of cash. We've been robbed a couple of times. Jeff was mostly sitting behind Claudia, in a little booth right inside the main door."

"When did Claudia vanish?"

"Soon after the second show started. Rita says she got the first show's take from Claudia and took it back to her safe, and that Claudia was still sitting there when she left. But Rita hates Claudia, because Claudia was about to leave Hooligans for Foxes, and I was going with her."

"Foxes is another club?" Claude nodded. "Why were you leaving?"

"Better pay, larger dressing rooms."

"Okay, that would be Rita's motivation. What about Jeff's?"

"Jeff and I had a thing," Claude said. (My pirate ship fantasy sank.) "Claudia told me I had to break up with him, that I could do better."

"And you listened to her advice about your love life?"

"She was the oldest, by several minutes," he said simply. "But I lo—I am very fond of him."

"What about you, Barry?"

"She ruined my act," Barry said sullenly.

"How'd she do that?"

"She yelled, 'Too bad your nightstick's not bigger!' as I was finishing up."

It seemed that Claudia had been determined to die.

"Okay," I said, marshaling my plan of action. I knelt before Barry. I laid my hand on his arm, and he twitched. "How old are you?"

"Twenty-five," he said, but his mind provided me with a different answer.

"That's not right, is it?" I asked, keeping my voice gentle.

He had a gorgeous tan, almost as good as mine, but he paled underneath it. "No," he said in a strangled voice. "I'm thirty."

"I had no idea," Claude said, and Claudette told him to hush.

"And why didn't you like Claudia?"

"She insulted me in front of an audience," he said. "I told you."

The image from his mind was quite different. "In private? Did she say something to you in private?" After all, reading minds isn't like watching television. People don't relate things in their own brains, the way they would if they were telling a story to another person.

Barry looked embarrassed and even angrier. "Yes, in private. We'd been having sex for a while, and then one day she just wasn't interested anymore."

"Did she tell you why?"

"She told me I was . . . inadequate."

That hadn't been the phrase she used. I felt embarrassed for him when I heard the actual words in his head.

"What did you do between shows tonight, Barry?"

"We had an hour. So I could get two shaves in."

"You get paid for that?"

"Oh, yeah." He grinned, but not as though something was funny. "You think I'd shave a stranger's crotch if I didn't get paid for it? But I make a big ritual out of it; act like it turns me on. I get a hundred bucks a pop."

"When did you see Claudia?"

"When I went out to meet my first appointment, right as the first show was ending. She and her boyfriend were standing by the booth. I'd told them that was where I'd meet them."

"Did you talk to Claudia?"

"No, I just looked at her." He sounded sad. "I saw Rita, she was on her way to the booth with the money pouch, and I saw Jeff, he was on the stool at the back of the booth, where he usually stays."

"And then you went back to do this shaving?"

He nodded.

"How long does it take you?"

"Usually about thirty, forty minutes. So scheduling two was kind of chancy, but it worked out. I do it in the dressing room, and the other guys are good about staying out."

He was getting more relaxed, the thoughts in his head calming and flowing more easily. The first person he'd done tonight had been a woman so bone-thin he'd wondered if she'd die while he did the shaving routine. She'd thought she was beautiful, and she'd obviously enjoyed showing him her body. Her boyfriend had gotten a kick out of the whole thing.

I could hear Claudine buzzing in the background, but I kept my eyes closed and my hands on Barry's, seeing the second "client," a guy, and then I saw his face. Oh, boy. It was someone I knew, a vampire named Maxwell Litton.

"There was a vamp in the bar," I said, out loud, not opening my eyes. "Barry, what did he do when you finished shaving him?"

"He left," Barry said. "I watched him go out the back

door. I'm always careful to make sure my clients are out of the backstage area. That's the only way Rita will let me do the shaving at the club."

Of course, Barry didn't know about the problem fairies have with vamps. Some vamps had less self-control when it came to fairies than others did. Fairies were strong, stronger than people, but vamps were stronger than anything else on earth.

"And you didn't go back out to the booth and talk to Claudia again?"

"I didn't see her again."

"He's telling the truth," I said to Claudine and Claude. "As far as he knows it." There were always other questions I could ask, but at first "hearing," Barry didn't know anything about Claudia's disappearance.

Claude ushered me into the pantry, where Rita Child was waiting. It was a walk-in pantry, very neat, but not intended for two people, one of them duct-taped to a rolling office chair. Rita Child was a substantial woman, too. She looked exactly like I'd expect the owner of a strip club to look—painted, dyed brunette, packed into a challenging dress with high-tech underwear that pinched and pushed her into a provocative shape.

She was also steaming mad. She kicked out at me with a high heel that would have taken my eye out if I hadn't jerked back in the middle of kneeling in front of her. I fell on my fundament in an ungraceful sprawl.

"None of that, Rita," Claude said calmly. "You're not the boss here. This is our place." He helped me stand up and dusted off my bottom in an impersonal way.

"We just want to know what happened to our sister," Claudine said.

Rita made sounds behind her gag, sounds that didn't seem to be conciliatory. I got the impression that she didn't give a damn about the twins' motivation in kidnapping her and tying her up in their pantry. They'd taped her mouth, rather than using a cloth gag, and after the kicking incident, I kind of enjoyed ripping the tape off.

Rita called me some names reflecting on my heritage and moral character.

"I guess that's just the pot calling the kettle black," I said, when she paused to breathe. "Now you listen here! I'm not taking that kind of talk off of you, and I want you to shut up and answer my questions. You don't seem to have a good picture of the situation you're in."

The club owner calmed down a little bit after that. She was still glaring at me with her narrow brown eyes, and straining at her ropes, but she seemed to understand a little better.

"I'm going to touch you," I said. I was afraid she might bite if I touched her bare shoulder, so I put my hand on her forearm just above where her wrists were tied to the arms of the rolling chair.

Her head was a maze of fury. She wasn't thinking clearly because she was so angry, and all her mental energy was directed into cursing at the twins and now at me. She suspected me of being some kind of supernatural assassin, and I decided it wouldn't hurt if she were scared of me for a while.

"When did you see Claudia tonight?" I asked.

"When I went to get the money from the first show," she growled, and sure enough, I saw Rita's hand reaching out, a long white hand placing a zippered vinyl pouch in it. "I was in my office working during the first show. But I get the money in between, so if we get stuck up, we won't lose so much."

"She gave you the money bag, and you left?"

"Yeah. I went to put the cash in the safe until the second show was over. I didn't see her again."

And that seemed to be the truth to me. I couldn't see another vision of Claudia in Rita's head. But I saw a lot of satisfaction that Claudia was dead, and a grim determination to keep Claude at her club.

"Will you still go to Foxes, now that Claudia's gone?" I asked him, to spark a response that might reveal something from Rita.

Claude looked down at me, surprised and disgusted. "I haven't had time to think of what will come tomorrow," he snapped. "I just lost my sister."

Rita's mind sort of leaped with joy. She had it bad for Claude. And on the practical side, he was a big draw at Hooligans, since even on an off night he could engender some magic to make the crowd spend big. Claudia hadn't been so willing to use her power for Rita's profit, but Claude didn't think about it twice. Using his inbred fairy skills to draw people to admire him was an ego thing with Claude, which had little to do with economics.

I got all this from Rita in a flash.

"Okay," I said, standing up. "I'm through with her."

She was happy.

We stepped out of the pantry into the kitchen, where the final candidate for murderer was waiting. He'd been pushed under the table, and he had a glass in front of him with a straw stuck in it, so he could lean over to drink. Being a former lover had paid off for Jeff Puckett. His mouth wasn't even taped.

I looked from Claude to Jeff, trying to figure it out. Jeff had a light brown mustache that needed trimming, and a two-day growth of whiskers on his cheeks. His eyes were narrow and hazel. As much as I could tell, Jeff seemed to be in better shape than some of the bouncers I'd known, and he was even taller than Claude. But I was not impressed, and I reflected for maybe the millionth time that love was strange.

Claude braced himself visibly when he faced his former lover.

"I'm here to find out what you know about Claudia's death," I said, since we'd been around a corner when we'd questioned Rita. "I'm a telepath, and I'm going to touch you while I ask you some questions."

Jeff nodded. He was very tense. He fixed his eyes on

Claude. I stood behind him, since he was pushed up under the table, and put my hands on his thick shoulders. I pulled his tee shirt to one side, just a little, so my thumb could touch his neck.

"Jeff, you tell me what you saw tonight," I said.

"Claudia came to take the money for the first set," he said. His voice was higher than I'd expected, and he was not from these parts. Florida, I thought. "I couldn't stand her because she messed with my personal life, and I didn't want to be with her. But that's what Rita told me to do, so I did. I sat on the stool and watched her take the money and put it into the money bag. She kept some in a money drawer to make change."

"Did she have trouble with any of the customers?"

"No. It was ladies' night, and the women don't give any trouble coming in. They did during the second set, I had to go haul a gal offstage who got a little too enthusiastic about our Construction Worker, but mostly that night I just sat on the stool and watched."

"When did Claudia vanish?"

"When I come back from getting that gal back to her table, Claudia was gone. I looked around for her, went and asked Rita if she'd said anything to her about having to take a break. I even checked the ladies' room. Wasn't till I went back in the booth that I seen the glittery stuff."

"What glittery stuff?"

"What we leave when we fade," Claude murmured. "Fairy dust."

Did they sweep it up and keep it? It would probably be tacky to ask.

"And next thing I knew, the second set was over and the club was closing, and I was checking backstage and everywhere for traces of Claudia, then I was here with Claude and Claudine."

He didn't seem too angry.

"Do you know anything about Claudia's death?"

"No. I wish I did. I know this is hard on Claude." His eyes were as fixed on Claude as Claude's were on him. "She separated us, but she's not in the picture anymore."

"I have to know," Claude said, through clenched teeth.

For the first time, I wondered what the twins would do if I couldn't discover the culprit. And that scary thought spurred my brain to greater activity.

"Claudine," I called. Claudine came in, with an apple in her hand. She was hungry, and she looked tired. I wasn't surprised. Presumably, she'd worked all day, and here she was, staying up all night, and grieved, to boot.

"Can you wheel Rita in here?" I asked. "Claude, can you go get Barry?"

When everyone was assembled in the kitchen, I said, "Everything I've seen and heard seems to indicate that Claudia vanished during the second show." After a second's consideration, they all nodded. Barry's and Rita's mouths had been gagged again, and I thought that was a good thing.

"During the first show," I said, going slow to be sure I got it right, "Claudia took up the money. Claude was onstage. Barry was onstage. Even when he wasn't onstage, he didn't come up to the booth. Rita was in her office."

There were nods all around.

"During the interval between shows, the club cleared out."

"Yeah," Jeff said. "Barry came up to meet his clients, and I checked to make sure everyone else was gone."

"So you were away from the booth a little."

"Oh, well, yeah, I guess. I do it so often, I didn't even think of that."

"And also during the interval, Rita came up to get the money pouch from Claudia."

Rita nodded emphatically.

"So, at the end of the interval, Barry's clients have left." Barry nodded. "Claude, what about you?"

"I went out to get some food during the interval," he said. "I can't eat a lot before I dance, but I had to eat something. I got back, and Barry was by himself and getting ready for the second show. I got ready, too."

"And I got back on the stool," Jeff said. "Claudia was back at the cash window. She was all ready, with the cash drawer and the stamp, and the pouch. She still wasn't speaking to me."

"But you're sure it was Claudia?" I asked, out of the blue.

"Wasn't Claudine, if that's what you mean," he said. "Claudine's as sweet as Claudia was sour, and they even sit different."

Claudine looked pleased and threw her apple core in the garbage can. She smiled at me, already forgiving me for asking questions about her.

The apple.

Claude, looking impatient, began to speak. I held up my hand. He stopped.

"I'm going to ask Claudine to take your gags off," I said to Rita and Barry. "But I don't want you to talk unless I ask you a question, okay?" They both nodded.

Claudine took the gags off, while Claude glared at me.

Thoughts were pounding through my head like a mental stampede.

"What did Rita do with the money pouch?"

"After the first show?" Jeff seemed puzzled. "Uh, I told you. She took it with her."

Alarm bells were going off mentally. Now I knew I was on the right track.

"You said that when you saw Claudia waiting to take the money for the second show, she had everything ready."

"Yeah. So? She had the hand stamp, she had the money drawer, and she had the pouch," Jeff said.

"Right. She had to have a second pouch for the second show. Rita had taken the first pouch. So when Rita came to get the first show's take, she had the second pouch in her hand, right?"

Jeff tried to remember. "Uh, I guess so."

"What about it, Rita?" I asked. "Did you bring the second pouch?"

"No," she said. "There were two in the booth at the beginning of the evening. I just took the one she'd used, then she had an empty one there for the take from the second show."

"Barry, did you see Rita walking to the booth?"

The blond stripper thought frantically. I could feel every idea beating at the inside of my head.

"She had something in her hand," he said finally. "I'm sure of it."

"No," Rita shrieked. "It was there already!"

"What's so important about the pouch, anyway?" Jeff asked. "It's just a vinyl pouch with a zipper like banks give you. How could that hurt Claudia?"

"What if the inside were rubbed with lemon juice?"

Both the fairies flinched, horror on their faces.

"Would that kill Claudia?" I asked them.

Claude said, "Oh, yes. She was especially susceptible. Even lemon scent would make her vomit. She had a terrible time on washday until we found out the fabric sheets were lemon scented. Claudine has to go to the store since so many things are scented with the foul smell."

Rita began screaming, a high-pitched car alarm shriek that just seemed to go on and on. "I swear I didn't do it!" she said. "I didn't! I didn't!" But her mind was saying, "Caught, caught, caught, caught."

"Yeah, you did it," I said.

The surviving brother and sister stood in front of the rolling chair. "Sign over the bar to us," Claude said.

"What?"

"Sign over the club to us. We'll even pay you a dollar for it."

"Why would I do that? You got no body! You can't go to the cops! What are you gonna say? 'I'm a fairy, I'm allergic to lemons.'" She laughed. "Who's gonna believe that?"

Barry said weakly, "Fairies?"

Jeff didn't say anything. He hadn't known the triplets were allergic to lemons. He didn't realize his lover was a fairy. I worry about the human race.

"Barry should go," I suggested.

Claude seemed to rouse himself. He'd been looking at Rita the way a cat eyes a canary. "Good-bye, Barry," he said politely, as he untied the stripper. "I'll see you at the club tomorrow night. Our turn to take up the money."

"Uh, right," Barry said, getting to his feet.

Claudine's mouth had been moving all the while, and Barry's face went blank and relaxed. "See you later, nice party," he said genially.

"Good to meet you, Barry," I said.

"Come see the show sometime." He waved at me and walked out of the house, Claudine shepherding him to the front door. She was back in a flash.

Claude had been freeing Jeff. He kissed him, said,

"I'll call you soon," and gently pushed him toward the back door. Claudine did the same spell, and Jeff's face, too, relaxed utterly from its tense expression. "Bye," the bouncer called as he shut the door behind him.

"Are you gonna mojo me, too?" I asked, in a kind of squeaky voice.

"Here's your money," Claudine said. She took my hand. "Thank you, Sookie. I think you can remember this, huh, Claude? She's been so good!" I felt like a puppy that'd remembered its potty-training lesson.

Claude considered me for a minute, then nodded. He turned his attention back to Rita, who'd been taking the time to climb out of her panic.

Claude produced a contract out of thin air. "Sign," he told Rita, and I handed him a pen that had been on the counter beneath the phone.

"You're taking the bar in return for your sister's life," she said, expressing her incredulity at what I considered a very bad moment.

"Sure."

She gave the two fairies a look of contempt. With a flash of her rings, she took up the pen and signed the contract. She pushed up to her feet, smoothed the skirt of her dress across her round hips, and tossed her head. "I'll be going now," she said. "I own another place in Baton Rouge. I'll just live there."

"You'll start running," Claude said.

"What?"

"You better run. You owe us money and a hunt for the death of our sister. We have the money, or at least the means to make it." He pointed at the contract. "Now we need the hunt."

"That's not fair."

Okay, that disgusted even me.

"Fair is only part of fairy as letters of the alphabet." Claudine looked formidable: not sweet, not dotty. "If you can dodge us for a year, you can live."

"A year!" Rita's situation seemed to be feeling more and more real to her by then. She was beginning to look desperate.

"Starting . . . now." Claude looked up from his watch. "Better go. We'll give ourselves a four-hour handicap."

"Just for fun," Claudine said.

"And, Rita?" Claude said, as Rita made for the door. She paused, looked back at him.

Claude smiled at her. "We won't use lemons."

THE JUDGEMENT

ANNE PERRY

The court came to order and the Judge entered, not with the shrill call of bugles or the roll of drums, but in silence and alone. His men-at-arms were outside, breastplates under their tunics as always, swords at the ready, and amulets at their necks. Since this was a trial for murder by witchcraft, perhaps this last was the most important.

The Judge took his seat in the high, carved chair, behind the ancient bench with its runes and symbols so dark with use they were almost impossible to read. He was a tall man, but beneath his voluminous robes his body might have been any shape.

The Prosecutor waited as everyone settled in their places. There was a big crowd, drawn by fear and excitement. He was impatient to begin, and he could see that the Judge was also. It was clear in his hard, clever face, even though he made no move to hasten the ushers. Perhaps he liked seeing them in their black robes, moving like shadows, or reminders of doom.

The Prosecutor shifted his weight from one foot to the other. He knew he would win. It was a simple case of a woman who had lusted after her brother-in-law. When he had rejected her, forcing her to face the truth of his loyalty to his wife, she had revenged herself by casting a spell which had caused his death. Murder by witchcraft could hardly be clearer. The trial was really only to demonstrate that justice was done. To begin with he had been impatient with the waste of time and the cost of it, until he had appreciated the deterrent effect on other women who might be tempted to such a thing. This new Judge was right to proceed, and publicly. Regrettably, it was a necessary performance. Of late too many people were ignorant of the reality of dark powers. They needed reminding of justice, and where it was breached, of punishment.

At last they were settled, and the Chief Usher read out the charge. The accused denied it. Her voice might normally be pleasant, her diction was beautiful, but now she was strained with fear. Good. So she should be. The Prosecutor looked at her curiously. She was quite tall. And slender. The weight of the chains on her must hurt. She was not beautiful, there was too much passion in her face. It was clever and wilful, perhaps what should be expected in one who turned to sorcery.

He stood up. "My fellow citizens!" His voice rang around the room. He surveyed them. After all, this was for their benefit, or it could have been done secretly. He was interested to see that there were as many women present as men. Some were in fine dresses of rich fabric decorated with embroidery, the heavy girdles around their waists were studded with gems, their hair braided with ribbons. Others wore plain browns and drabs, hair tied back with scarves, as if lately come in from some form of work.

The men too were of every variety, knights-at-arms, clerks in brown jerkins with ink-stained fingers, students and artisans with callused hands. He saw at least one apothecary—now there was an art that at times verged too close to that of the sorcerers! And of course there were many farmers and labourers. The dead man had been a farmer, a rich one.

He called his first witness, Stroban, the dead man's father. Stroban moved forward from the front bench and into the Square of Testimony, straightening his shoulders with an effort. Grief had aged him in a few terrible days. His face was bleached of colour, his grey hair seemed thinner, drawn across his skull like an inadequate protection. He looked at the accused just once, and his outrage was naked in his eyes. Then he turned to the Prosecutor. He was there to see justice for his dead son, and he would not let himself down by losing his composure.

The Prosecutor asked his name and circumstances. He answered clearly in a low voice in which pride and sorrow were equally mixed.

The Prosecutor pointed to the accused where she stood, body stiff, face averted as though she found it too difficult to meet his eyes. "And who is she?" he demanded.

"Anaya," Stroban replied. "The widow of my daughter-in-law's brother. She came to us in her time of need, and we took her in and treated her as our own." His voice cracked. He struggled to control it. "And she repaid us with envy, rage, and murder!"

There was a ripple of horror around the room, a mixture of hunger and fear.

The Judge leaned forward, his face grave, the lines around his mouth deep and hard. "That is what we are here to test, and to prove, aye or nay."

"Of course, my lord," Stroban acknowledged bleakly. "It is right that judgement should be seen. It is the law, and necessary to a just and civilised life."

The Judge nodded. "Justice will be served, I promise you, and great and everlasting justice, deeper than men will easily grasp."

The Prosecutor permitted himself to smile. The Judge was a proud man, even a little arrogant, and he would frequently interrupt where it was not needed because he liked the sound of his own voice. But he would rule correctly. The Prosecutor would one day be a judge like him, with his strengths, but not his weaknesses, not his pomposity or his conceit. Curious how quickly one could see that.

"You took her in and gave her a home?" he said aloud, to confirm it for the court.

"Yes," Stroban agreed. "It was no less than our duty."

The Prosecutor flinched. That sounded a little cold and self-righteous. It was not the image of the bereaved family he had wished to display. "How long ago was this?" he asked hastily.

"Just under a year."

"And how did she behave?" He must move them on to think about the accused. He glanced at her, and saw no contrition in her face, no respect, only what seemed to be fear.

"At first, with meekness and gratitude," Stroban answered. "All gentleness, modesty, and obedience." His face reflected the hurt of her betrayal.

The Prosecutor felt an overwhelming anger rise in him. Of all crimes witchcraft infuriated him the most, it was the culmination of everything evil that deceived and destroyed. It denied honour, and humanity. He looked at the Judge and saw a like anger in his high, thin face, the disgust and revulsion that he himself felt, and the knowledge that he had it within his power, at least this time, to punish it as it should be punished—with death. Witches might have black arts, but they were still mortal, and once they were exposed, they could feel pain like anyone else.

He controlled his face and his voice with difficulty, and only because he was certain of the outcome.

Stroban was less certain. All his life he had known right from wrong. Any man did, if he were honest in heart. And could there be any virtue greater than to know truth and judge rightly? It was the cornerstone of all virtue. Too often evil prevailed. Had it not done so in his own house, his beautiful son would not now be lying dead. Bertil, whom he had raised so carefully, taught every detail of honour and righteousness. And then this woman, with her cleverness, her inappropriate laughter, her wild thoughts, had come into their home, taken in by charity, and first betrayed them by trying to seduce Bertil away from his wife; and then when he had rejected her she had threatened to kill him. And when he had still refused, she had cast her spell, an act of deliberate murder.

The Prosecutor was speaking again. "How long did she behave this way, feigning love and obedience?"

"She never stopped," Stroban said, with disgust for her deceit.

The Prosecutor looked at the Judge's face. Stroban had not been duped because of his own innocence and charity, his inability to imagine such duplicity. The man was self-righteous, too quick to judge and condemn. It was a cold fault, an ugly one.

But the Judge would be shown the truth, then it would be the time to act. There must be law. Rules must be made and kept, by everyone. Without rules there was chaos, and that was truly terrifying, the gateway to all darkness. Even the Judge must obey the law.

The Prosecutor wanted more details. "Did she work hard around the farm? And the house? Was she truthful, as far as you know? Did she respect you and your wife? Did she treat you with the courtesy and gratitude that she owed you?"

"Oh yes," Stroban replied. "She was very careful." He knew he must speak the exact truth, whatever it was. He had committed no wrong, so it could not harm him or his family.

The Prosecutor's eyes widened. "Your choice of words suggests that you think she planned something evil from the beginning. Is that so?"

Stroban hesitated for a moment. He believed that she had, but it was only in the hindsight of what she had done. He had not known it then. He looked at her standing in her chains and wondered how he could have been so blind. It was his own innocence that had blinded him.

"No," he admitted aloud. "I should not have implied that. I do not know what was in her mind. But she was attracted to poor Bertil from the start, that was plain. At the time I believed it was only recognition of his goodness. Everyone liked Bertil." Emotion overcame him, and he was unable to regain control of himself for several minutes. He saw pity in the Judge's eyes, and admiration, but neither would have anything to do with his decisions.

"Please continue," the Prosecutor prompted. "How did the accused show this affection, precisely?"

Stroban forced himself to steady his voice. "She helped him around the farm."

"How?"

"She was clever." He said the word so it was half a curse. "She had ideas for improving things. And she was clever with figures, and measurements." He said the last bitterly. It was measurements she had used to kill Bertil, although he still did not know how.

"She improved your yield?" the Judge interrupted, leaning forward over the ancient bench, his sleeve hiding some of the runes on it. "She made life easier for you, better?"

Stroban felt a surge of anger. He was making her sound good! "For a while," he admitted. "Oh, she was clever!"

The Prosecutor was annoyed. It showed in his expression and the nervous clenching and unclenching of his fists. This was his territory, and the Judge was trespassing. "Were you grateful for this help?" he cut across. "Did you wish it?"

"At the time, of course we were," Stroban said.

"All of you? Your wife Enella and your daughter-in-law, Korah, as well?"

"Of course."

"You all trusted the accused?" He pointed to where she stood, her face white, her eyes hollow and frightened even though her head was still high. Did she yet realise that there was no escape for her?

"Yes," Stroban answered. "Why should we not?"

"Indeed. Tell us what happened to change your mind?"

Stroban felt his stomach twisting with the pain of memory, and yet he was on the brink of finding justice. It was up to him, his word, his saying what was right and true. He must be exact.

"There was a quarrel between Korah and Anaya, the accused." He avoided looking at her now. "I didn't know what it was about at the time . . ."

"Korah will tell us," the Prosecutor assured him. "Please go on."

Stroban obeyed. "A few days later there was a more serious quarrel. That same evening Anaya said that if Bertil did not do as she had told him to, then the barn roof would cave in and kill him." He could barely say the words. The scene was carved indelibly in his mind, Anaya standing in the kitchen, her hair wound in a copper red ribbon, the sun warming her face, the smells of cooking around them, the door open to the yard beyond and the lowing of the cattle in the distance. It was another world from this. They could not then have imagined the horror that awaited them.

The court was silent, faces still with fear.

"And how did Bertil reply to her?" the Prosecutor asked.

"He said she was wrong," Stroban whispered. "My poor son! He had no idea." His voice caught in a sob. "He didn't believe in witchcraft."

There was a shudder around the room. People shifted in their seats, closer to loved ones.

"But you do?" the Prosecutor insisted.

Stroban was angry, and afraid. He looked at the Judge and saw anger in him too, at the stupidity of the question, perhaps? Then he saw something else in the high-boned, curious face, passionate one moment, ascetic the next. It was a long, breathless moment before he understood that it also was fear. He had tasted the power of sorcery, and he knew there was nothing to protect ordinary men except righteousness and the exact observance of the law.

But if the Judge knew that, really knew it, then there was hope for them. He squared his shoulders and lifted his chin. "Of course I do! But I know that just men, obedient men, can defeat it!"

There was a murmur of admiration around the room, like a swell of the tide. Faces turned to the accused, tight with hatred and fear.

"Had you ever thought before that the barn roof would collapse?" the Prosecutor asked.

"Of course not!" Stroban was angry. "It rests on a great post, thick as a tree trunk!"

"Was anyone in the barn when this happened, apart from your son?"

"No, just Bertil, and one of the oxen."

"I see. Thank you. The Defender may wish to ask you something."

Stroban turned to face the young man who now rose to his feet. He was a complete contrast to the Prosecutor. Far from being arrogant, he looked full of doubt, even confused, as if he had no idea what he was going to say or do.

And indeed he did not. The whole proceeding was out of his control. When he had spoken with Anaya earlier he had believed her when she had said she was innocent. Now he did not know what to think, nor did he have any faith in himself to achieve a just trial for her. Perhaps the Judge would help him? But when he looked at the Judge, his long, pale face seemed as utterly confused as he was himself.

The Defender turned to Stroban, cleared his throat and began. "We are deeply sorry for your grief." He hesitated. He must say something to the point, but what? "Where was the accused when this tragedy happened?"

Stroban's face was a mask of anger, his voice high-pitched. "You say 'tragedy' as if it were a natural happening! It was witchcraft! She made the roof fall in, exactly as she told him she would, if he did not submit to her lust. But he was a righteous man, and he refused, so she killed him!"

There was a shiver of horror around the room. People reached for amulets.

The Defender turned to the Judge for help, but the Judge did nothing. He seemed just as lost and overwhelmed. The Defender turned back to Stroban. "I asked you where was she?"

"I don't know," Stroban said sullenly. "Out in the fields somewhere, she told us."

"Not in the barn?"

"Of course not! She didn't need to be there to make it happen. Don't you know anything about sorcery?"

"No, I don't. Perhaps you would be good enough to instruct me?"

Stroban's cheeks flamed. "I know nothing either! What do you think I am? But it is powerful and wicked, and all good people who love truth and the law must fight against it with every strength they have. We must see that justice is done. It is our only protection."

There were nods of agreement, a mixture of fear and an attempt at assurance.

The Defender knew he would accomplish nothing with Stroban. It would be better to wait for his wife.

But when the Prosecutor called Enella she echoed exactly what her husband had said, almost in the same words. The Prosecutor sat down again, wholly satisfied.

The Defender rose. “You agreed that the accused was very fond of your son,” he began, not quite sure where he intended the question to lead. He glanced at Anaya, and saw a strange kind of peace in her eyes. He turned back to Enella. “In what ways did she show this?”

Enella was confused. “Why . . . the usual ways, I suppose.”

“And what are they?” he pressed.

“She . . . she talked with him easily, comfortably. She made him laugh, without telling the rest of us what it was about.”

“You felt excluded?”

“No! Of course not!” Now she was confused as well. She had been tricked into saying something she had not meant to.

“Why not?” he asked. “It sounds as if you were excluded.”

She looked at Stroban, then away again. “It was exactly as my husband said, she wanted him for herself, in spite of the fact that he was married to her dead husband’s sister, whom she should have loved and honoured. It was because of Korah that Bertil took Anaya in in the first place. Only a wicked woman would be so ungrateful!” Enella was afraid of uncertainty. She liked order. It was the only way to be safe.

"It sounds from what you say as if Bertil also liked her," the Defender pointed out. "Are you certain that she was not merely responding to him? After all, he was her host, so to speak. The head of her household."

Enella was afraid. Stroban was not helping her. She looked at the Judge.

The Judge leaned forward over the bench, his face tense and unhappy. He stared at the Defender. "I cannot see where you are leading. Stay on the known path, if you please."

Enella relaxed again. The Judge was a decent man, a fair man. There was no need to be afraid after all.

"I'm sorry, my lord," the Defender apologised. He was confused again. He looked at Anaya where she stood perfectly still. Her face was white, as if exhausted by plunging from hope to despair, and back again. Her shoulders drooped, as if the courage of a few moments ago had slipped from her. He had promised her that he would do his best, and so far he had been pathetic. He must do better.

He took a step towards her, waving his hand. "We have heard that Anaya," he used her name self-consciously, "liked to make Bertil laugh. She helped him in his work, because she was clever, and inventive. Is that true?" He knew that Enella would agree that it was, her husband had already said so, and she would never contradict him.

"Yes," she said unhappily.

"She made new suggestions for efficiency and skill, things that had not been done before?" he pressed, beginning to see a tiny light of hope.

There was only one possible answer, to have denied it would have been ridiculous. "Yes."

"So she was cleverer than Korah, or than any of you?"

"Well . . ."

"Or you would have thought of them for yourselves, before she came?"

"Well . . . yes, I suppose so."

The Defender was beginning to feel better. He looked at the Judge and saw a spark of hope in his eyes also, a slight straightening of his shoulders and easing of the muscles of his jaw. It gave him courage to go on. He felt less alone. "Surely it must be true?"

Enella said nothing.

The Defender was sorry for her, but he could not let her deny it.

The Judge looked at her, his face gentle. "You must answer," he told her.

"Yes," she said very quietly, her face filled with unhappiness.

"Thank you," the Defender acknowledged. "So Korah had to have seen it also?"

"I don't know!" It was a lie, and the scarlet guilt flooded up her face. She must have felt its heat. "I imagine she did."

"Perhaps she was angry? Could that be what the quarrel was about?"

"I don't know!" That was the literal truth, the letter of the law if not the spirit. She hid in the safety of that, looking to the Judge for protection, and from the easing of the rigidity of her body, believing she received it.

The Defender thanked her and gave her leave to go.

The Prosecutor called Korah, handsome, angry, thin-lipped. She walked into the Square knowing exactly what she was going to say. It had been sitting in her heart like a black weight since the first time she had seen Bertil laughing with Anaya and realised that while loyalty would hold him to Korah, but, if not yet, then soon, it would be Anaya he loved, Anaya who touched the man within and awoke his heart and his dreams. In that day her hatred was born.

The Prosecutor faced her, arrogant and angry. She faced him squarely, meeting his eyes. He would not treat her as he had cowardly, obedient Enella. Korah was not funny or imaginative, or beautiful, but she understood people. She could see right through the façade, the pretences, to the weakness within. And the Judge would help. She had been watching him, the high, thin face, the tight mouth. He was just like her. He understood what it was like to be mocked, to be left out, even in your own home. He could see the need for justice. It was not revenge, it was what Anaya deserved, not for witchcraft—there was no such thing—but for theft.

"Anaya is your brother's widow, and after his death you took her in and gave her a home?" The Prosecutor was repeating the important facts, just to remind the crowd, and the Judge.

"Yes, I did," Korah answered. Never say more than you need to, that was the way to make mistakes.

"And she repaid you by helping in the house and on the farm?"

"Yes. She was very skilled at it." Be generous. It sounded better than grudging praise. And it was the truth.

"Better than you?"

"In some ways, not in others." Don't let them see the envy. Don't look at Anaya in case your thoughts are there in your face, in spite of all you can do. She looked instead at the Judge. He understood; it was obvious in his expression, the eyes, the lips. Perhaps he too had been betrayed? It must have been long ago. He was dried up now, desiccated, withered inside.

The Prosecutor was talking again. "Was your husband a handsome man, charming?"

"Yes." Oh yes, that was true. "Everyone liked him. It was far more than looks. It was his manner, his honesty, his warmth, his laughter, his kindness." All that was so painfully true. It hurt to say it now for all these prurient, superstitious people peering at her. Damn Anaya! They should burn her! Let her feel the fire on her body, consume her flesh and destroy it, even if they could not make it burn her soul on the inside.

"So you were not surprised when your sister-in-law was attracted to him?"

In spite of herself, Korah's eyes were drawn to Anaya, and for an instant they looked at each other. Korah saw faith struggling with fear of pain, of failure, of utter loneliness, and victory was like honey on her tongue.

"No," she answered. "I believed she would honour her place as my sister and my guest. I had no idea she had . . . powers."

The Prosecutor had seen the exchange. "Bertil rejected her?" he asked.

"Yes. He was very distressed by it. He found it grossly dishonourable. He was revolted."

"What did Anaya do?"

Korah smiled very slightly, just a tiny movement of the lips. "She said that if he did not change his mind and come to her, then the barn roof would cave in and crush him to death." No one could catch her out in that. They were not the exact words, but the meaning was the same. Timour had heard her say it, and he could testify. He was so transparently honest, everyone would believe him.

"And did he change his mind?"

There was a silence in the room as if no one breathed. The sunlight outside seemed a world away.

"Of course not," Korah said. "I don't think he was afraid, but even if he had been, he would rather have died than give in to such a thing."

A hundred voices in the room murmured approval, and sympathy.

Anaya stood with her eyes closed, as if needing to summon all her strength just to remain upright.

"It seems we have lost an exceptionally fine man with his death," the Prosecutor said with relish. "Perhaps evil always seeks to destroy that which is purest and best."

The Judge seemed about to say something. He drew in his breath, then let it out again in a sigh, as if some inner resolution had prevailed.

"Finally, Mistress," the Prosecutor said, "how long had that barn stood with that roof safe and secure?"

"Seventy years."

"Thank you." He looked smug, totally satisfied with himself.

The Defender took his place. He seemed even more confused than before.

"I have nothing to ask you."

She stood down, glancing at the Judge's pinched, unhappy face, and for an instant seeing her own future in it, old and alone, eaten by bitterness and self-disgust. Then she drove it from her mind and returned to her seat beside Enella, but a coldness remained in the pit of her stomach.

The Prosecutor called Timour, who confirmed all that Korah had said. He looked trustingly at the Defender as he approached. He felt sorry for all of them, especially Anaya. He had liked her, as he knew Bertil had. She had seemed funny and kind and brave. He had had no idea that she had any harm in her, still less that she had knowledge of the black arts. He still found it hard to believe. But he did know barns, and he knew oxen. He said as much when the Defender asked him.

"Oh yes. It's my trade," he agreed.

"Did you see this barn after it had fallen in?"

"Yes. I wanted to know what had happened. It's important, in case it should happen again." He looked at the Judge to see if he understood. He seemed to. He had the air of a brave man, not only a strength in his face but a gentleness as well, as if he expected the best in people. He was the sort of man Timour liked, wise without arrogance, kind without sentiment. "I saw it before, you see," he explained. "They had been keeping oxen in it for a long time, my lord. Big beasts, and very heavy, very powerful. They like to lean against the posts and rub their backs, scratch them, as it were. If you don't keep an eye on them, sooner or later they'll dislodge the pole from its base. I warned Bertil about it. He was a good man, and my friend, but he did put things off." He glanced at Stroban an apology. "I'm sorry, but that's true. Anaya saw it, and she warned him too. But he was always going to do it tomorrow. I suppose when tomorrow finally came, it was too late."

There was silence for a moment, a realisation, a wakening from a dream both good and bad. It was the Judge who asked the question, not the Defender. "Could the ox have pushed against it while Bertil was there, and knocked it over when it was at the most vulnerable?"

"I suppose it must have done," Timour answered. "I ran out just as the roof buckled and caved in. I got bruised by some of the falling timbers. He should have put it out before he began to work, but he can't have."

"Witchcraft!" Stroban cried out, rising to his feet, his face flushed. "It's still her fault!"

"No!" the Defender said with sudden strength, whirling round, his robe flying, his arm outstretched. "A man delayed mending his barn until the post was seriously weakened. It is a tragedy. It is not a crime." He looked to the Judge, raising his eyes to the high seat, the dark runes carried in the wood. "My lord, I ask that you pronounce Anaya innocent of this poor man's death, free these people of the fear of sorcery, and allow them to grieve for their loss without fear or blame. She did not threaten him, she warned him. And tragically, he did not listen. If he had done, we should not be here today mourning him, seeing witchcraft where there is only jealousy."

Stroban looked desperately at the Judge and saw a man filtered by the details of the law and unable to see the greater spirit of it, a man who understood loss but not love. He was a small man, who could in the end become a hollow man.

Enella looked at the Judge and saw a man who kept to the safe path, always, wherever it led, upward or down, and there was an emptiness in it that nothing would fill.

Korah saw what she had recognised before, only this time it was not for an instant. It would always be there, whether she looked at it or not.

The Prosecutor was angry. He saw a Judge whose arrogance had allowed him to lose control of the court. He did not know how it had happened, or why victory had inexplicably become defeat.

Timour and the Defender both saw an upsurge of optimism. Hope had come out of nowhere, and vanquished the error and despair.

The Judge pronounced Anaya innocent. The court was dismissed, and people poured out into the dark, gulping the sweet air, leaving the room empty except for Anaya and the Judge.

He moved his right hand very slightly, just two fingers from the surface of the bench. The chains fell away. She stood free, rubbing her wrists and stretching her aching shoulders.

"You did well," he said quietly. He was smiling.

"I doubted," she answered. It was a confession.

"Of course you did," he agreed, and as he spoke his face changed, it became wiser, stronger, passion and laughter burned in it, and an indescribable gentleness. "If it were easy, it would be worth little. You have not yet perfected faith. Do not expect so much of yourself. For lessons learned hastily or without pain are worthless."

"Will they understand?" she asked.

"That they were the ones on trial, and that the judgement was your own? Oh yes. In time. Whether they will pay the cost of change is another thing. But there is love, and there is hope. We are far from the end." His cloak shimmered and began to dissolve. She could no longer see his shoulders, only his strong, slender hands and his face. "Now I have another charge for you."

She looked at him, at the white fire around him. All she could distinguish was his smile, and his voice, and a great peace shone within her. "Yes?"

the sorcerer's assassin

SHARON SHINN

When you work at a school for mages, I've learned, it's wise never to leave your room unless you've cloaked yourself in a reflecting spell. That way, as you walk the long, high corridors of arched stone and stained glass, you can feel relatively safe in the knowledge that rancorous or embarrassing spells aimed your way (accidentally or otherwise) will simply bounce off your own enchantment and go sticking onto the perpetrator instead. I can't tell you the number of students I've passed in these halls who have suddenly bloomed into a seven-foot-tall lotus or shrunk to an agitated frog. Yes, of course, I could with little effort reverse any such hex cast on me, but it's so much easier to saunter out into the world knowing I am immune from ill-trained apprentices or maliciously inclined pranksters.

Professor Morben, it was clear, had come to class that morning garbed in no such protection.

I stopped at the doorway of the wide, clean room where he taught Illusions and Transmogrification. Ten or twelve students were huddled against the back wall, wearing their lilac apprentice's robes and looking totally devoid of magic. Professors Dernwerd and Audra were standing over a shape that looked very much like a man who had crumpled to the floor. Dernwerd's thin gray hair was standing up any old which way, as if he had been summoned from the mirror before completing his personal grooming. Audra, of course, looked perfect as always, her dark red hair wound into a tight bun, her gold robes hanging precisely over her sharp, narrow shoulders.

They both looked up at me when I stepped into the room. "He's dead, Camalyn," Dernwerd said in a shaky voice.

I was briefly annoyed. How many times had I told the other teachers to address me as "Headmistress," at least in front of the students? Then the words registered. "Dead?" I repeated. "Morben? Is *dead?* That's not possible!"

Audra looked at me with her cool green eyes. She's only a couple of decades younger than I am, but she looks at least fifty years my junior, and that's only one of the many things I can't stand about her. "Take a look for yourself," she invited. "But I wouldn't advise you to get too close until we've ascertained what happened."

I crossed the room in the stately way I've cultivated and came to a halt a few feet away from the corpse. Yes, there could be no doubt about it. Morben was dead. His face had a riven, petrified look, his mouth gaped in a silent scream, and his eyes gazed up at some unbearable horror. His hands were clenched around his throat as if to choke out his own life or claw at spectral hands bent on that very task. He did not move or breathe or radiate any life heat at all.

I had hated the man, but I had certainly never expected him to come to an end like this. I stared down at him. "What happened to him?"

Dernwerd gestured at the students. "They said he was in the middle of a class on Transmogrification when he suddenly started shrieking and pointing at something on the ceiling. They all looked, of course, but didn't see a thing there. Then he started grabbing at his neck and contorting all around as though someone was squeezing the life out of him. Then he dropped to the floor and he died. In minutes, they said."

I glanced back at the students, a room away but obviously listening to every word. "Is that true?"

They looked at each other and nodded. "Just like he said," confirmed one girl who looked about twelve. I know that magic folk age differently than mortals do, and I'm 105 myself, so everyone looks young to me, but I cannot believe we are now admitting *children* to the school. She was probably eighteen and a very knowing girl, but she looked so young and so innocent that I moved a little to shield her eyes from a view of the body. "He screamed and screamed, until he started choking, then he kept making these terrible little grunting sounds. Like he was trying to tell us something. But we couldn't see anything. We couldn't do anything. It happened so fast."

I looked back at Morben, ghastly and terrified. What could possibly have killed one of the most powerful wizards in the kingdom? Despite Audra's caution to stand clear of the body, I had decided to take a pace closer when the corpse abruptly disintegrated into a smoking pile of black ash. I stepped back hurriedly and brushed some cinder from my sleeve.

"I think we'd better cancel classes for the day," I said, keeping my voice steady to disguise my sudden shakiness. "Time to convene a council of mages."

The Norwitch Academy of Magic and Sorcery had been founded three centuries ago and enjoyed great prestige and prosperity ever since. I was the seventh wizard to ascend to the top position in the school, a feat I had accomplished thirty-eight years before, and the first to preside over an investigation of murder. Not a distinction I particularly wished to claim.

A staff of twenty professors reported to me, and between us we taught a student body of four hundred students. A countless number of cooks, laundresses, gardeners, and stableboys also lived on the premises, making sure life at the school ran smoothly. Thus, in theory, there were close to five hundred suspects in this unsettling murder case.

In actuality, however, the number could be narrowed down to five without any trouble at all. There were, in the entire kingdom, only half a dozen wizards with the knowledge and power to cast a death spell that actually worked. All six of them worked at the Academy, and one was now dead.

The other five of us sat in my office and looked at each other with expressions of mistrust and wonder.

"So!" I said briskly, folding my hands before me on my ornate desk. "I suppose all of you have heard the dreadful news by now. Morben is dead, and someone killed him, and we need to try to discover who and why."

"The why is simple enough," Audra said with some contempt. She sat in one of my stiff high-backed chairs as if it was a comfortably stuffed divan, and her gold robe molded itself to her long legs. Dernwerd, Borrin, and Xander couldn't keep their watery old eyes off her. "He was a foul-mouthed, lecherous, mean-spirited hack, and everybody hated him."

"It's true that he was a difficult man, but you needn't speak so harshly," Dernwerd mumbled in his irritating, apologetic way. As if he thought that even in death Morben might reach out to slap him if he didn't talk nice.

"Yes, but to disapprove of him and to kill him are two very different things," Xander said. Xander was a lean, bald, punctilious scholar who would argue the most minute point of history or spellwork till you wanted to run screaming from the room.

"Frankly, I'm surprised he hasn't been done away with long before now," Borrin drawled. Supercilious, wealthy family background, north-country accent—Borrin does think he's the most elegant of the wizards, though I'm pretty sure he uses magic to keep his hair silver and his figure trim. I can respect his abilities, which are formidable, but not his vanity.

You will be thinking by now that I dislike almost everyone in my employ, and you would be right. In fact, I am a terrible misanthrope, and my attitude is even worse when it comes to wizards and warlocks. Call me a misosorcerer and be done with it! But I inherited all five senior members of my faculty when I joined the school, and I was under contract to keep them. Trust me, otherwise I would have ousted Morben when I first came on board, and I might have fired the other four while I was at it. Though honesty compels me to admit that all of them, even Audra, are ferociously talented mages.

And all of them have the ability, if not the inclination, to kill a man by magic.

"Well, he's dead now," I said. "And it seems obvious that one of the five of us murdered him."

They all looked at each other and at me, and none of them said a word.

"The students didn't recognize the spell they described, but I did, and I assume you did as well," I went on. "It can be found in the Hazelton *Grimoire,* though a variant without the screaming is indexed in Mortensen's *Spellbook,* and only the five of us have the knowledge to *unlock* either of those volumes, let alone the strength to speak the enchantment. So one of us killed him. Why?"

Dernwerd was on his feet, pointing at Audra. "You're the one who always hated him!" So much for his usual conciliatory manner. "I heard you! Just yesterday in the hall! I heard you tell him that if he touched you again, you'd turn him to ice and iron!"

"And I would have, but he didn't," Audra said furiously. "Aren't *you* the one he embarrassed in front of his whole class last week when you couldn't recapture the igliat and had to get Morben's help? He said you had the skill of a Rank Five wizard and shouldn't be allowed to teach advanced classes."

Dernwerd's face was the same gray color as his hair. "How did you know that?"

She shrugged one thin shoulder. "A couple of the students told me. They thought it was funny."

Borrin was smiling in that detestable way, and Xander gave him a long, thorough look. "You smile now, but you didn't think it was so funny when Morben called you an up-country upstart with imaginary bloodlines," he said in his painstaking way. I had no doubt that he had reproduced the quote with shattering accuracy.

Borrin stopped smiling. "My family's older than the kingdom, and if anyone's a sorcerer-come-lately it's Morben with his questionable antecedents and his rough-and-ready magic."

"And, anyway," I said to Xander, "you were none too fond of him, either. You were quite public in your hatred for him once he published that paper about the error you made in your *Treatise*."

The bald man glared at me. Borrin was laughing again. "And you, Camalyn?" Borrin said. "Why did you despise the estimable Morben? Because he told the school board that you were an aging spinster with a poisonous mind and a dried-up heart? Because he told them no female should ever be head of Norwitch Academy, but if they were going to make that mistake, they should at least choose one who could claim to be a *woman*."

Audra snickered. Dernwerd and Xander looked embarrassed for me. I looked at Borrin and wished him dead. "So one of us killed him," I repeated, "and we all had a reason. Now we have to determine who had the chance. I want each of you to write down a diary of where you've been since midnight last night, with names of witnesses who can substantiate your claims. I will begin the investigation."

"What about you?" Borrin said. "You have the skills, and you have the temper. Who will investigate you?"

I pointed at Audra. "Let the *womanly* woman of the group have that privilege," I said coldly. "Though you may all give her whatever assistance you desire. I expect your reports by this afternoon. Now you can go."

All four of them were quick to turn in accounts of their recent activities, and I handed over my own schedule to Audra when she came by my office. I spent a little time reading their reports, but in truth I didn't have much hope that I would learn anything. A good wizard can appear to be in two places at one time; even a bad one can set up a spell in a remote location so that it's triggered by an action or a phrase. How could I possibly check their alibis and prove definitively that one of them was responsible for this crime? Or even—interesting thought—that two or more of them had been involved?

I shut my eyes and leaned back in my well-padded chair, reviewing the case. Well, to be truthful, I had had more reason than any of them to want Morben dead. He had recently gone to the school board to complain about me—my attitude, my abilities, my age—and to suggest himself in the role of headmaster instead. I don't suppose any of them knew that I had managed to audit his entire presentation illicitly. I had planted a magical seashell in the council room and linked its listening ear to another shell set up in my office. It was like being in the room with the rest of them without actually having to see their stern and self-righteous faces. I found myself disliking the board members as much as I disliked Morben.

But I hadn't included that information in the report I gave Audra.

Which led me to wonder what the others hadn't told me.

Going on pure instinct, I'd have said the likeliest killer was Audra herself. Morben had lusted after her ever since she'd joined the Academy, and being stalked for more than forty years could wear on the patience of the sweetest woman, which we all knew Audra was not. Moreover, she had always wanted to teach his specialty classes in Illusions and Transmogrification, but he was not about to give them up, so she was stuck with Travel and Time Manipulation, which were useful though much less glamorous skills. Distaste and envy could have combined to make her want to see Morben dead.

The men had fewer incentives, I thought. Dernwerd, in any case, was a whiny and ineffectual man who might smolder with hatred for a hundred years before he brought himself actually to lash out at someone. Though I'd seen him level a mountain once, with utter grace and precision, so I knew he had more power than his personality might predict. Xander never seemed to pull his head out of his books long enough to develop any kind of emotional reaction, good or bad, to anyone else alive, so I found it hard to believe he would have nurtured enough animosity to hunt Morben down. Borrin, though. He was smart enough, good enough, and nasty enough to kill a man, and the insult to his family name would probably have been sufficient to send him seeking revenge.

I wrote them all down on a piece of paper, in descending order of probability: *Audra, Borrin, Dernwerd, Xander.* After thinking about it a minute, I squeezed another name between Audra's and Borrin's: *Camalyn.*

That still left Audra as the most likely murderer.

We spent two days canvassing the students and checking Morben's bedchamber and classrooms for any kind of evidence, but found nothing that incriminated anyone. There was no point in suspending school any longer, so we allowed classes to resume the following day. The school board members were all unhappy that the murder was still unsolved, but frantic to resume the educational process so parents didn't start pulling students out. Therefore, none of them made a fuss when we opened the classrooms again.

All was relatively serene for a week, and I began to grow a little more cheerful about the whole thing: *Well, Morben's dead, and we have a murderer in our midst, but that killer has done us all a favor, really, so maybe we should just let the whole thing go and get on with our lives.* Unrealistic, you'll say. Absolutely, I'll agree.

About ten days after Morben's death I was heading down the hall between my Alchemy class and my Protective Spells seminar when I heard a sound of hysterical shrieking. Of course, I ran in that direction, as did the other five hundred people on the school property. I noted that Audra came puffing up from the southern stairway, and that Dernwerd and Xander arrived at the same time, as if they had been consulting together when the cries were raised.

The commotion was coming from Borrin's Animal Languages classroom. We rushed inside as if by hurrying we could affect the outcome of events that had already been put in motion. Naturally, we could not.

The scene greatly resembled the one from ten days earlier. Students cowered against the back wall of the room and a wizard lay dead on the floor, face contorted in horror, hands clamped around his own throat. But this time I was not about to let myself be thwarted by the spell. I muttered a command of my own, and the body remained intact. No smoking pile of ashes. Gruesome though it was, we would be able to examine the corpse for evidence.

The other three wizards had come to stand beside me and were staring down at Borrin with many emotions on their faces, none of them grief. They were angry, and they were afraid, for what can kill two wizards can kill three, or six. I raised my voice to address the students. "Clear the room, please," I said. "The professors and I must talk."

As soon as the door had closed behind them, the accusations started.

"You!" Dernwerd screeched, pointing at Audra. "You did this! I was with Xander all morning, I know he and I are innocent, but where were you before you came running up to investigate the alarm?"

"I was in the archives with many junior professors nearby," she said icily. "I did not speak to any of them, but I'm sure one or two will remember seeing me there. And as for the two of you being guilt-free—who's to say you didn't execute this little scheme together? I would think that would be a nice, convenient way to operate."

Dernwerd boggled at her. Xander shook his bald head. "And who's to say it's only the three of us who might have engineered this death?" he asked quietly. "For who saw Camalyn before she arrived on the scene? Where had she been earlier in the morning?"

"Yes, Camalyn!" Dernwerd exclaimed. "Explain your actions, please!"

"I would be much more likely to dismiss you than kill you if I wanted to see any of you gone from here," I said in a hard voice. "But it is very clear that we now have a murderer in our midst who is working his or her way through the senior staff. One of the four of us. Trust me,

I want to identify and destroy this person, but my first priority is safety—for the students at this school and the master wizards who remain alive."

"And what do you propose?" Audra sneered. "That the four of us stay always in sight of each other, watching and waiting? A bad idea, I think! Whoever has the strength to kill us one by one might easily have the ability to kill three of us at once. We should at least scatter throughout the halls and make his life more difficult."

Xander gave her a searching look. "So—you would rather be unobserved, Audra, would you?" he asked slowly. "What actions are you hiding? Why so secretive?"

"Why so trusting?" she shot back. "Perhaps I feel I have a better chance to protect myself if you three bumblers aren't nearby to hamper me."

"For the moment, I see no practical way for us to shadow each other day and night," I said, mostly just to stop the bickering. "Those of you who wish to keep a fellow company may do so. If you want to spy on each other," I added with some malice, "I will not stop you from doing that, either. I will examine the body and see what evidence it might yield."

"Oh, no, you will not!" Audra exclaimed. "I will stand here and watch every threadbare clue you lift from Borrin's corpse, or every false clue you plant there when you think none of us are looking."

Xander and Dernwerd exchanged uneasy glances. "Yes—she's right—I think we had better stay too,"

Dernwerd said apologetically. "In case one of us notices something another one overlooks—"

"Fine. Stay. And help," I snapped. "Let us get this autopsy under way."

But we found nothing helpful except the glimmer of magic. And even it bore no signature we could trace. Eventually I summoned the gardeners and told them they were turned gravediggers. Borrin would be buried beside the trellis of calysian roses that bloomed through all seasons. A better end than he deserved, actually, but it did not seem to be the time to be raking up past differences.

None of us heard from our murderer again for three more days. Again, I had permitted classes to resume, though everyone crept through the hallway with a sort of hunched and hunted gait, as if expecting at any moment horror would incorporate out of the very air. I was fairly certain the students and the staff had no reason to worry, but I was just as sure our renegade would eventually strike again at one of the senior wizards.

I was right. The killer came for me.

I had stepped outside for a breath of winter air and was walking along the lovely stone promenade that was attached to the second story of the school and overlooked the gardens. Little to see in the gardens at that season but hardy evergreens and hopeful brown stalks that, in a few months, would be animated by an even more ancient and powerful magic than mine. I always loved gardens in winter. They made me believe that even old and ugly and withered creatures possessed the potential for beauty and rebirth.

I had completed my first pass down the promenade and was just pivoting to make the return trip when I felt the unmistakable frisson of sorcery skitter across my skin. I paused, one foot on the floor, one foot lifted to step.

All around me, unfolding and refolding in infinite permutations, I saw reflections of myself caught in the exact same pose. I knew instantly what had happened, of course. Someone had cast a multiplying curse on me, assuming that I would never have gone out in the world unprotected, but also assuming that I had arrayed myself in a different kind of enchantment altogether. For instance, it might be supposed that I had summoned an artillery spell that was designed to fire off damaging shots as soon as it was activated by someone else's magic. A multiplying curse goes on and on and on without end—I would have been igniting so many deadly explosions that within minutes I would have died in my own detonations.

Never had my assailant expected that I would have kept my simple old reflecting spell in place. So this replicating curse, while impossibly annoying, was completely harmless. All it did was show thousands of copies of me, millions, putting down my foot and looking around, trying to gaze through my own reflections to determine who had accosted me.

I admit I was not surprised when I was finally able to make out Audra standing on the promenade before me, her eyes closed, her lips moving, as she quickly invoked a different bit of magic. I moved rapidly myself, tossing up a wall of protection that should be able to frustrate even the most virulent curse, for a while at least. Then, through my own still, watchful horde of sentries, I peered at her, trying to guess what she might do next.

She was gesturing more forcefully. Her red hair was unbound and whipping in an ensorceled wind, and her gold robes clung to a body that was more voluptuous than I remembered it being. I had always believed Audra to be constructed of bones, spite, and magic, but clearly dislike had colored my perceptions.

Or desire had colored someone else's.

I looked more closely. Last time I had seen her, Audra's hair had not been quite so luxuriant, nor so long. Nor was she usually this tall, and her angular face was far from being beautiful in the normal run of things. And, may I say, I am not in the habit of rating other women's physical attractions, but in my opinion, she generally had none. At the moment, her bosom was very well endowed.

This was not Audra. This was someone's idealization of Audra.

I knew of only one truly gifted illusionist who had also been in love with the red-haired witch. Apparently Morben was not dead after all. We had never had a chance to inspect his body, I suddenly remembered. We had assumed that the original death spell was what had caused the corpse to flare to ashes, but that had just been part and parcel of the overall illusion. There had been no body to examine because there was no body. Morben had projected the whole scene of assault and death, then caused the final image to vanish with a flick of his fingers. How could we have been so stupid?

I had just been so happy he was dead.

But if I didn't show some ingenuity immediately, I would be the one dead, and Morben would be the one who was happy. I could feel him testing my wall of protection, flinging first one angry spell and then another against my magical shield. He was very good at mayhem; he would be able to find a way through it eventually. And then every single copy of Camalyn the Headmistress would fall to the stone floor, choking on death and fury.

I considered the situation, tilting my head to one side.

All my reflections did likewise. I was maintaining two simultaneous sets of magic, the reflecting spell and the spell of protection. Morben, meanwhile, juggled two of his own, the illusion of Audra and the attack on me. That level of magical use had probably drained both of us to an approximately equal level.

But if I could reduce my expenditure of energy to one spell only, I should be stronger than my enemy. I would have to work very fast, of course. I would have to know exactly what I was doing before I made a single move.

Morben's curses hammered at my shield. I concentrated on holding the wall in place while conjuring and dispersing other bits of magic. My mirrored images all raised their hands before them, as if to plead for mercy or feel for an unseen door. I murmured a word, and all my doppelgängers fell away.

The counterfeit Audra whipped around to face me, her beautiful mouth stretched into a disdainful smile. "One of you or a thousand of you, it does not matter," Morben said in Audra's voice. "I will slay you all."

I had never gotten much pleasure out of bandying words with Morben, and I did not bother now. I merely extended my right hand and spoke a single word. "*Stone.*"

The other wizard turned to a statue with its mouth half-open and its hands lifted as if to strike. He did not move again.

I stood there a moment, smiling, then resumed my habitual reflecting spell. You could never tell where the next danger might come from, or when. It was not possible to be too careful.

To tell the truth, I had expected a more emotional reaction from the school board and my fellow wizards once it was discovered who the killer was and how I had vanquished him. Something along the lines of, "Oh, Camalyn, you're so wise, we're so grateful, you've saved us all" would have been entirely appropriate, I thought. Instead, the head of the school board merely said, "I suppose you'll be wanting funds to hire some new instructors." My remaining staff quarreled amongst themselves over who had been most delinquent in overlooking the obvious clues that pointed to the notion that Morben was not really dead.

I was not surprised when they ultimately decided I was most to blame. "Had Camalyn figured this out sooner," Xander said, "Borrin would not be dead."

I could not be entirely sorry that my deductions had been so slow.

The corollary event that probably made me happiest about the whole affair was how angry Audra was that the cautionary statuary on the promenade looked just like her, with a few enhancements. "You could have turned him back into *Morben* before you turned him into stone forever," she said a few days after the incident was concluded.

"I could have, if I had wanted to risk dying for your vanity," I agreed. "I only had time for one spell. I chose to incapacitate him, not de-beautify him."

"What if he breaks free of enchantment?" Dernwerd asked in a fretful voice. "What if he comes back to life and kills us all?"

I shrugged. I wasn't too worried about it. A wizard's spell generally will last for that wizard's lifetime, so *I,* at least, should be dead before Morben had any reasonable chance of resurrection. "Get out the sledgehammer and shatter him to bits," I said. "Grind him into dust and let the wind blow him away. It's all the same to me."

"But are we just to leave him like that forever?" Xander asked. "It seems so indecent, somehow. What kind of lesson does that present for the students?"

"Not to try to kill the Headmistress," I said over my shoulder, for I was bored with the conversation and already walking away. "I don't know that they need to learn anything else while they're here at Norwitch."

And, come to think of it, I'm not sure any of them did.

the boy who chased seagulls

MICHAEL ARMSTRONG

The old man walked along the beach on his lifelong mission to collect trash and other cast-off stuff. In town the children called him the Beachcomber, or Old Man, or (not to his face) Creepazoid, but he had his own name, he thought, a name he would share if anyone asked. Hardly anyone did, and so only the beachcomber knew his true name.

Uncle, he thought of himself. I am Uncle.

Uncle walked the beach with steps firmer and longer than on the often icy streets of the town, an Alaska fishing town, hard on its luck and struggling to keep profit ahead of pride. On the beach he could walk as his true self, ancient and unbowed to time. Not whole, though. The beach had taken pieces of him and only rarely gave them back.

He used an old bamboo staff, crushed smooth at the end and split in parts, for balance and defense. Like almost everything about him, he found it on the beach—given to him by the beach, he liked to think. Uncle wore old tennis shoes with heavy socks, canvas duck pants cut off below the knees, red long johns, a wool shirt, a rumpled old dark green rain slicker, and a big floppy wool hat. His white beard hung to his chest, and his white hair poked out from under the hat.

Uncle carried a battered old canvas back slung around one shoulder, a plastic grocery bag inside for wet or disgusting items he found on the beach. He saw it as his own special mission to collect trash. Secretly, he looked for treasure, but he found that if he had it as his stated purpose to collect trash he would find treasure that much more easily. And he had to collect everything.

Yes, Uncle had his rules. He must pick up all plastic, anything of human manufacture, unless it was so heavy he couldn't carry it; and then he flung it above the high-tide line so that someday someone else could pick it up. Glass bottles he broke and ground into the rocky sand, to be turned into beach glass.

Of beach glass he had some rules, too. Only worn beach glass could be picked up. No edge should be shiny, no surface unground. Pieces smaller than a fingernail should be left to return to sand. Intact glass floats, of which he had found only a dozen in all his life, he could take. Broken floats must be returned to the beach.

Paper that would rot away he could leave if he had no room to carry it, unless he found the paper offensive, as with most fast-food wrappers. Uncle did not see it as his mission to clean up trash near parking lots or trash left by teenagers at beach parties. He picked up the faraway trash and left other trash for good citizens or bad boys on community service to haul away. He would not pick up gross diapers or tampons, used bandages, or anything similarly disgusting.

Of natural treasures, old bones he could take, except whale bones, and seashells and interesting rocks. Sometimes he made little sculptures, like spirals of gray rock split with quartz. Uncle did not take feathers, not off the beach, except feathers of birds who stayed the winter. Certainly he did not take eagle feathers, not because that was against the law—he did not give a shrew's ass about the law—but in respect for the eagle. He called the eagle "Uncle," like him, for that is what his name meant, and the raven "Grandfather." Even though ravens wintered, he never, ever touched their feathers. Eagle feathers he might move, binding them to the highest branch of a driftwood log, or sticking them point down into the beach.

Of seagull feathers, he never saw them, and so didn't touch them, even though they were there. Uncle and seagulls did not get along, not since that time long ago.

On one of his walks he saw the boy chase seagulls. As an old man, an elder, Uncle saw it as his duty, right, privilege, and honor to correct the behavior of boys. Sometimes he hit them, although he hadn't done so in a long time, and sometimes he yelled at them. In his old age, though, he had come to berate them through jokes and stories.

The boy ran ahead of Uncle on the low tideflats, out where the seagulls clustered in great flocks. The boy ran carefree in the fading summer, that month before the huge storm tides that would wipe the beach clean. Already big swells had rolled in, bringing in trash from far out to sea: soap bottles, plastic lids, broken buoys, and tangled nests of fishing line. Uncle had a bagful of trash and headed home to his driftwood beach shack up a ways on the Spit. The boy, no more than ten, ran on the flat sand, jumping over puddles and great rafts of kelp. He saw the seagulls and ran toward them. The seagulls held their ground until the last minute, then roared up in a great flight of cackling and rustling, settling down a hundred yards away. The boy did this again and again, each time making Uncle madder and madder. What had the seagulls done to the boy? Didn't they deserve their rest?

Soon the boy's path intercepted Uncle's. Usually kids turned away from Uncle, but this boy who chased seagulls also dared to challenge the old man. He came up to Uncle with that nasty gleam in his eye, that puny little chest thrust forward and his chin high in the air. Oh, Uncle had seen hundreds of punks like him, and they did not scare him at all. He could sweep out with his bamboo staff and knock them off their feet so fast they wouldn't think it happened.

Uncle thought of doing so right then. A boy who chased seagulls like that deserved a good beating. In his meaner days, he would have done just that, only there were laws against old men beating up boys, and while Uncle didn't care for the laws, he did care for the inconvenience. So instead he told the boy a story.

"Hullo, Beachcomber," the boy said.

"Hullo, Boy Who Chases Seagulls," Uncle said.

"Ha!" The boy loved that, glad someone had noticed his mischief.

"Why do you chase seagulls?"

"Because it's fun."

"You wouldn't think it fun if you knew what happens to boys who chase seagulls."

"Oh, crap," the boy said.

"What is your name?" Uncle asked him.

"Travis," he said.

"Well, Travis, I knew a boy who chased seagulls once, and you know what happened to him? The seagulls ate him."

"Crap," the boy said again.

"No, no, this is true," Uncle said, smiling. "I bet you."

"What?"

"If you don't believe my story, I will give you this," and he opened up his hand and showed him a rare blue piece of beach glass.

Travis grinned. "OK, tell me your damn story."

Uncle saw that grin and knew he had him hooked.

"This was long ago," Uncle said, "back when the sea ran thick with fish, and even though people fished with sail-boats and oars, they caught ten times as many fish as today. A fisherman could work eight runs of salmon a summer, two weeks straight each run, and make enough to live on the whole year—and live in style, even though everything cost more then.

"On one of those fishing boats, a beautiful strip-built boat named *Mystery,* a boy about your age fished with his father, older brothers, and uncles. A boy grew up fast then and could became a man in one summer, his thin shoulders and puny muscles turning broad and strong in one month. The boy had another name, one his parents had given him to honor a grandfather back in the days when men had silly names, so out of embarrassment the boy insisted everyone call him 'Buster.'

"When on land and walking upon beaches, Buster loved to chase seagulls. He thought them scummy birds, trash birds, because they ate fish scraps and chased each other. They shat on roofs and rocks and trucks and sometimes people, and they smelled. Buster hated seagulls and did not understand their importance to the sea, to fish, to how his family made their living. He did not understand their power.

"So, when walking on the beach and letting himself be a boy and not a soon-to-be man, he chased seagulls. Oh, he loved the sport. He would creep up on huge flocks, for there were thousands more seagulls back then, as there were more fish (but not as many eagles), and he would scatter them. He would do this for hours, stalking them, never letting them rest, until the seagulls, disgusted, flew elsewhere, or the tide came in.

"One day when the *Mystery* was out fishing, casting its nets close to a nearby island on a low tide, the boy went up to the bow to pee over the edge. No one saw him leave the men at the stern, hauling in nets, and because the boy had a reputation for being lazy, no one missed him when he didn't come back, for what happened was this. While on the bow peeing, his cock hanging out of his underpants and his green rain bibs undone and flopping down, the boy lost his balance and fell into the sea. He would say later that he didn't lose his balance, a seagull flew by and pushed him in, but what seagull could be so strong?

"The men at the back didn't hear him splash in, didn't notice his disappearance, so busy were they hauling in nets and pulling out fish. If you've ever picked nets—you have, haven't you, Travis?—then you'd know how only the fish matter, and how it's easy to forget everything else.

"Buster fell in headfirst, which saved him, for the cold so stunned him that it made him lose his breath, and he didn't suck in water. The cold northern ocean engulfed him, like a bear squeezing him, and he couldn't breathe, couldn't think. His rain pants caught a bubble of air that kept him afloat. He kicked off his rubber boots when they filled up with water. When he came up to the surface, he screamed and yelled and gasped for air.

"No one heard him, of course, what with the seagulls screeching around the boat. Soon Buster lost his strength for yelling, but gained it for breathing. He sucked air, warmer than the water, and though he couldn't feel his legs or feet, his chest felt warm. If he'd known anything about human physiology, he would have known that what happened was all his blood had been shunted from his limbs and to his body core, and that's what kept him alive.

"Buster drifted away from the *Mystery,* toward that island. When he saw the island, he saw that he would have to make it there and out of the water. He didn't have to swim far or fast, for the tide as much as his own strength pushed him in. He fetched up on a sandy beach.

"He gasped and coughed on that sand, out of the water and warming up quickly in the midsummer sun. Buster might have been cruel, but he wasn't stupid. He knew he would have to get to a higher beach, because the tide would eventually come in—yes, you know that, don't you, Travis? See, the tide on this beach is already coming in, but I'm not moving, and I'm sure you're hoping this old man will finish the story before your feet get wet.

"So, Buster crawled up that beach. It was all he could do, crawl, and it seemed to take him hours to make the journey, although it was but a few minutes. He kept passing out from the chill, but every time he felt like drifting to sleep, a seagull would swoop down and nip at him.

"At first he thought they were saving him, as indeed they were, only they also nipped at his flesh and took little bites, once they had torn away his rain bibs and his sweatshirt. The seagulls harassed him and drove him higher up onto the beach, to his own safety, and their justice.

"For up on the beach, by a long line of sea wrack from the last tide, a line of fresh kelp and dead crabs, a thousand seagulls waited for Buster. He crawled up to the high-tide line, hoping it would be high enough, and collapsed.

"And the seagulls took him. They ripped at his flesh, at his back and legs, tearing out a thousand chunks of skin and muscle. They bit off the ends of his fingertips, ate his ears, ate the calluses on his feet and one of his eyes. They ate the tip of his nose and part of his lips. It was as if the seagulls knew how much to eat of him without actually killing him, so that he would suffer to the end of his days, half-blind, half-crippled, face ruined.

"Only, the seagulls' feast saved him. By then the tide

had begun to come in, his father and brothers and uncles had hauled in their nets, and it happened that his father looked toward the shore of the island and saw this great cloud of seagulls. He thought they might have found a whale. Back in those days, fishermen also took whales, and even a beached whale could be worth something. Buster's father took out his big mariner binoculars, looked to shore, and saw Buster's flailed back, dripping red, and finally realized Buster had fallen overboard and washed up on the beach.

"His father and uncles took a little dinghy up to the beach and rescued Buster. They wrapped him in a blanket, soon soaked with blood, and bathed him in fresh ocean water. The salt stung him so hard he couldn't cry, and it healed his wounds. Later, the town doctor stitched up the worst of the wounds as best he could. Without good fingers, though, Buster couldn't fish, and with so ugly a face and lips that could not even kiss, he never married. The only thing he could do was pick up trash and sell junk, and that's what he did until the end of his days.

"Which is why, Travis, you shouldn't chase seagulls."

The boy looked at him, stunned, and for a moment Uncle thought he might have reached him. Then the boy laughed, and Uncle knew his story hadn't worked. He shook his head.

"So what happened to Buster?" Travis asked. He might not have understood, but at least he appreciated a good story.

"Buster decided he had to redeem himself to the seagulls. So mean had he treated them, though, it became a difficult task. He scrounged fish scraps and saved them for the seagulls, then saved them for the eagles to eat so they wouldn't eat the seagulls. Buster began walking the beaches for trash and junk, junk to sell or use or salvage. Sometimes when people lost things on the beach or in the sea, they would pay Buster to find them for him, and often he did.

"One day after Buster had become a young man, he found a bit of pink flesh on the beach, flesh that looked like no flesh he had ever seen. He put it up to what was left of his nose to smell it, and amazingly, it *became* his nose. The flesh just sort of oozed onto his face, and where he had not had a nose, he now did, although it stayed pink for a long time, and even when it tanned, always remained slightly lighter then the rest of his face.

"Many months later, he found another bit of flesh, one of his fingertips. Over time, over many, many years, bit by bit he regained the parts of his body the seagulls had eaten. He realized that what happened was that the seagulls had shat him out. The seagull crap took time to gather together and become that which the seagulls had eaten. And then, of course, it took time for the flesh to wash up on the beach, and for Buster—he long ago quit using that name, though—to find those small parts of his body. It took many bags of trash, junk, and some treasure for him to haul off, but there you go."

Travis glared at him now, become again a surly boy. "Ah, that's just a story," he said. "It's not true." He held out his hand for the bit of blue beach glass.

"Oh? You think not?" Uncle pulled off his gloves, finger by finger, and showed Travis his wrinkled hands. "See these fingers? See how the tips look a different color? And see my lips, how what you think is scar is just that part of my lips the sea gave back? And see my nose?" Uncle lifted up the corner of his hat, then, showing the boy his empty eye socket. "And see my lost eye, the eye I have searched for ever since that day long, long, ago when the boy who chased seagulls learned his lesson."

"Creepazoid!" the boy yelled, and ran away before Uncle could whack him with his bamboo staff.

Uncle watched the boy run back up the beach, toward town. Along the way, Travis deliberately veered from his path to run through a flock of seagulls, only one or two of whom grudgingly flew up. They had grown tired of the boy's game.

Uncle turned and continued on his way, back to his tiny driftwood shack heated by coal, back to his single bed, his single room, and the junk and treasure he scavenged and sometimes sold. As the sun moved down below the bluff above town, one last flicker of light caught a shiny something on the beach. Uncle reached down and picked it up. At first he thought it might have been a child's marble, ground cloudy by the beach, but when he held it up to inspect, the marble rolled into his empty socket and became his eye.

Uncle looked at the world in stereo again, the world no longer flat but wider, although a bit fuzzier with the cataract in his old and weathered eye. Well, he thought, that's the last of it, the last bit of flesh returned from the sea. His cabin and his bed awaited him, and he wondered if he'd bother to make a fire for the night, or if he even needed to.

Must have made my peace with the sea, he thought, with the seagulls.

And Buster, born as Percy, now known as Uncle, went home, perhaps to die, perhaps to live another day, but never, ever, ever to chase seagulls.

palimpsest

LAURA ANNE GILMAN

"That had better be coffee."

"Hazelnut. Double."

"You'll live." Wren's arm reached out from under the blanket and snagged the cup out of her partner's hand. Without spilling a drop, she raised herself on her elbows and took a sip.

"God. I may be human after all." She peered out from under a tangle of mouse-brown hair at the man standing in the dim light of her bedroom. He looked broad-shouldered and solid and reassuringly familiar. "What time is it?"

"Nine. A.M.," he clarified. "Rough night?" Sergei sat down on the edge of her bed, forcing her to scoot over to make room.

"No more so than usual. The Council came down

hard on the piskies who were dragging people under the lake, so there've been some minor temper tantrums in protest, but other than that everything's quiet. Well, quiet for them, anyway."

There had been the equivalent of a gang war in Central Park earlier that year between water and earth sprites. Fed up, the city's independent Talents—lonejacks—and the Mages' Council had declared truce long enough to make sure things didn't get out of hand again. Wren, like all lonejacks, distrusted the Council on principle, and the Council and their affiliates thought lonejacks all were troublemaking fools, so it was an uneasy truce to say the least.

Wren took another sip of the coffee and decided that there was enough caffeine in her bloodstream to move without breaking apart. She got out of bed, cup still in hand, and staggered to the dresser to pull out a clean T-shirt.

"You know if the *Cosa* ever did get itself organized . . ."

"Bite your tongue." She ran one hand through her hair and peered at herself in the mirror. "Oh, I look like hell. Thank God I don't have another stint of babysitting for a couple of days. I could sleep for a week . . ."

Suddenly his presence there clicked, and she turned to glare at him, the effect in no way diminished by the fact that she was naked save for a pair of pink panties.

"Sorry, Zhenechka. We've got a job."

Wren closed her eyes tightly, seeking balance, then kicked back the rest of the coffee with a grimace and handed the cup to him. "Shower first. Then details."

She stopped halfway to the door. "Is it at least going to be fun?"

"Would I sign you up for anything boring?"

"The last time you said something like that, we spent two nights in a Saskatchewan jail. And if you say 'it wasn't boring,' so help me I'll fry your innards."

The sound of the shower started up, and Sergei allowed himself a faint smile. "Wasn't boring."

Under the pounding of steaming hot water, Wren swore she could feel the particles of her body coming back into focus. She ducked her head under the stream of water, then reached for the shampoo, massaging it into her scalp with a sigh of pleasure as the deep herbal scent wafted through the air. She could rough it with the best of them, but after a night wrassling with earth spirits peevy at everything that moved, a little luxury was nice. *And if the coffee's any indication, this may be the last luxury I get for a while. He only buys the Dog's coffee when he wants to soften me up.*

Rinsed, dried, and dressed, she walked out of the bathroom drawing a comb through her hair, wincing at the tangles. Her partner leaned against the counter in her tiny kitchen, drinking a mug of tea and reading the newspaper. "All right, you know you're dying to tell me. So spill."

"Seven grand down." He gestured to the counter where the coffee machine was just starting to send out scented steam. "Another ten when you retrieve their package."

"We're working cut-rate this week, I see." They had three price scales. High-end was the stuff that was snore-worthy: divorce settlements, insurance reclamations. Situations that required thinking and ingenuity were slightly cheaper. Sergei knew, by now, what would pique her interest, and was willing to dicker a little less sharp for them. And third . . .

Don't think about the third. If you think it, they'll call.

Third was working on retainer for the organization known as the Silence. Wren had been with them for a little more than a year now, Sergei for far longer than that. Human, nonmagical, and utterly without mercy or compassion, the Silence were nonetheless one of the Good Guys. She thought. She hoped.

"So, what's the deal?"

"Stow-and-show. Special interest group, wants nine-tenths of a particular display." Translation: Several someones, acting in concert, wanted her to steal something—possession being nine-tenths of the law—from a museum, the "stow-and-show."

"You have got to stop watching those god-awful heist movies. Life's not a caper, Serg." The coffee machine finished perking, and she grabbed a mug from the sink and filled it. "Paperwork?"

He jerked his chin at her kitchen table, and she noticed the sheaf of papers awaiting her perusal.

"They're organized, I'll give them that."

"Organized, *and* chatty. Guy wanted to tell me every detail of his life, his job, and the weather in Timbuktu."

Coffee in hand, Wren sat down at the table and drew the blueprints toward her. "And how is the weather there, anyway? Oh Christ on a crutch, the Meadows." She had hit them twice in four years—by now she and the alarm system were old friends. "And still people loan them exhibits. I just don't get the world, I really don't. What's the grab?"

"Painting. Smallish, should be easy enough to stow in the tube. In and out, seventeen minutes, tops."

"I can do it in eleven, if it's in the main gallery." It wasn't ego if you really were that good. And she was. Possibly—probably—the best Retriever of her generation.

He waited a beat, then dropped the other shoe. "And we got a Call."

She heard the capital letter in his voice, and her head lowered to rest on her crossed arms on the table. "Of course we did. Because my life just wasn't full to the brim with joy already."

"Beats unemployment."

"Easy for you to say, Mister Stay-at-Home-and-Cash-the-Check."

Which wasn't fair, she knew. Sergei had warned her about working for the Silence. They wanted first call on her time, always and ever. But it had seemed a worthwhile trade-off at the time.

And their checks always, but always, cleared.

"You going to need to charge up?"

"*Now* you ask?" They were sitting in the car—a yellow sedan, mocked up like a cab, the quintessentially invisible car in Manhattan—outside the Meadows. Although she knew the answer, Wren reached deep inside, touching the roil of current that always rested within her, the sign of a Talent. A gentle stroke, and it uncoiled, sparkling like glitter in her veins. "No, I'm fine. Soaked up a bit when the last batch of storms rolled through, in case things got ugly in the Park."

She had loved storms since she was old enough to lurch against the windowsill. *"You're a current-user, kid. You're always going to crave the storm."* Her mentor's voice, years and lifetimes gone. You could recharge current off man-made sources, and there were lonejacks who preferred that. Safer, more readily accessible, and no hangover if you pulled down too much. But Wren went to the wild source every chance she got.

She didn't have much chance to rebel, these days.

"If you draw down too much, remember that there's a

secondary generator over here." And his index finger stabbed the blueprint on the seat between them.

"Yeah, saw that." They'd been over the plans half a dozen times already. But it made Sergei feel better if they rehashed everything just before she went in. Normally he wouldn't be anywhere near the scene on a simple grab like this, but the transit workers had gone on strike, and she couldn't risk hailing a real cab to get home. So he would drop her off, go drive around for a while, and come back for her.

"Try not to pick up any long-distance fares while I'm gone."

"Not even if they offer to tip like a madman," he promised.

She laughed, touched his cheek for luck, and slipped out into the darkness.

In some ways, the strike was a nice bit of luck. In her dark grey tracksuit and black sneakers, if stopped by anyone she could claim to be heading home from a late night at the office. A knapsack slung over her shoulder held a lightweight dress and strappy heels to back up the story, plus a thin, strong nylon rope coiled in an inside pocket, her lockpick set, and a wallet with realistic-looking identification and enough cash to get home for real should something go wrong.

Pausing just beyond the reach of the closed-circuit cameras, Wren took a deep breath, let it out. Ground. That was the key. Focus. Center. Ground.

As though she had grown from the earth, Wren felt the weight of its comfort rise up through her, from bedrock into flesh and bone. Soothing the serpent of energy and coaxing it up her spine, into her arms, down her legs. It was like an orgasm, a muted one, pleasure sparking every nerve ending until she was completely aware of everything around her, but not so much that she was overwhelmed by it. *Balance. Balance . . .* There was a thin line you had to ride, when you directed current. It wasn't enough to be able to sense it, or to be able to direct it. You had to convince it to do what you wanted, when you wanted.

Taking the faintest hint of current, she lifted her hand, drawing the camera's attention. It was like weaving without a loom. Flickers left her fingertips as she concentrated on the circuits and wires of the camera system. Too much, and you burned it out, setting off alarms. Too little, and a sharp-eyed watchman might spot her. Just a hint of static, something that could be brushed off, so long as it didn't go on for too long. Just long enough for her to move, crouched low and flowing across the grounds like the low-flying bird she was named for, until she reached the relative safety of the decorative overhang. *God bless old buildings.* The Meadows had started life as a mansion, and still boasted any number of odd architectural details that created enough shadows for Wren to wrap herself in.

Letting her heart rate slow down to normal, Wren pictured the assignment in her mind. It was a small thing, barely twelve-by-twelve, set in a severe silver frame. Part of a traveling exhibit of paintings that were as of yet unattributed but considered by a number of experts to be "rediscovered" works by various Impressionist masters. The art world was wild over the find; Sergei had been to see the exhibit twice even before they got this gig. If she knew her partner, he'd want to hold on to the painting for a few days until they handed it back, just to have one of the so-called Fabulous Finds in his possession.

Actually, if she'd been prone to liking artwork, she thought she might want to own something like this too. The colors were almost alive, creating a wash of light on the landscape that reminded her of the photograph Sergei had in his own office, the black-and-white nature photographer, the guy who took all those pictures of national parks.

Art critique later, she told herself. *Clock's tick tick ticking . . .*

The thing about museums is, they weren't stupid. They knew that technology was fallible, and that humans were fallible. But most of them also had serious budget restrictions. The Meadows had a top-of-the-line electrical alarm system. It would probably have stopped any casual intruder, or at least alerted the police to the incursion. But the Board of the Meadows had one serious disadvantage. They had never heard of current, the magical kind, or the *Cosa.*

Magic wasn't the fairy dust and wild imaginations science liked to claim. It was real, and tangible . . . if you were part of the small percentage of the human population able to sense it. An even smaller percentage of those humans, like Wren, were able to direct the current into anything useful.

And Talents like Wren, who honed her skills for the specific purpose of larceny, were called Retrievers.

A light touch to the door, and she felt the tingle that meant elementals were around, drawn to the current that was bound into electricity, no matter what form. A quick push of current bridged the gap in the alarm system long enough for her to open the door and slip inside. She started to move in the slow-slide fashion she had perfected for not creating footfalls, when she stopped and returned to the lock. Placing her hand on the alarm pad, she waited. Elementals had the reasoning ability of inbred hamsters, but you could use them, if you knew how. She did.

Come on, you know you're bored with that stale, man-made electricity . . . come taste some of mine . . .

They came to her tentatively at first, then swarming in their eagerness. Natural current "tasted" better to them. She let them feed for a few seconds, nibbling around the edges of the current curling up from her belly, twining around her spine. *All right. Earn your keep.* She visualized clearly what she wanted them to do. A faint hesitation, and the swarm was off, splitting into a dozen different directions as they moved along the museum's state-of-the-art wiring.

A pity they couldn't call back to warn her if someone else was in the hallways; but if a person didn't have current, elementals didn't know he or she existed.

The painting was in a little alcove off gallery #11, in a space that had probably once been a servant's room. Or a closet. What did she know? Wren thought, listening with part of her Talent to the sounds of the elementals causing chaos in other parts of the building. She grew up in a double-wide trailer, for Pete's sake. They didn't even have any mansions in Redwater.

Palms held over the frame, and the current surged, creating the illusion again that the alarm hadn't been breached. Moving quickly, she fit a small ceramic knife into the frame and slit the painting carefully along four sides, sliding it out and rolling it up. Tucked into an aluminum tube, the tube stowed in her backpack. And then it was time to go. She checked the digital readout on her knapsack, far enough away from her body that the current didn't futz it too badly. Fourteen minutes. *Damn. Getting old, Valere. You're getting old.*

By the time she made it out to the edge of the museum's property, it was almost twelve thirty. She perched in the vee of a large oak and contemplated the street. The empty street.

"Dammit, Didier . . ." She'd had to duck and wait while a guard went by her; too close, that one. They were getting smarter. She'd have to put a no-go on any jobs here for at least two years. Maybe three.

Not for the first time she wished for a cell phone. But even if they hadn't been too risky—too easy for someone to check the last few numbers dialed—she still couldn't carry one. No cell phone, no PDA . . . even the odd watch was prone to strange fluctuations under current, and when she pulled down a surge, all bets were off.

Another fifteen minutes, and she had to accept the fact that Sergei had probably been forced to call it a night. The glitches she had the elementals set off might have caused a patrol car to take a swing by, even though none of it had been enough to trigger an actual alarm.

"Good thing you wore the comfy sneakers," she told herself, swinging herself down from the tree and landing with lazy grace on the grass. It was going to be a long walk back.

It might have been the night air. Or the current still running high in her system. Or, as Sergei claimed, just a natural-born stupidity. But at the time, the idea to kill two jobs with one evening seemed just a matter of common sense and practicality. She had to walk by the site anyway, so why not?

"Why not," Sergei said over his tenth mug of high-test

tea, the first five of which had cooled while he was waiting for her, "is because a) you were carrying a retrieved object. And b) because you hadn't done anything more than a cursory glance at the job write-up."

She knew he was mad then, when he called it a job instead of a situation.

"And c) because you got *caught!*"

Wren winced, fighting the urge to duck under the diner's table. "Not so much caught," she protested meekly. "More like . . ."

"Who's there?"

Wren swore, wrapping herself in current and fading into the shadows. The store was a hodgepodge of clichés, down to the moth-eaten *thing* stuffed and mounted on the counter, its crystal eyes reflecting light back at her. At least, she hoped it was just crystal reflecting light . . .

"I said, who's there?" An old man to match the shop stomped downstairs, a megapowered *X-Files*-quality flashlight in one hand. Wren closed her eyes so she wouldn't reflect the light. The beam flashed across her face, passed on . . . then came back.

"I know what you're here for," the old man cackled. "But you can't have it. Can't, can't can't!"

Nobody said anything about the guy being a Talent, she thought with irritation, then common sense reasserted itself. He wasn't a Talent, or a seer, or anything that would have allowed him to sense what she was or what she intended. He was just old-fashioned bugfuck. Crazy had a way of messing with the brain in ways even current couldn't work around.

"Yeah, old man?" Her voice was low, dangerous. She'd copied it from *Blue Angel,* practicing until she had it down just right. If anyone reported her to the cops, they'd get laughed out of the station for claiming they'd been robbed by Marlene Dietrich.

"Yeah. It's mine. Mine I tell you. I bought it, I got it, and I'm going to keep it."

Any moment Wren expected him to break into a round of "mine, my precioussss." If he did, she was out of there, and the Silence could keep their damn retainer that month.

"My staff, mine. Going to make me a wizard. Going to teach me how to talk to the birds."

"I think you're halfway there, old man," Wren said, relieved that he was nattering about something other than her goal. And if the staff that he was talking about actually was an Artifact—an item used like a battery to store current—the Silence would just have to hire her to come back and get it. Sergei's cat would have better luck working a manual can opener than the man in front of her actually accessing current.

"What's that? You, stop there. Who are you? How did you get in here?" The hand not holding the flashlight came up, the dark shape unmistakable even to someone as gun-shy as Wren. A sawed-off shotgun.

Think quick, Valere!

"I'm a djinn, come to gift you with a treasure," she said, punting madly. Maybe, in her dark clothing, the shimmer of current still wrapped around her, visible or no, she'd be able to pull this off. "A painting, through which magic you might transport yourself instantly."

A combination of Bugs Bunny cartoons and *Star Trek* reruns, but he leaned closer, the gun not focused quite so threateningly as a minute ago.

Moving carefully, she withdrew the tube from her knapsack, having to tug it free when it snagged on the dress's folds.

"All shall be yours . . . for one simple gift in return."

The old man checked himself, glaring at her suspiciously. The shotgun began to rise towards her face. "What's that?"

"A trifle, a trinket. One of no use to mortals but great significance to djinn." She was dancing as fast as she could, the sweat crawling under her scalp and running down the side of her face and back of her neck. "A bell, a silver bell with a golden clapper, a bell that does not ring. You have such a thing, I am told. Give it to me, and the magic painting shall be yours."

"You traded one job for the other." Sergei was trying, really trying, to be his usual hard-assed self.

Wren reached across the diner table and snagged the pseudocream in its little tin pitcher; poured it into her coffee until it went from mud to diluted mud. "Hey, no problem. I'll just go steal it back."

She drank her coffee, pretending not to hear the muffled, pained noises coming from her partner.

"Oh . . . hell." Disgust dripped from every word as she stared down at the body of the pawnshop owner. Someone had staved in the back of his head with his own staff. There was a moral in there somewhere, but the smell of stale blood and feces was rising off the body, and she didn't want to waste time thinking when she could be working. Wren wrinkled her nose, wiping her palms on her jeans as though there was something sticking to them. "If I'd wanted to see dead bodies, I'd have gone to work for the morgue, dammit."

Ten minutes since she'd walked in the door. Daylight retrievals usually weren't her thing, but it wasn't as though the guy was in any shape to report her.

She risked another look down. Even less shape, now.

Normally working current just required an internal adjustment and some finely focused concentration. But there were times that shortcuts were useful, and words were the surest way to focus current fast, if a little dirty.

"Picture gone missing

hands not meant, not deserving
Retriever reclaims."

It wasn't great verse, but it didn't have to be. It just had to be meaningful, in form and function. Her mother loved haiku, and so using that form made her think of her mother, which made the form meaningful. And she *needed* to get that picture back. Which made the content meaningful. And . . . there it was. Her hands itched as the current she had generated reached like a magnet to lodestone, forcing her forward, stepping over the old man's body, to where the painting was tacked up with thumb pins—*Sergei's going to shit*—on the wall behind the counter.

"Looks like the old boy was trying to make a getaway . . . pity he didn't make it." She took the painting down, the tingling fading once she made contact with the spelled item. She looked around for the tube, but didn't see it. Refusing to muck around any longer, she pulled the scrunchie out from her hair, letting the ponytail fall loose, and wrapped it around the rerolled painting. She was ready to get the hell out of there, but something made her look back over her shoulder to the body lying on the floor.

"Ah . . . hell." She sighed, tucking the roll under one arm and retracing her steps. Stooping low, she put her hand out, palm down and flat. A hesitation, a centering, and then she touched the corpse. Spirits fled in the moment of death, unless there was a damn good reason—or a very strong spell—holding them in place. But while the animus might be gone, the body still had current caught in the biofield every living being generated, the natural electricity that made Kirlian photography possible.

"What? No! No, mine, mine, mustn't take, mustn't . . ." a fast-moving figure in front of him, angry, full of rage. "Where is it? She didn't have it on her when she left, which means you have it, now where? Where. Is. It?"

Whimpering, then another heavy blow. The old man spins under the force, falls to the ground. "Useless old fool . . ."

The sound of something whistling down a shock of red-flaring pain, and . . .

Nothing

Wren came out of the connection like a dog shaking off water, breathing heavy. "Damn damn damn *damn!*" He'd been killed for the painting. Killed . . . and she might have been . . . No time to think about it, she'd already stayed too long. Not that she was worried about cops showing up to investigate: Poor bastard had been dead a day at least.

Her eyes narrowed at the thought. "Ah . . . hell." Nobody deserved to rot like that. Slipping out the front door, she wiped the handle clean, then uncoiled a narrow rope of current from her inner pool and reached out with it, brushing the surface of the burglar alarm.

The loud wail of the alarm covered the sound of her bootheels on pavement, moving in the general direction of away.

The painting remained untouched on the coffee table where Wren had tossed it when she came in the door to Sergei's apartment. Wren was curled up on the sofa, while Sergei paced back and forth in front of her.

"Who the hell are we working for, Sergei? Because I get the feeling there's something they didn't tell us. Something that almost got me killed. And did get that poor bastard—"

"Bob Goveiss."

"Bob, killed. So give."

"Yes. That's what doesn't make sense."

"What?"

"The violence." He shook his head. "Those paintings were on loan from the French government. The same government that's about to splinter apart from the inside, which could have awkward repercussions on the current political scene."

"So sayeth CNN, amen," Wren said, but she was listening. "And . . . ?"

"And, the organization that hired us was planning on holding that painting hostage, to force the various factions to come back to the table."

Wren stared at her partner. "Okay, huh?"

He paced back and forth, gesturing with his hands as he spoke. "It's rare, but there have been a number of cases where an item is taken to force two sides to cooperate or risk being shown in public as the destroyer of a priceless work of art. Most recently in the theft of a Chagall painting: A ransom note was sent demanding peace in the Middle East before the painting would be returned. A useless demand, really, but it made a splash in the news."

Wren considered that, a small smile appearing on her face. "I like that," she said finally.

"Yeah. It does have appeal. But it doesn't always work. Anyway, it still doesn't make sense. Why would anyone who knew about the heist want to—"

"Play a round of Kill the Retriever?"

"Yes."

"Dunno. That's your job to find out. I'm going home before I forget what it looks like, catch some sleep before my next turn playing peacemaker. Call me when you find out anything." She got up, stretched, looked at her partner. "But do me a favor? Lock the doors when I leave. And don't be careless."

Sergei shook his head, his squared-off face softening as he smiled. "I'm always careful, Zhenechka."

Wren thought briefly of the nasty little gun he carried on some jobs, and shuddered. "Right. Better them than us and all that jazz." She kissed him good bye, rubbing her cheek against his five o'clock stubble, and let herself out.

The next evening he caught up with her on Park duty. A piskie had decided to pick on her, spluttering insults on her paternity, her maternity, and the general state of her underwear. Since piskies were, on average, twenty inches high and five pounds soaking wet, Wren's reaction was closer to embarrassed annoyance than anything else. She kept trying to kick it, but it would dance out of the way and come back a few moments later, still talking.

"Goid, you're annoying," she said to it.

"And you could use a drag into the lake. Wanna try?"

"Remember what happened last time you tried dunking a lonejack?"

Clearly it did, dancing back again until it was just out of reach. "Annoying human. Spoil all our fun."

"Be glad that's all I'm spoiling, you bothersome little wart."

"Want me to shoot him?" Sergei asked, falling into step beside her.

"You got a bullet small enough?"

"I hear tell that's all he's got," Goid crowed, then bit its tongue with an audible yelp when Sergei turned to glare at it. It was no secret in the *Cosa* that the Wren's partner had little love for the fatae, the purely supernatural creatures of the *Cosa Nostradamus.*

"Scoot," he said to it. Goid scooted.

"Damn. Next time the *Cosa* calls, you can answer, okay? What's up?"

"Nothing." His voice was sharp, and she could practically feel the irritation rising off him, now that the distraction of the fatae was gone. "As in, not a god-damned thing. As in, my contact seems to have disappeared."

"The rest of the payment got deposited?"

One or two of the lines in Sergei's forehead eased out. "The rest was deposited this afternoon, soon as they got their hands on the painting."

"Well then." Wren let out a little sigh. "What's a possible attempt on my life, so long as we're paid."

He cast a sideways look at her. "You mean that?"

They walked a few more paces along a tree-shrouded path, ignoring the faint giggles and rustling branches following them. "No," she said finally, on a sigh. "No, I don't. Not after . . . I felt him. And I felt him die. I can't walk away from that."

"Right. Lowell did a rundown on this organization for me. They check out clean, he says—but he was very surprised that they had the money to pay us. Not a dime in their collective kitty, and no fund-raisers going on in their name."

"Breaks my heart, it does." She didn't like Sergei's assistant, but the twit did know how to do his research. "So they hocked the furniture to pay us?" The giggles got louder as they reached a particularly large tree, and Wren put a hand on Sergei's arm to stop him. "Hang on."

She slipped out of her sneakers and planted her bare feet in the grass by the side of the road. Safely grounded, she opened herself to the current of the world around her. Colors swirled, electrons danced, and she sorted through the information tugging at her senses until she was able to discern the slightly off pattern twined around the tree. A tendril snaked out, stroking the ends of the pattern, then retracting in a flash as the pattern snapped out, attempting to snare her within its own tendrils.

She came back to herself with a blink, after confirming that the trap had been sprung. A chorus of disappointed "awwwws . . ." trailed after them as she slipped her shoes back on, and they walked on.

"Okay. So: no money. And yet they manage to scrape together seventeen thou to pay us. So what's the deal? They borrow the money from someone to pay for the retrieval, then that someone decides they'd rather have the painting than the promise of money?"

He shot her a sideways glance. "Maybe. Or it was never actually the organization who wanted it, at all. We might have been set up."

"But then why make the final payment? I mean, we're tough, but we're not that tough. Are we?"

"More to the point, do they think we are? If so, not a bad thing."

"Also besides the point, your ego aside." And she squeezed his hand to soften the words. "Ignore who hired us for a minute. Who went after me? Did that same person kill poor old Bob? What do we have? An organization, poor as proverbial church mice, that still manages to retain us to retrieve an object that they claim they're going to use to force political unity.

"Okay, here's a question for you."

Sergei nodded, indicating he was listening.

"Why did they bother to tell you what they'd be using it for?"

He let out a huff of breath. They walked in silence through the park, past human joggers running in pairs, and the occasional biker in bright spandex zipping through at high speeds. If any of the fatae were still watching them, they were being quieter about it.

"I've been wondering about that too. At first I thought the guy was just a talker. But then I started to think maybe his verbal diarrhea had a purpose. The assignment was the kind of thing you can't help talk about, because it's so different from the usual. But we don't talk about clients outside the office . . ."

"You would have if I'd turned up dead. Especially if they'd done it in such a way to suggest that, rather than waiting to be handed the painting, they'd stolen it from us."

Sergei stopped like he'd walked into a wall. "Chyort! Stolen it back, then used it to make peace. With your blood. Damn straight I would have talked. I would have blackened their reputation until they couldn't stand under the weight of it."

"And the talks would be undermined by doubt, maybe just enough to break them."

Sergei started swearing again, alternating between Russian and English, until Wren was certain that she could see blue current sparking and shimmering in front of his mouth.

"We're going to have to do something about them using us like that," she said thoughtfully, almost to herself. "Bad for business, otherwise . . ."

Sergei had called the dinner date, his voice on the answering machine filled with such glee she could only imagine the retainer he'd managed to con out of someone. She wasn't in the mood to party, her brain still filled with the annoyance of having been tricked into getting involved in politics, not to mention the attempt on her life, but dinner was dinner was dinner, especially if Sergei was buying. She threw herself into the shower, grabbed the first summer-weight dress she could find that wasn't wrinkled, and threw it on. Things had changed enough in their relationship over the past year that she slicked on lipstick and mascara, and tied her hair up in a looked-more-complicated-than-it-was knot before heading out the door. Not that any of that was going to turn her into a raving beauty, but Sergei appreciated the effort. And she appreciated his appreciation.

They were regulars at Marianna's, to the point where

Callie, the waitress, didn't even bother getting up to show her to their table. Of course, it wasn't that large a place, either. She could see Sergei sitting in the back the moment she walked in. And he was grinning like he was about to choke on wee yellow feathers.

"You're scaring me. What?"

"I had a little chat with an old friend of mine who was shocked, shocked to hear that criminals had their hands on any part of the 'Fabulous Finds.' A few hours later, this job came in. Since we are, after all, the only team who could pull something like this off . . ."

He slid a piece of paper across the table to her. She picked it up, noting first the weight of the paper, then the fact that it was letterhead stationery; and then her mind took in the words, and she started to laugh as Sergei called Callie over to open the wine.

"The Meadows Museum board would like to make use of your services to retrieve a painting that went missing from our premises on the night of July 14 . . ."

Getting paid to take back what they took in the first place, *and* undercut any attempt the organization might make to go ahead with their plan anyway.

"I love this job," Wren said, raising her glass.

"To karma," Sergei agreed. "To karma, and the joy of being the boot that gives it a kick in the ass. *Zdorov'ye!*"

the death of clickclickwhistle

MIKE DOOGAN

"Is it dead?"

Probationary Intern to the second assistant undersecretary Oscar Gordon looked around for the speaker, but the hallway outside the delegates' quarters was empty. Even in a small, busy spaceship, the crew was giving the alien diplomats a wide berth.

"Up here, mudfoot," the voice said.

Gordon looked up. A pale, thin young man was standing on what was, to Gordon, the ceiling, his left hand wrapped around a gripfast to keep himself from floating away.

"Is it dead?" he asked again.

Gordon shrugged. "How can I tell if it's dead if I don't know what it is?"

The man sighed, flipped himself off the ceiling, tumbled through the zero gravity to another gripfast, and oriented himself with Gordon.

"Mudfoots," he said to the air. Then, to Gordon, "It's in contact with the deck, isn't it?" He didn't wait for an answer, instead raising his voice, and saying, "Computer, is the object on the deck near the location of my voice an organic?"

"It is," a voice drawled out of the air, "if you mean the other object besides Probationary Intern to the second assistant undersecretary Oscar Gordon of the Federated Planets' Corps Diplomatique."

Gordon laughed. "I guess starspawn don't know everything," he said to the young man.

"Probationary Intern Gordon," the voice drawled, "name-calling with ship's fourth officer John Carter isn't really an occupation for a member of the Corps Diplomatique. You humans should get along better, whatever your superficial differences."

Gordon recognized the justice of the computer's rebuke. His command of diplomacy wasn't all that it should have been. He'd only graduated from the academy at Alpha Cen six months before, and this was his first real assignment.

The sentient races were having a big powwow on Rigel A1101, called Ricketts by the humans who lived there. Protocol prevented any extraterrestial ships from approaching the inner system that held Ricketts, so the

Chuck Yeager had been assigned, along with a dozen other ships, to meet the arriving interstellar vessels, pick up their legations, and ferry them to Ricketts. This was hardly a plum assignment, so the Brahmins had assigned the lowest-ranking and least-well-connected diplos to the ships.

Gordon looked at the young man hanging in front of him. He's one of the reasons I don't like spaceflight, he thought. So at ease in zero G, and so superior about it. Look at his uniform. Plain gray silk without an insignia on it. How does anyone tell who's an officer out here?

His own uniform, the uniform of a very junior diplomat, was a thousand times nicer. Rainbow bodysuit, lavender cloak and spats, yellow gloves and boots. He might be short and dark and even a trifle plump from an endless round of practice state dinners, but compared to the other young man, who was long and pale from years of no-gravity spaceflight, he looked like a million credits.

Say what you want about the Corps Diplomatique, he thought, we know how to dress. Even if the magnetics he needed to keep from floating away in zero gravity did ruin the drape of his cloak.

"You are quite correct, Computer," the young diplomat said aloud, bowing slightly to the ship's officer. "Can you tell me how this object got here?"

The object, somehow thoroughly anchored to the deck, was an oval, thicker in the middle than at the ends, its surface divided into segments by snaky lines. To Gordon, it looked like the shell of an earth tortoise with the leg and head holes filled in.

"I can," the voice drawled. "It was rolled out the hatchway leading to the diplomats' quarters. I'll show you."

The air in front of the two humans congealed into a replica of the hallway. The hatch opened, and the object rolled out on its side, wavered and fell, ever so slowly, to the deck, where it remained.

"Attila the Hun!" Gordon said. "If it came out of the diplomats' quarters, it's my problem. Computer, can you tell us who moved it here?"

"No can do. Before any of the alien species came aboard the captain ordered me not to snoop in their quarters. Something about diplomatic immunity."

More likely worried about the Xtees bringing bug detectors and catching him red-handed, the young diplomat thought. Gordon looked at the object on the deck. "Computer, we didn't take on any aliens that look like this, did we?"

It was Fourth Officer Carter who answered.

"We took on thirteen species, all oxygen breathers, none of which looked like that." He closed his eyes for a moment. "But one that could. It's a Husker."

Gordon snorted. "That's no Husker, starspawn," he

said, flipping his cape so that the synthmaterial rippled. "They're eight feet tall, and they have all those arms, or fronds, or whatever they are."

"Which one of us was it that smoked spatial geometries, mudfoot?" the ship's officer asked. "Oh, that's right. It was me. That's a Husker."

The Huskers were a recent contact. They were from a system in Clarke's Cloud, a raft of stars in toward the center of the universe. Or so they said. They called their home star "the sun" and their home planet "Earth," just like every other sentient species, which drove the translation program crazy. It also made it hard to locate their home planet. They were officially designated Unknown Origin 37s. But they looked like nothing so much as walking—sort of—talking—after a fashion—stalks of corn. So it didn't take fifteen minutes after first contact for some wag to hang the nickname on them.

The young diplomat opened his mouth to argue, but the computer interrupted. "Fourth Officer Carter is right. Look."

A full-grown Husker appeared in the air in front of Gordon's nose, then folded itself slowly this way and that until what was left was an object like the one on the deck.

"Vlad the Impaler!" Gordon said. "How am I going to explain this to Second Assistant Undersecretary Tulk?"

"Who's that?" Carter asked.

"My boss in the Corps Diplomatique," Gordon said.

"Aren't you going to have to explain it to the chief Husker first?"

Gordon's answer was cut off by a throat-clearing noise.

"Actually, fellas," the computer said, "there's a more pressing problem."

"What's that?" the young diplomat snapped. "And why in the name of Jeffrey Dahmer do you talk like that?"

The computer's drawl sounded aggrieved. "There's no need to keep using foul language," it said. "This is the authentic dialect of pilots from time immemorial, and is thought to have started with the mid-twentieth-century test pilot this ship is named for."

There were several loud sniffs, followed by silence.

"Whatever you do, don't irritate the computer," the ship's officer said. "The HAL 2750s are touchy as a hair trigger, and if it gets a case of the sulks, we won't be able to get anything out of it for hours."

"Ted Bundy!" Gordon said. "You mean I've got to apologize to a machine?"

Carter nodded.

The young diplomat thought about refusing, but he was in a tight spot and needed all the help he could get. So he sucked in a deep breath, and said, "I'm sorry, Computer. I didn't mean to offend."

"Thanks for that handsome apology, Probationary Intern Gordon," the computer said. "I'm pleased as punch you gave it, because I've got something important to tell you. The internal temperature of the object near you that we believe to be an Unknown Origin 37 has been rising steadily."

The two men looked at one another.

"Uh, computer," Carter said. "What is the significance of this information?"

"Why, Fourth Officer Carter, I'm surprised at you," the computer said. "Given your physics studies, you should know what happens when heat builds up in a self-contained vessel."

"Jack the Ripper," Carter said, "the thing's going to explode."

"Explode?" Gordon said. "It isn't bad enough one of my diplomats is dead, it's got to explode, too? How do you think that's going to look on my record?"

"Computer," the ship's officer said, "can you tell me what the force of this explosion will be?"

The computer displayed some numbers in front of Carter, who gave a low whistle.

"We've got to get that thing out of here before it goes off," he said, "which will be when, Computer?"

"Thirty-three minutes," the computer said.

The young diplomat turned, grabbed the edge of the Unknown Origin 37, and heaved. Nothing happened.

He looked at Carter, who wasn't exactly rushing to help.

"It's stuck to the deck," he said. "Can't you give me a hand?"

"Not a lot of muscle to lend," the ship's officer said. "Haven't been spending much time at gravity recently. But I've got something better. Computer, have engineering send us a couple of hands and their decking tools. Tell them it's an emergency."

In a matter of minutes, two young men who didn't look very different from Carter turned up. Unlike him, however, they were wearing powered exoskeletons.

"Subengineers Seamus Harper and James Scott," one of them said. "What's the trouble?"

"This object," the ship's officer said, "is going to explode in about half an hour."

"Twenty-eight minutes," the computer said.

"Okay, twenty-eight minutes," Carter said. "The explosion is likely to be powerful enough to be inconvenient."

"You want us to disarm it?" one of the engineers asked.

"Can't," Carter said. "It's organic. Biological. For some reason it's building up heat. Enough heat and ka-blooie."

"Roger that," the other engineer said. "We'll just pull up the deck plate it's hooked to and carry it . . . well, what do you want us to do with it?"

"Space it, and fast," Carter said.

"Hold on," the young diplomat said. His normally dark complexion had turned almost as white as those of the ship's crew. "You can't just space a diplomat from another species. There will be letters of protest. Speeches in the all-creatures assembly. There might even be an exchange of notes!"

"And just what do you think will happen," the ship's officer asked amiably, "if this thing explodes and damages some more of the Xtees?"

Gordon thought about that. Finally, he said, "Go ahead and get rid of it."

The two subengineers slapped screwdriver tips onto the end of their power arms and began unbolting the deck section. As they worked, Gordon took out his hushphone and spoke into it for a few minutes.

"Shouldn't you go confer, or whatever it is you do, with the Husker delegation?" Carter asked, after the young diplomat ended his communication.

"I thought about that," Gordon said. "But I don't want to be haggling with a diplomat many grades my senior over this. Enough time would pass for a hundred of these things to go off before I got anywhere."

Carter gave him a considering look. "Well, at least you're not completely stupid," the ship's officer said. "My old granny always told me it was better to ask for forgiveness than permission."

"Besides," Gordon said, "I just sent a laser burst to the office on Ricketts. Maybe I'll hear from Tulk before I have to meet with the Unknown Origin 37s."

Carter laughed.

"Not likely," he said. "Bureaucrats are the same everywhere. Nobody on Ricketts is going to want to touch this mess for fear they'll get some on them."

The two men watched the engineers take up bolts. When they had finished, they fitted their power arms with grapples, pulled up the section of deck containing what was perhaps a dead Husker, and prepared to carry it off.

"Couldn't we just stick that in a stasis tube until we figure out something better?" the young diplomat asked.

The two engineers looked at one another.

"Not enough time to modify one, even if we knew how," one of them said.

"But if you're worried about spacing this," the other said, "well, if we could get it open and vent the heat, we wouldn't have to."

They looked at one another again.

"Electrical charge," one said.

"Low voltage should do it," said the other.

The ship's officer cleared his throat.

"I said space it," he said.

"Yes, but then you would, wouldn't you," said one of them. "You're not an engineer."

The two of them moved off, balancing the deck plate between them.

"Computer," Carter said, "maybe it would be a good idea if you kept an eye on those two. Say, an on-command display?"

"Right you are, Fourth Officer Carter," the computer said.

Carter looked at Gordon, and said, "You're the diplomat. Now what?"

Gordon gave a theatrical sigh. There wasn't any help for it but to start taking his medicine. He could see the end of the career he'd just started staring him right in the eye.

"Now, I guess I'll have to go talk to the Unknown Origin 37 delegation and see if I can find out what happened," he said. "We're just assuming that this is a dead member of the delegation, after all. Would you like to come along?"

"Love to," the ship's officer said. "Just let me get a power suit. And, Computer, why don't you join us? I'll explain it to the captain."

Carter was back in a few minutes wearing an exoskeleton, and the two of them proceeded to the hatchway.

"I don't know what your experience with other species is," the young diplomat said, "but we have some in this group that are a bit exotic by human standards."

"I'll keep that in mind," Carter said as he undogged the hatch.

The diplomats were housed near the *Chuck Yeager*'s center of mass, where it was easiest to maintain gravity. Each had quarters suitable to its environmental needs, but most came from planets with atmospheres and gravities not far off Earth normal. When humans first mastered interstellar travel, they were surprised by two things:

the diversity of the sentient life-forms they encountered and the similarities in the planets that supported them. There were a number of theories about why this was, the dominant one being that the universe has a wicked sense of humor.

The *Chuck Yeager* wasn't a cruise ship, so the individual quarters were small. But there was one fairly large common area, and when the two humans stepped through the second hatchway door, that's where they found themselves. It was empty.

"Who cut the cheese?" Carter asked.

"Excuse me?" Gordon asked.

"It's a piece of old Earth slang," Carter said. "Old Earth studies are a hobby of mine. I was referring to the smell."

The young diplomat tapped his nose. "I'm wearing filters. But I think one of these creatures is a flier that uses methane emissions to help keep itself aloft."

The ship's officer rubbed his upper lip vigorously.

"Methane emissions," he said. "You mean the thing . . ."

His sentence was cut short by the arrival of an Xtee. It shot out of the entrance to a hallway at about five feet off the deck, banked sharply, and headed for the two humans. It had a vaguely human face, a long, sharp beak, and four stubby appendages on each side of its body, all of which were flapping furiously. It looked like a cross between a Leprechaun and a penguin.

As it sank toward the deck, the creature emitted a loud noise from its rear. It immediately regained height and speed.

"Ah, Saddam Hussein," Carter said, "it's a Gaspasser."

The creature shot toward the two humans. Gordon couldn't tell if it was under control, but decided to take no chances. He hit the deck. The Gaspasser flew over, headed directly for the ship's officer.

"Screw diplomacy," Carter said, and walloped the flying creature with a power arm. The Gaspasser tumbled beak over butt, righted itself, wobbled on, hit the far wall, and fell to the deck, where it lay with its stubby appendages still flapping feebly.

"Adolf Hitler, Carter," Gordon said. "What if you've killed it? Don't you think one dead Xtee diplomat on my record is enough?"

"Don't worry about it," the ship's officer said, "I've run into things like this before. They usually aren't that easy to hurt."

He strode over to where the Gaspasser lay, picked it up, and lofted it into the air. The beat of its wings picked up, it emitted an even louder noise from its rear, and shot off toward the hallway from which it had come.

"Whew!" Carter said. "Imagine what the atmosphere on that thing's home planet is like. You haven't got an extra pair of nose filters, do you?"

The young diplomat shook his head.

"How did you encounter an Xtee on this tub?" he asked.

"Oh, I get around," Carter said vaguely. "Where are the Huskers, anyway?"

Gordon decided not to push it. "They're down here," he said.

The two humans walked through the common area and down the hallway, which ran in a circle around the ship. They passed a series of compartments, each with a hatchway. Some were open, some shut. The closed hatches had small windows in them. Carter and Gordon stopped to look into each compartment.

"Enough to make you want to dig up Charles Darwin and slap him silly, isn't it?" the ship's officer said.

Gordon nodded. The creatures in the compartments seemed to be living proof that there was no rhyme or reason to sentience or planetary dominance.

The first compartment contained a group of wicked-looking lizardlike creatures with long snouts that had several eyestalks at their ends.

"These are from Enid IV," the young diplomat said.

"Yeah, I know," said Carter. "Peepers."

The next compartment held what might have been a coatrack covered in spiny balls that seemed to leap away from the coatrack, then snap back. No telling, Gordon thought, if that's all one creature or a whole bunch and the coatrack is some sort of transport.

"From somewhere in the Echo systems," Gordon said.

The ship's officer nodded. "Tether balls," he said.

In the next were a collection of what appeared to be dogs of various types. Their door was open. Most of them were sitting around a green-topped table, playing a card game. Several seemed to be smoking cigars.

"From Canus III," the young diplomat said.

"Mutts," said Carter.

One of the Mutts was lying on the floor, licking between its hind legs. It raised its head, and growled, "What are you looking at?"

The pair moved on.

"Was he doing what I think he was doing?" Carter asked.

"That's nothing," Gordon said. "You should take part in their traditional greeting ceremony."

The next compartment contained the Gaspassers.

Next to them were what appeared to be a herd of cuddly lambs, until they smiled and showed rows of razor-edged teeth. When they lifted their feet, the humans could see they were taloned and not hooved.

"These are from somewhere down space, toward the core," the young diplomat said.

"Cute little devils, aren't they?" Carter said. "You can see why they're called Lambchops."

The Huskers were in the next compartment. Their door was closed. Gordon rang the doorbell with great reluctance.

The door flew open, and a Husker stood in the doorway. It gave off a series of squeaks and squawks.

"What the hell do you want?" the human's translation program asked. The translation program was wired into each of the Xtee compartments, and was supposed to be able to translate among the aliens as well as between alien and human. Gordon had his doubts.

"Not exactly the most diplomatic opening, is it?" the ship's officer said.

"It's probably the program," Gordon said. "We haven't got all of the bugs worked out of it."

"Oh, sure, say it's my fault," the program said. "Shoot the messenger."

"We were wondering if all the members of your delegation are accounted for," Gordon asked the Husker.

The Husker listened to the squeaks and clicks that came from the translation program. The middle of its body rotated away, then rotated back.

"We're all here," it said.

This wasn't the answer Gordon was expecting. He didn't know what to say next.

"Ship's fourth officer John Carter," Carter said. "I'm afraid we'll have to come in and take a census."

The Husker's midsection swiveled away, then back again.

"Under the rules of diplomacy, this is our sovereign territory," it said. "I'm afraid I can't let you pass."

"I'm desolated to have to tell you that the safety of

the ship is involved," Carter said, "and that takes precedence over protocol."

The Husker went into its swivel routine again.

Gordon opened his mouth, but closed it without saying anything. The ship's officer was a bold and smooth liar. He could have a real future in the Corps Diplomatique.

The Husker stepped back without speaking. The two men entered the compartment. The ship's officer made a show of counting the inhabitants. "We brought twelve of you on board," he said, "but there are only eleven here."

"I am John Smith, the leader of this delegation," the biggest Husker said. "You are correct. John Doe is missing."

"John Smith?" Gordon said. "John Doe? Is that the best you can do?"

"It's not my fault," the translation program said. "These are common names on this species' home planet, and that's the way they translate."

"Why don't you just leave the names in their language?" the young diplomat said. "Fewer distractions."

Which was how the two humans learned that it was Clickclickwhistle who was missing, according to Clicksquawksqueal.

"We think we know where Clickclickwhistle is," Carter said. "Computer, would you show us the Unknown Origin 37 we removed from the deck?"

The computer threw up a scene on the opposite wall. The Huskers seemed to see in the same spectrum as humans, so Gordon figured they should be able to follow what was going on. Unfortunately, what was going on was that the two subengineers had the Unknown Origin 37 on the shuttle deck, the section that was open to space. There were wires running from it to a console some distance away where the subengineers stood in space suits.

"Computer!" the ship's officer yelled. "Stop whatever they are doing immediately!"

Too late. One of the space-suited figures threw a switch, and there was a tremendous explosion. Pieces of Unknown Species 37 flew everywhere. The two subengineers were blown backward and dangled at the end of tethers, their suits leaking air in dozens of places. Other space-suited figures began moving their way.

Carter began whispering into the left forearm of his powered exoskeleton.

"Is this the way you treat visiting diplomats?" Clicksquawksqueal demanded. "You blow them up?"

Gordon moved closer to the ship's officer, who seemed to have finished whispering. For a reason Gordon couldn't quite name, the Huskers suddenly seemed much more dangerous.

"We didn't blow up Clickclickwhistle," he said. "We found him all folded in the hallway outside the diplomats' area and his temperature was rising. Our computer told us he would explode on his own. Why is that?"

"All folded up?" Clicksquawksqueal said. "What do you mean?"

"Show him, Computer," Gordon said.

The computer projected a photograph of the Unknown Origin 37—or, rather, the late, lamented Clickclick-whistle—in front of Clicksquawksqueal. The creature did the same swiveling routine as the doorman and was silent for several minutes.

"Clickclickwhistle was in decommissioned pose," Clicksquawksqueal said. "He would have expanded to the universe on his own."

"Decommissioned pose?" Gordon said.

"Hey, I'm doing the best that I can," the translation program said.

"Is that how your species disposes of its dead? Explosion?" the young diplomat asked.

Clicksquawksqueal swiveled and was silent again.

"It is," it said at last, "it is our way of returning our biological material to the planet."

"Well, I'd hate to walk through one of your grave-yards," Gordon said.

"Graveyards?" Clicksquawksqueal said. "What are graveyards?"

"Perhaps we should turn our attention to what happened to Clickclickwhistle," the ship's officer suggested. "When did you see him last?"

Gordon thought about strangling the starspawn. The demise of an alien diplomat in his keeping was the last thing he wanted to talk about.

Clicksquawksqueal seemed to share that sentiment. It

swiveled and was silent for so long that Gordon thought perhaps it'd gone to sleep.

"Clickclickwhistle was an adventurous sort," the Husker said when it had swiveled back. "He went out exploring and never came back."

"Weren't you worried?" Gordon asked.

The swiveling was shorter this time.

"Define worried," Clicksquawksqueal said.

"Never mind," Carter said. "Perhaps it would be better if we discussed this in more comfortable surroundings. Will you and your colleagues follow me?"

He turned his exoskeleton and walked out the hatch into the hall. Gordon was right behind him. "What do you think you're doing?" he hissed at Carter.

"Solving a mystery," the ship's officer said. "Watch and learn."

After a few minutes of what had no doubt been furious swiveling in the compartment, Clicksquawksqueal emerged, followed by the rest of the Huskers.

The two humans led them down the hall. When they reached the Lambchops' quarters, one of the creatures was standing in the hatchway.

"Where's the party?" it asked.

"No party," Carter said. "We are simply going somewhere more comfortable to continue our discussion with the Unknown Origin 37 delegation about the demise of one of its members."

"Cool," the Lambchop said. "Mind if we tag along?"

Gordon opened his mouth to tell the Lambchop, as diplomatically as possible, to mind his own beeswax, but the ship's officer beat him to the punch. "Not at all," he said. "The more the merrier."

"What are you doing?" the young diplomat demanded in a fierce whisper. "Do you think I want the whole galaxy knowing about the blot on my record?"

"I said watch," Carter said. "I didn't say talk."

He stopped his exoskeleton opposite the hatchway to the Gaspassers' quarters. He pressed the doorbell. No response. He tried the handle. Locked.

"Computer," he said.

The hatchway popped open. The Gaspassers were all huddled in one corner.

"We're having a meeting," Carter said cheerfully. "Diplomats love meetings. Come along."

Without waiting for a reply, he moved on. When he reached the door to the Mutts' compartment, he stopped again. "If you creatures can tear yourselves away from your card game for a minute, there's a discussion in the common room you won't want to miss."

"Says who?" one of the Mutts growled.

"Believe me, you'll want to be there," Carter said pleasantly, "and so will the Unknown Origins next door."

"Josef Stalin!" Gordon said. "Are you going to invite the entire diplomatic corps to this meeting?"

"Nope," Carter said. "That's it."

With that, he led his group down the rest of the hallway and into the common room.

"Table," he said, and a long, rectangular table rose out of the floor.

"Chairs," he said, and chairs rose to line the table.

"This is normally the ship's conference room," he explained, striding to the head of the table. "Please, take a seat."

The Lambchops and Huskers all sat on one side of the table. As they sat, the chairs shaped themselves to fit their anatomies.

"Now," Clicksquawksqueal said, "perhaps you can explain what we're doing here."

"Not just yet," Carter said. "Let's wait for the other delegations to arrive."

"You're pretty confident they're coming," said Gordon, who'd taken a seat next to the ship's officer.

"It's my winning personality," Carter said. "It's irresistible."

Sure enough, a minute later the Gaspassers came into the room, trailed by the Mutts. They took seats facing the Lambchops and Huskers.

"Thank you for coming, gentle creatures," Carter said. "In the interests of universal harmony, it is truly an honor to welcome you to this historic meeting aboard . . ."

"Get on with it," a Mutt that looked like a border collie snapped, "I've got a full house waiting back at the game."

"Yes," said one of the Lambchops, "you said you had something to reveal about the death of one of the Unknown 37 diplomats. Let's not spend more time than we have to in such odiferous surroundings."

"Who you calling odiferous, you cotton-covered assassin?" the collie barked.

This started all the Lambchops and Mutts bleating and barking. The Huskers rustled their fronds, and the Gaspassers emitted noises that indicated that they were about to become airborne.

"Oh, great," Gordon said to Carter, "you're starting a riot. Well, why not? They can't drum me out of the Corps Diplomatique twice."

"Silence," the ship's officer thundered, his voice enhanced by speakers in the exoskeleton. "I can have the walls lined with Federation Marines in a heartbeat."

That seemed to make an impression. "Now," Carter said, "we know that the unfortunate Clickclickwhistle left the Unknown Origin 37s' compartment and never came back. We know that he was, what was the word, decommissioned inside diplomat country and was rolled through the hatchway into the outside hall. So we know that the culprit is a member of one of the diplomatic missions."

"What?" the border collie snarled. "You're accusing one of us of murder? I won't stand for that."

"If you don't calm down," Carter said, "I'll send for a rolled-up newspaper. Now, before we go any further, perhaps the leader of the other Unknown Origin delegation can explain why one of its members is missing."

That caused a flap among the Gaspassers, who chirped and whistled at one another, then at Carter.

"Missing? No one is missing from our delegation," one of the Gaspassers said.

"Now, now," Carter said. "Do you take us for chumps? Computer, how many of this species came aboard?"

"Twelve, just like all the other delegations," the computer drawled.

"And how many do you count now?"

"Eleven."

The heads of the Gaspassers all bobbed as they tried to count each other. The other delegates seemed to be trying to count them, too.

"Do you mean to say," Clicksquawksqueal said, "that one of that species was involved in the decommissioning of Clickclickwhistle?"

"What sort of a charge is that, you overgrown bush?" the border collie howled.

"Who are you calling names, bitch?" the head Lambchop bleated.

In the next instant, all of the Lambchops and Mutts were standing in their chairs snarling and snapping. The Huskers were standing and shaking their fronds at the Gaspassers, who in unison emitted loud noises and rose into the air. Clicksquawksqueal slammed a frond down on the table.

And it cut right through the tabletop.

"George W. Bush!" Gordon shouted, "that tabletop is high-density alloy."

The Gaspassers shot across the table at the Huskers. One pair of their appendages was moving so fast they looked like circular saws.

"Tanglefoot!" yelled Carter, and every alien froze in place.

"That's a neat trick," the young diplomat said. "How'd you do that?

The ship's officer smiled. "Oh, just a precaution," he said. "When I went to get this exoskeleton, I took the opportunity to ask engineering to modify a couple of stasis fields so they'd work on the Xtees. Later, I got on the communicator concealed in here"—he waved his left power arm—"and ordered the stasis projectors installed in the floor of the deck above us. The computer is controlling them."

"Well, I hope you know that subjecting diplomats to stasis without their consent is a violation of several all-creature protocols," Gordon said. "Not that it matters to me. I've lost not one but two alien diplomats. My career is over."

"Oh, I don't know about that," Carter said. "Computer, why don't you release oh, say, the border collie-looking Mutt and the Lambchop with the biggest mouth."

The aliens came out of stasis yelling at one another,

but when they saw what had happened to their colleagues, they stopped.

"You can't do this to us," the Lambchop said. "When we report this to your Corps Diplomatique, both of you will regret it."

"Oh, I don't think so," the ship's officer said. "I just thawed you two to see if you want to come clean."

The Mutt and the Lambchop looked at one another, then back at Carter. Neither made a sound.

"No?" Carter said. "Then why don't you two sit quietly while I explain what happened to my young friend here? Now, then, Probationary Intern to the second assistant undersecretary Oscar Gordon, let's pretend. Say you're a species in toward the core of the universe, and you're engaged in an all-planets donnybrook with another species in your neck of the stars. Let's call you, oh, I don't know, Lambchops, and your opponents Mutts."

"You and your opponents are pretty evenly matched, and each of you is always looking for an advantage. That includes sending out long-range teams, searching for new military technologies.

"Within a few years of each other, you both encounter the Federation of Planets. They won't sell you weapons, but you figure if you get to know your way around, you'll find some member species that will. So you send out spies disguised as diplomats, traders, what have you.

"Then you get word from your spies that there's going to be a big meeting. You hear your opponents will be there, too. One of the items on the agenda will be the little tiff you're having. You know it will take some time to make arrangements for the meeting that are satisfactory to diplomats representing more than five hundred species. And it's taken, what, forty years to make the arrangements and get everybody together?

"So you could use two things. Allies. And, in case things don't go your way, weapons. You know the Federation forces won't let you bring weapons to the conference, at least not anything they recognize as weapons.

"But you've got an edge. You use mechanical weapons in your fight with the Mutts, but you also use biological weapons. And you figure that you might be able to get some of those weapons past by having them posing as diplomats from a new species."

"How am I doing so far?" Carter asked the Lambchop.

"Eat dirt, you bald ape," the Lambchop replied.

"I must be pretty close," Carter said. "So you need something a little more sophisticated, and, just as important, something your opponents have never seen before. So you modify some plant life you found somewhere and, voilà, you have the Unknown Origin 37s, also known as the Huskers."

With a snarl, the Lambchop leaped toward Carter. It hit the intervening stasis field and was knocked to the floor.

"You mean, Clickclickwhistle wasn't an alien diplomat, it was a weapons system?" the young diplomat asked. "How did you figure that out?"

"I've had occasion to see military hardware once or twice," Carter said, "and I didn't like the look of those fronds the minute I saw them. But what convinced me was the explosion. Giving his biological material back to the planet, my eye. I know a fragmentation bomb when I see one."

"Bahhhd, bahhhd species," the border collie taunted. "We'll have to report these miscreants to the proper authorities."

"Not so fast," Carter said. "I'm not finished. You see, one of the reasons you and your opponents have been at war so long is that you are pretty evenly matched. So it's no surprise when they have exactly the same idea as you do."

"What?" said the Lambchop, which had shaken off the effects of its collision with the stasis field and climbed back into its chair. "They brought weapons, too?"

"That's right," Carter said, "the Gaspassers. I suspect that when we check, we'll find that their first contact was within months of the Huskers'. So when you sent Clickclickwhistle out on whatever errand it was on, it ran into one of the Gaspassers. Was it out doing some snooping, too?"

"I'm not saying anything," the border collie whined.

"No matter," Carter said to Gordon. He gestured to the aliens in stasis. "This little display here shows me everything I need to know. Maybe the Gaspasser couldn't control its flight too well in the different gravity. The one we saw was certainly having trouble. Maybe Clickclick-whistle did something that led it to attack. Whatever happened, it struck the Husker in some vital spot with something, its beak or one of those saw-blade appendages. And Clickclickwhistle *est mort.*"

"But what happened to the Gaspasser?" Gordon asked.

"I'm guessing the Huskers are bred so that when they take a fatal hit, they fold up immediately to form a fragmentation bomb," the ship's officer said. "The Gaspasser couldn't free itself in time, and ended up inside the bomb. And remember, it was full of methane."

"So when Clickclickwhistle exploded, the Gaspasser did, too?" the young diplomat asked.

"Precisely, my dear Watson," Carter said.

"Who's Watson?" Gordon asked.

"Never mind," Carter said.

Nobody said anything for a minute.

"Interesting theory," the border collie yapped, "but how are you going to prove it?"

"Well, I've got some proof already," Carter said. "The computer monitored shortwave communications between the Lambchops and the Huskers, and between you and the Gaspassers. Probably the Lambchops telling the Huskers what to say to us humans, and you ordering the Gaspassers to this meeting. And then there's the fact that few species but you Mutts could put up with a weapons system that smells like that."

"Hardly conclusive," the Lambchop said.

"I know," Carter said. "That's why you two are going to confess."

That set them both to protesting, but Carter waved a power arm at them. "The jig's up, fellas," he said. "If you don't confess, we'll have Federation cruisers in your systems within a month. You won't be able to warn your governments, because I'll just have the computer put you back in stasis. Then Probationary Intern to the second assistant undersecretary Oscar Gordon and I will depart. We'll block off this room, drop the stasis fields, and deal with whoever survives."

"Personally, I hope it's a Lambchop or two. The crew hasn't had fresh meat in a while."

That brought a gasp from the Lambchop.

"But I don't want to be speciesist about it. The Mutts aren't really dogs, so they might taste just fine, too."

A snarl from the border collie.

After their confessions had been recorded, the weapons systems moved to a safer place, and Marine guards stationed in the diplomatic area, Carter and Gordon went to visit the two subengineers in the infirmary. Harper and Scott, who were mostly encased in healing gel, had some pretty wicked-looking wounds, but didn't seem to have learned much from their brush with death.

"It's like I told him," Harper said, "we just needed

slightly lower voltage and everything would have been fine."

Gordon and Carter left the infirmary, the former walking gingerly and the latter propelling himself along the hallway from gripfast to gripfast.

"I guess I'd better be getting back to the diplomats," Gordon said.

"Yes," said Carter, "I don't think the destruction of a couple of alien weapons systems is going to mar your record. Particularly since my report is going to play up your role in preventing the introduction of dangerous weapons into the all-creatures assembly. You might even get the 'probationary' taken off your title."

"That'd be nice," Gordon said. He was silent for a moment, then said, "Don't take this the wrong way, but how does someone so young have so much knowledge and authority?"

The ship's officer laughed. "The whole idea behind the Mutts' and Lambchops' plans was that everyone would take things at face value," he said. "You're still doing that. I've spent much of my life in zero G. No gravity, no wrinkles. I might look sixteen, but I'm old enough to be your father. Maybe your grandfather."

"And you're not really fourth officer of the *Chuck Yeager* are you?" Gordon said.

"Yes, I am," said Carter, "but only for this trip. I've been fourth officer on several ships, as well as other things. But I imagine you can guess my real occupation."

The two humans reached the door to the diplomats' area. Gordon stood awkwardly, not knowing what to do next. Carter did a backflip and sailed off down the hall.

"Take care, mudfoot," he called.

"You, too, starspawn," Gordon replied, then turned and let himself through the hatch.

Cairene Dawn

JAY CASELBERG

The fog had been up again that morning, just like it was most mornings—that greasy Nile mist clinging to everything, making you wonder what strange, mystical land you might be in. Then the sound of car horns and traffic, the grind and burr of a population on the move would filter through, redolent with its own smells, none of them particularly pleasant. For a while though, you could imagine you were in another place, a place of magic and power. But then Cairo *was* a strange and mystical place, a melting pot of nations and cultures bound to make you wonder what was real.

Perhaps it was that inability to pin things down that first drew me to that seedy, smelly city, heavy with its own exotic sounds and sensations. Nobody belonged in

Cairo, not even the Cairenes, but it had been like that since the dawn of history. You see, the dirty and the grubby have their own particular tang. Some people like it.

Me? I'm Agamemnon Jacques. I can curse my parents for that one. Most people just called me Jacques. I prefer it that way.

That afternoon, I was sitting in a bar, waiting for a client. Not so unusual, but this was no ordinary bar. This was Harry's Pub, nestled in the heart of the Marriott, way up on the eastern side of Zamalek, playground of the well-to-do. Next door lay the grounds of the Gizera Sporting Club and all around the marks of the wealthy. The hotel might have been a part of a chain now, but the marks of its past opulence were all around me. It had been a palace once. It was still full of liveried staff, still spoke swank, and in my dusty, pale street suit, I felt somewhat out of place. Still, Cairo's pretty forgiving if you've got the money. So, I sat there in one corner of Harry's Pub, listening to the voices, Arabic, German, French, trying to pick who it was I was here to meet. I needn't really have bothered.

The woman walked into the place and owned it with her presence. She wore a pale green-blue tailored suit that shimmered as she moved. Dark hair framed a pale, high-cheekboned face, sharp and soft at the same time. There was no hesitation. She scanned the room, spied me sitting at my solitary table, and headed straight for me. As she stood across the table from me, looking down with an assessing gaze, I looked back, knowing right away that this woman was really someone.

"Mr. Jacques?" she said. Her voice was deep and rich, a slight accent tingeing those couple of words. It wasn't anything I could identify right off. Something exotic.

"Yeah, that's me," I told her. "But just call me Jacques."

She nodded, pulled out a chair, and flowed into it—there was no other word—all smooth and fluid in a single movement. She crossed her legs and folded her hands neatly in front of her. A drinks waiter appeared a mere breath later. I'd had to wait.

"Tea," she told the waiter. "And whatever Mr. . . . um . . . Jacques's pleasure is."

I lifted my glass, and the waiter nodded, turning away with his tray clutched to his chest. The quick backward glance at my companion didn't go unnoticed. So, I was not alone. She was some woman all right.

"Madame Fouad," I started. "You said something in your call about a matter of grave importance . . ."

She lifted a finger to still me. "Be patient, Jacques," she said.

This was a woman used to commanding people. I went back to my scotch, watching her over the rim of my glass. The waiter came and went, fussing for a moment with the pot and glass of tea, until she waved him away with a brief word of thanks. She lifted her glass, holding it between thumb and forefinger, took a delicate sip, and set the glass back down. Her nails were painted the same lapis as her suit.

She gave a brief smile. "It is amusing that we should use the word 'grave' I think," she said. "It is my husband, Ossie, Mr. Jacques."

"Just Jacques," I repeated. "What about him?"

She folded her hands in her lap and looked down. "I fear something has happened to him. He has not been seen for several days."

"And what makes you think something has happened?" People went missing all the time in Cairo. Often, they just showed up again a few days later. There were plenty of diversions if you went looking for them and you had the cash, but then you'd kind of expect that from the playground of the Middle East. There was Dubai of course, but Dubai wasn't Cairo. Sitting there, looking at her, I couldn't imagine what could make her husband want to stray.

Slowly, she lifted her gaze to meet mine. "This has happened before," she said slowly. "I speak from experience. It's the family business you see. Ra Industries. My brother-in-law has always been jealous. He has always wanted the greater share of what we do. Ossie has always been the one in the way of his plans. The last time it happened, it got so bad that he killed Ossie. Murdered him. It was months before we found his body and had him resurrected. I don't think Seth has learned. His ambition drives him too much. Of course Ossie forgave him, but I think that it is not enough."

She caught me in the process of pouring the remaining contents of my old glass into the new, and I managed to slosh some scotch over the table. Slowly, I put the glass back down, not really believing that I'd really heard what Madame Fouad had just said.

"He killed your husband?" I stared at her.

"Yes. Locked him in a coffin and threw him in the river. It was a very nice coffin, but it's the principle of the thing. I have no doubt something similar has happened again."

I stared down at my glass, toying with it as I worked out what I was going to say. "I see," I said slowly.

Great line, Jacques. Now, you get all sorts in my business, and you hear some things, but I just wasn't ready for this. I thought I did a pretty good job of covering what was going through my head. She was an attractive woman, seemed to be in control, someone who looked like she was used to having a handle on a situation. I was prepared to listen. Like I said, you hear all sorts in my line of work, particularly in a place like Cairo. The Egyptians are generally a superstitious lot, and you can use that. But I just couldn't swallow a lot of the stuff they believed.

Madame Fouad continued, and I found myself being drawn deeper by the rich tones of her voice.

"His brother, Seth, has always had designs on the

family business. With Ossie gone, his way would be clear."

"But what about you, Madame Fouad?"

She fixed me with a firm gaze. "This is Egypt. We may have become enlightened over time, but this is still Egypt, and I am still a woman."

I nodded. "What sort of business is it?"

She regarded me steadily with those wide, dark eyes, and I found myself having problems keeping my attention focused on the matter at hand. "All sorts of things, Mr. Jacques. Import/export. Other holdings. We have a diverse range of interests. You might say we deal with bits and pieces of everything. But the nature of our business should not concern you."

I was prepared to accept that for the time being; I could do some digging on my own.

"So why me?"

And that was the question. I could see no reason why someone like her would bother contacting someone like me. She had to have the resources at her disposal to pick anyone she wanted.

"I need discretion," she said, her gaze unflinching. "If word of this should get out . . . You are someone outside our usual circles. I very much doubt you would have had previous dealings with my brother-in-law. Perhaps with some of the people he employs from time to time, but no . . . you are not the . . . usual type."

"Hmm, you're probably right," I said, quite prepared to take her word for it at that moment.

"I am certain that I am," she said, lifting her glass for another sip of tea.

I glanced around the bar, but there was no one in earshot.

"My rates, Madame Fouad . . ."

She gave a dismissive wave of her hand. "Are unimportant."

And that was that. There was some more small talk, and when prompted, she handed over a faded photograph showing her husband, Ossie, in traditional Egyptian garb. Maybe it had been taken at a party somewhere. He was darker than she, but a good-looking man, all the same, sporting a small dark beard. I studied the photograph, then slipped it away inside my jacket. She fixed me with that deep gaze of hers, and I found myself wanting to help her in any way I could, whether she was half-crazy or not . . . or whether I was half-crazy too. She stood, apparently satisfied that our business was done for now.

"Madame Fouad," I said. "How will I . . . ?"

"I will be in touch with you," she said, then turned, heading for the exit. She dealt with the check on the way out with a flash of gold.

I sat there for a while longer, savoring the amber burn in my glass while I worked out what my next move would be. She hadn't given me a whole lot to go on, and I hadn't even thought to get her first name.

The light fell golden across the spans of the 25 July Bridge. The early-evening muezzin calls floated above the city, urging the faithful to prayer. Boats cruised up and down the stretch of brown-green water before me, tinged brassy with the fading sun. I walked past the rank of black-and-white taxis, their drivers waiting to haggle with the well-to-do tourists, looking for three, four times the going rate, heading away from the Gizera Sporting Club, up toward the bridge.

I had two choices. It was either the City of the Dead or the Khan el-Khalili, where the stallholders would be starting to set up for the evening's trade. But the Khan was no ordinary souk. You could get just about anything you might want at the Great Khan, if you knew where to look, and me, I knew where to look.

I might just have given Madame Fouad's statement more pause for doubt; but to be honest, I needed the work. The flash of gold goes a long way to shutting up that little voice in the back of your head, and in Cairo the dead are as much a part of everyday life as the living. Look at the City of the Dead. The locals have taken up living among the tombs and mausoleums. Not only among, but inside them too. The dead have a life of their own in Egypt, and had since the dawn of time. It was a part of their culture. And I thought I could live with it, especially if someone like Madame Fouad was footing the bill.

So, I stood there on the banks of the Nile, the wash of garbage and traffic wrinkling my nose, the shouts and car noise swelling around me, and the only question running through my head was where I should go first. Maybe that was wrong. Maybe I should have listened, but there's so much noise in this grand old city that sometimes you don't know what might be the little bit that counts.

A little way up the street, I hailed a cab. He wanted too much, clearly taking me for a foreign tourist, and I walked away. I fared a little better with the next one. He only wanted double the standard rate, but this was Zamalek, so I agreed and climbed into the front seat next to the driver as was the custom. In my Western garb I was going to stand out anyway, but anything you could do to mark yourself as not too removed could only help.

The driver was good at what he did. Meandering in and out between the trucks and buses, his hand pressed flat against the horn. Sometimes I really wished drivers in Cairo would use their lights in the burgeoning dark or late at night, but I just had to trust to the fact that this cab was probably more valuable than the driver's life. It was in his own interests to keep us in one piece.

On the way, I pulled out the faded photograph and

studied it. A good-looking Egyptian guy looking like he was out of his proper time. I hadn't heard of Ra Industries before, as far as I could remember. Ossie was a common enough Egyptian diminutive, but Seth, now that was different. Maybe their parents, like so many others of their class, had had them schooled abroad, wanting them to move above and beyond their roots. Sometimes a name is a simple enough step upon that path. I slipped the photograph back into my inside pocket and tried to avoid watching the near misses as we weaved in and out of the traffic. Maybe, just maybe, Madame Fouad had been speaking metaphorically. That didn't make sense though, at least not then.

My driver dropped me at the Midan Hussein and I left him there with a quick *shukrun.* I could have entered the Khan farther down Al Azhar Street, but I liked the long walk up Muski, past the perfumers and the costumes and the bits and pieces designed to trap the unwary tourists. The scents, the sounds, gave me a transition into that canvas-covered other world that is the Khan proper. My goal was farther north, but walking up past the twinned mosques, past the goldsmiths and copper shops of al-Muizz li-Din Allah took me away from modern Cairo, into another time and another place. Everywhere there was noise; the hawkers, the touts, the blare of radios and other music. Everywhere was the smell of another era, another reality. It was almost as if I had stepped into another age.

I had a couple of contacts in the Khan. One was back in the narrow winding streets that sold antiquities, real and fake, but my main guy, Ismail, plied his trade up in the street of coppersmiths. Keeping one eye open for pickpockets, I headed in that direction, pushing past the streams of native Egyptians and tourists both. I was looking out for familiar faces, too—signposts to the subtle trade that might be going on around me, beneath the veneer of market commerce. I'd learned the faces, the ones that mattered, but on that evening, most of them were strangely absent.

I stopped in front of Ismail's tiny store, peering inside at the shelves of burnished copper, the piles of pots and jugs stacked haphazardly in the front. There was no sign of him. But then, as if he sensed my presence, a stained curtain twitched in the back, and a familiar pockmarked face peered out.

"Zhaik, Zhaik, it is you, my friend. You come to see me."

I glanced up and down the street, then grinned. "Ismail, you old crook. How are you?"

A big yellow grin greeted my statement. "Allah willing, I am well, Zhaik."

"And business?"

Ismail rocked his head from side to side. "Ah, you know." He came to the front of the store and peered round the corner. He glanced across at the stall across the street with narrowed eyes, tossing his chin at the stallholder opposite. The man gave a quick nod, and after a quick glance up and down the street, Ismail beckoned me inside.

Behind the stained curtain sat a simple table and a couple of chairs. A dirty stove sat with a pot of tea upon it. Ismail pulled down a couple of tea glasses, wiping them with the hem of his robe as he gestured to one of the seats. He planted the glasses down, pushed a bowl of white sugar lumps into the center, and reached up to turn on a radio that sat atop a battered fridge in the corner. Satisfied, he poured two glasses of tea and sat, pulling his off-white galabiya around himself.

"So, Zhaik," he said, suddenly all business, peering across at me with yellowing, watery eyes.

"I've got a new case," I told him. I dug into my pocket and drew out the photograph, slipping it across the table so he could see it. Ismail picked it up and peered down, his eyes narrowing. He shook his head.

"You're sure?"

He slid the photograph back. "Yes. I am sure. *Aiwa.*"

I slipped the picture away again. "Well, his wife says he's gone missing."

Ismail shrugged, as if this was no news, something that happened every day, and he was right.

I leaned forward. "No, there's something about this one," I told him. "You should see the wife. We find him, and I think it's going to be worth the effort." I rubbed my thumb and first two fingers together in front of his face.

Ismail looked up at me, his eyes narrowed, then he grinned. "Is good, Zhaik."

"Yes, is good," I said. "Anyway, they're loaded, but she wants to keep it quiet. She said something really weird though. She said her brother-in-law had killed him before, and she thought he might have done it again."

Ismail's grin suddenly faded and his eyes widened. "What is this woman, Zhaik?"

I frowned. "Madame Fouad. That's her name. I didn't get a first name. Her husband's name—the guy in the picture—his name's Ossie."

Ismail gave a slight shake of his head.

"Anyway, it's all to do with the brother, or so she says. It's all to do with the company, Ra Industries. The brother's name is Seth."

Ismail suddenly sucked air through his teeth and shook his head. "I cannot help you, Zhaik."

"Come on, Ismail."

He leaned forward, close enough that I could smell his breath, his body. "Is bad business, Zhaik. You walk away, yes."

"What are you saying?" I said, leaning back.

He shook his head again. "You go now, Zhaik. You go now."

I was about to protest, but Ismail sliced the air with his hand. I didn't understand, but Ismail had been useful to me in the past, and I didn't want to upset the relationship. Whatever I'd said had struck a nerve in places he didn't want me to be. Sometimes their damned superstitions went a little too far. I wondered what it was this time.

I bid him a quick good bye, and left him there slowly shaking his head, not even bothering to finish my tea.

For the next few days I pursued my own inquiries. I hit a wall in every direction. I could find no record of the Fouads or anything to do with Ra Industries. Every way I turned, at the merest mention of those names, the shutters came crashing down. The dusty streets and alleyways of Cairo guard their secrets well, but I'd never seen anything like this. Usually a few Egyptian pounds is enough to loosen lips. Not this time. I was left scratching my head, grinding my teeth with frustration, dreading the call from Madame Fouad, knowing I had nothing to give her.

Two days later the call came. It wasn't Madame Fouad. It was Ismail.

"Zhaik," said the breathy voice at the other end of the line. "You must come. I have something for you."

"What is it, Ismail?" There was something in his voice—no banter, all seriousness.

"You must come, Zhaik." The line went dead.

I jumped in a cab and headed for the Khan, not even bothering to haggle over the price. Ismail was waiting for me when I got there.

"What have you got?" He looked nervous, jittery. He shook his head, beckoning for me to follow him into the depths of the marketplace. He didn't even bother checking that someone would look after his store.

Ismail lead the way, pushing past stallholders and browsers alike. I knew the section. One of my other contacts plied his trade from a small antiques store in the very area, but the store Ismail led me to was unfamiliar. Ismail ushered me inside a small shop, cluttered with statuary, tomb fragments, and papyri. He closed the door firmly behind us. A moment later, we were joined by a small, rotund sweaty man, with a full black beard and thick glasses.

"This is Ali," said Ismail. "This is his shop."

I nodded.

"Come, come," said Ali.

He led us into another back room. This one was far cleaner than Ismail's. On a small table in the room's center, sat a bundle, wrapped in newspaper and tied up with string. Ali reached across, retrieved a knife, and cut the string; then waved me toward the package. Looking from one to the other, I gingerly reached forward and started unfolding the newspaper. I swallowed and stepped back. What lay revealed was a foot. I reached forward and prodded it with the tip of one finger. It was a foot all right. I peered closer. Neatly manicured nails, slightly dark skin, and a clean cut at the ankle.

"Where did you get this?" I said.

"A local fishermen. It comes from the river three days ago."

Three days ago? It looked recently removed. Very recently removed.

"What's happened? Where has it been kept?"

"Ali has had it here. I hear about it. I talk to him. I call you, Zhaik. He has it here maybe two days, I think."

But that was impossible. Sitting wrapped in newspaper for a couple of days in the Cairo heat, a severed foot wasn't going to look like that. I reached out and folded the newspaper back over, swallowing back my disbelief.

"At least put the damn thing in a fridge," I said.

There was nothing to indicate that this was who I was looking for, but somehow, deep inside, I knew it was. I turned away from the table, one hand massaging the back of my neck. One foot did not a body make. This was probably a matter for the Cairo police, but I didn't want to involve them yet. I turned back to Ismail.

"Get him to keep it here. Ask around. See if anything else has shown up. Until then . . . I don't know."

The next thing to turn up was a head. There was no doubt about who it belonged to. I couldn't deny the possibilities any longer.

Right on cue, that evening, the call I was dreading came. I heard her voice on the end of the line, and my heart sank.

"I have some bad news," I told her.

"Yes, what is it?" she said, her voice calm, her tone even.

"We think we've found your husband."

"We? What is this 'we,' Jacques?"

I paused at that. "I use a couple of contacts, a couple of people who work for me, Madame Fouad. I can trust them."

"All right. So tell me."

"Well, we haven't exactly found all of him."

"I see. What have you found?"

"So far, only a foot and his head. I'm sorry, Madame Fouad."

Her next statement blindsided me completely. I expected tears. I expected wailing. "Ah, very good, Jacques," she said. "You have truly earned your fee."

I held the phone away from my ear, staring at it in disbelief. Slowly, I brought it back to my ear.

"Madame Fouad?"

"Did you hear me, Jacques?"

"No, I'm sorry . . ."

"Make sure to keep the pieces you have safe. Continue searching. I have faith in you, Jacques. I will be in touch to arrange collection of what you have."

The connection went dead, and I lowered the phone.

Over the next couple of weeks, the word went out, and one by one, pieces of the body turned up. A cowherd brought in one. A local farmer another. A tourist guide yet another. Every piece, wrapped in leaves, or newspapers, or blue plastic bags were all in the same perfect condition, as if they'd been severed mere minutes before. I didn't understand it. I didn't really want to. Ismail, his pockmarked superstitious face filled with knowing, seemed to accept it as if it was something that happened every day. Every couple of days, Madame Fouad called, monitoring the progress.

Of course we paid. We paid in bits and pieces for the bits and pieces, and the word spread. By the end, we had fourteen individual parts. We had the whole Ossie Fouad in pieces, all except for one. And maybe he didn't need that piece anymore. After all, according to my research, he already had a son, a healthy young man called Horace, all set to take over the company when his own time came. I met him when he and his mother came to collect the pieces.

A good-looking young man, with his father's skin, he leaned in close to me as he bundled the neatly wrapped pieces of his father's corpse into the back of a truck.

"We cannot thank you enough, Mr. Jacques," he said. "But I would keep out of sight for a while. Your fee should look after you. After my father's resurrection, my uncle will not be pleased. He doesn't take kindly to failure. I would give you this word of caution. My uncle Set does not forget and his reach is long. Watch for him in the darkness."

Set? I had thought she'd said Seth.

I looked over at his mother, watching me with her dark, intelligent eyes, the barest smile upon her lips, and I felt a chill despite the evening's heat.

I heard a few rumors later that the Fouads never did find that missing piece. I wonder from time to time how Ossie might feel about that. Ismail told me that she, Madame Fouad, had had a replacement fashioned from gold, right down the street from his little copper shop. Maybe that was true, maybe it wasn't, but I wasn't going to take the trouble to find out.

All I knew was that somewhere inside Ra Industries, there was a man called Set Fouad, a man who didn't forget easily. I wasn't even sure if he was a man, but I knew I didn't want to meet him anytime soon. For now, I was keeping my head down. Maybe I'd move. Maybe Alexandria. Maybe Athens. Somewhere like that. I needed to raise the cash first. If I never heard the name Ra Industries again, I'd be happy.

Do you know what a jackal sounds like in the fog of a Cairo dawn?

Justice Is a Two-Edged Sword

DANA
STABENOW

It was the first day of the Tattoo Fair, and the town square was bustling with vendors and performers from the nine provinces of Mnemosynea. Pthalean playwrights were rehearsing songs and skits with Pthersikorean dancers. From a dais two feet square a Kalliopean poet was declaiming in iambic pentameter what appeared to be an epic concerning the life of Okeon, the god of the sea, who had five wives, seventeen children, and a great deal of domestic discord that played out, as one might expect, on the hapless humankind living onshore. Next to the dais the poet's clerk was doing a brisk trade in autographed scrolls.

A Palihymnean had a booth built of shelves of sheet music featuring every hymn written in praise of the gods from Atonis to Tseuz. Foreseers from Yranea set out star charts, some rolled, some mounted on poster board, next to wicker baskets full of fortunes tied with red satin ribbons, and shuffled their prefiguration cards in preparation for their first customers, girls looking for true love, farmers looking for rain, merchants looking for a reading on the futures of surcoats (long or short?) and breastplates (functional or ornamental?). As her mount picked his way through the debris field of wagons, tent poles, heaps of canvas and crates of goods, Sharryn pointed out one Pthalean stand-up comedian rehearsing an act that had a troupe of tragic actors holding their sides. "We should get tickets to that performance. Anybody who can make a Mnelpomenean laugh has to be funny."

Crowfoot grunted and nudged her destrier through the crowd.

Sharryn looked at her with affectionate exasperation. "When last did you take the time to laugh that hard at something that silly?"

Crowfoot's destrier whickered agreement, and the swordswoman cuffed her mane without force. "Less of that from you, Blanca."

Blanca rolled an eye at Pedro, the sturdy brown pony bearing Sharryn, who tossed his head and snorted. "Even they agree with me," Sharryn said. A bit grimly, she added, "And after Epaphus we could both use a little amusement."

Crowfoot, ignoring the reference to the events in the

provincial capital the day before, scanned the marketplace over the heads of the jostling, energetic crowd. "Where is this inn you keep on about? The road has left me dry as a bone."

Sharryn brightened. "Makarios's?" She craned her neck. "There, the red brick building on the corner." She smacked her lips. "Wait till you taste Makarios's lager. It truly is the stuff of the gods."

"Careful, one of them will hear you." Crow was only half-joking. She looked at Sharryn out of the corner of an eye. Her partner's eager expression indicated that there was more of interest at the inn than mere beer.

They urged their mounts alewards. Weary of the road and their last Assideres, they were both mildly annoyed to find their way blocked by a small knot of shouting, gesticulating townspeople. The knot grew into a group, then into a crowd, with no way out or around save to walk their horses right over the top of it. That of course would be unacceptable behavior for two of His Most Serene Majesty's chosen, so they didn't, however greatly they were tempted.

"A full tankard of cold, crisp lager," Sharryn said, staring sadly in the direction of the inn. "I can practically smell it from here."

"Lead me to it," Crowfoot muttered. "Goodman," she said to one of the townsmen standing at the fringe of the crowd, and had to raise her voice and repeat herself to be heard over the uproar.

He spared her an impatient glance, then looked again, his eye caught by the crest on the breast of her tunic and by the hilt of the sword protruding from the sheath strapped to her back. What he had been about to say changed to a deferential, "Swordswoman," accompanied by a bow of the head. He looked for and found Sharryn, almost hidden by the bulk of the destrier, took in the same crest on the same tunic and the staff in her hand, and said, bowing again, "Seer."

"Goodman," Sharryn said pleasantly. "What's all the fuss about?"

"It's nothing, Seer. A fight."

Crow surveyed the growing crowd, exchanged a raised eyebrow with Sharryn, and said, "A fight with a large audience. Is this part of the festival? Does one buy a ticket?"

"It's nothing," he repeated, with an involuntary look over his shoulder. "A fight over a girl, merely."

Crow stood in the stirrups and saw a tangled ball of two men crash into the side of a cart loaded with nuts. The cart went over, the nuts went everywhere, and the vendor burned his hands catching the brazier. The two men were forcibly separated by a couple of stern townsmen, and stood revealed to be a young, slight man with dark hair, dressed in the charred leather apron of the smith, and a much larger man of roughly the same age, towheaded, pale-skinned and lantern-jawed, wearing a fletcher's gauntlet. One of the townsmen, fists on his hips, surveyed the two pugilists with palpable scorn, addressed them with what appeared to be a pithy homily, and set them to work to right the nut vendor's cart and recompense him for his lost revenue. The crowd began to disperse, but Crow saw the looks exchanged by the two young men and thought that there would be more trouble before long.

"Were you making for the inn?" She looked down to see the eyes of the townsman fixed on her.

"We were."

"Allow me to lead you there." He accomplished this with no unnecessary pushing and shoving, Sharryn noted with approval, but a tap on the shoulder, a nod, and a smile; and then there was the massive shadow of Blanca looming behind him, before which people naturally fell back.

They were dismounting in front of the inn when a big burly man burst out of the door, crying loudly in a strange tongue, and swept Sharryn up into a comprehensive embrace. It was returned with enthusiasm. Crow busied herself with an unnecessary adjustment to the left stirrup of her saddle. Blanca snorted. Pedro whinnied. The townsman looked a little startled.

After a while Sharryn came up for air, pink-cheeked and bright-eyed. "This is Makarios," she said.

"I should think so," Crow said.

"Zeno!" Makarios roared. He had a robust baritone that was easily heard over the noise of the crowd. A sharp-featured boy with untidy dark hair and a sly grin scrambled from beneath a forest of legs. "Master Makarios?"

"Take the pony and the destrier to the stables. Water them, feed them, groom them, clean their tack." He cocked an eye at Crow. "Anything else?"

She shook her head. The boy gave her a quick grin bracketed with mischievous dimples, but his hand on the halters was steady and sure, and Blanca and Pedro allowed themselves to be led away without complaint.

"Makarios," Sharryn said, "this is Crowfoot, my Sword."

"So I see. Well, well." He eyed the townsman. "How did you happen to fall in with such rabble, Cornelius?"

Cornelius grinned. "They needed an escort through the crowd." He hooked a thumb over his shoulder.

Makarios remembered his duties as host. "You must be thirsty, come in, come in! Sofronia! Beer!" He unceremoniously dislodged a dozing patron from a large table comfortably close to the fireplace and disappeared for a moment, to reappear again with a tray loaded with meat rolls, cheese, and fruit. Crow's stomach chose that moment to growl, loudly, which made Makarios grin and shove the platter closer to her. Her mouth was full when Sofronia, a plump woman with red cheeks and thick gray hair in a plait hanging to her waist bustled out with four tankards in one hand and an enormous earthenware pitcher in the other, which, pour as they would, never seemed to empty. Makarios grinned at Crow when she noticed this. "You're drinking on the king's coin, aren't you?" and she had to admit that they were. The lager was cold and crisp, tasting of sun on grain, and good, rich earth, and deep, clear water.

Sharryn polished off the last crumble of cheese and sat back with a satisfied sigh. "That was worth the ride." She smiled at Makarios, who was looking at her with love in his eyes.

Cornelius drained his tankard and went to refill it, but the pitcher was empty this time. "Sofronia!" Makarios bellowed. "Knock the bung out of another keg!"

"You don't have to get me drunk," Sharryn told him.

His smile could only be described as lecherous. "Yes, but it's more fun when I do."

Cornelius burped. "Excuse me, Sword."

"The name is Crowfoot, Cornelius."

She had unbuckled the sword. It rested against the arm of her chair. He eyed it. It was almost as tall as he was. "Do you mind if I ask how heavy it is?"

He was angling for an invitation to test the heft and balance of the weapon. She ignored the bait, more out of a care for his health than for any proprietary feel for the sword. "Heavy enough for justice," she said, and wished the truth sounded less sanctimonious.

"Of course, of course," he said hastily. Cornelius was square-jawed and solid, with dark hair neatly combed over dark, steady eyes, jerkin and leggings made with quality but not luxury, knee boots well traveled.but also well kept. He wore a guild badge with a Catherine wheel embroidered on it. A trader, then.

"You recognized us," Crow said.

He nodded. "I was trading in the capital two years ago when the king announced the Treaty of the Nine, along with the Charter of Mnemosynea and the conditions thereof."

"And what do you think of it?"

He gave her question serious consideration, ignoring for the moment the din rising in back of them as the common room filled with the evening crowd. "If it will bring peace to the Nine Provinces and safe roads to get my goods to market, I'm for it."

"And do you think it will?"

Their eyes met for a long moment. "I don't know."

The corners of her mouth quirked. "I don't either, Cornelius."

Night had fallen, and, at a look from Makarios, Sofronia lit the oil lamps hanging from brackets on the walls with a snap of fingers. Crow decided to stretch her legs in the direction of the stables, a glance enough to keep Cornelius in his seat. Sharryn made a face at her just before Makarios pulled Sharryn toward the stairs.

Blanca and Pedro had been brushed to a dull gleam, their hooves looked as if they had been polished, and both had buckets of water and troughs of hay and grain in their stalls. In the third stall down, she found Zeno industriously polishing the metal bits of her tack. Made of the finest steel from the king's forges, they shone silver in the lamplight, Sofronia's evening lighting task having apparently extended to the outbuildings. Crow wondered if that included the necessary. She hoped so; one of the less pleasant aspects of being continually on the road was trying to find an unfamiliar outhouse in the middle of the night.

"There must be some magic in your polish, boy," she said. "That bridle hasn't looked that good since we left the capital."

He gave a proud nod. "My Talent is for horses, and anything to do with them."

"You're young to know that." It happened, though, and often enough not to occasion more than idle comment.

Everyone in the Nine Provinces was born with the gift of magic. What kind and how much was usually revealed to them at the onset of puberty, but sometimes it happened earlier. Crow herself had been thirteen when she felt herself drawn to a former soldier who had lost a leg in battle and stumped into her village on a wooden replacement, there to buy out the local stable and begin an ambitious breeding program. He had found her on the back of a fiery-tempered mare, sans bridle or saddle, and his first and last glimpse of her for the afternoon was her gripping the mare's black mane as both of them went over the fence and disappeared into the forest at a gallop.

She had apologized when she brought the mare back. He eyed her for a long, uncomfortable moment before stumping over to the wall where his sword hung, still in the scabbard in which he had last sheathed it. He pulled it free and in the same motion sent it hurtling at her. It spun, point over hilt, to smack into her open palm. She had gazed at it in astonishment, unable to remember raising her hand.

She smiled now, remembering doughty old Nicodemus and the long, sweaty hours of schooling in the training area he built in back of the barn. Riding, horse care, use of sword and shield and knife and quarterstaff and longbow and crossbow and a hundred other weapons that she would probably never encounter. "But if you lose your sword and your shield and the only weapon you can lay hand to is a Yranean war club," Nicodemus had said, "then you'd better by the gods know how to use it."

Her mother had wept when her daughter's Talent had been revealed. Her father had been proud, especially when she was named head of her own cohort in the last war. She was an only child, and her mother still yearned for grandchildren, making visits home a nightmarish progression of eligible suitors. Her village was too near the capital, it made visits home too easy, so when the king had called for volunteers to bear the Swords of Justice she had seen a job that would keep her on the road for the better part of every year. She'd been second to sign up, and still took a certain amount of pride in the fact that she had been the first to pass successfully through the Ten Trials of the Sword.

Zeno was regarding the sword with a fascinated eye. "It's beautiful. My friend Elias is a smith, but he does nothing like that."

"All the Swords come from the Magi Guild's forge," she said. "They do good work."

They grinned at each other, and he went back to polishing. "How do you get to be a Sword, anyway?"

"Didn't your mayor publish the Treaty and the Charter?"

He hunched an impatient shoulder. "Who has time for all that reading?"

She sat down next to him in the straw, setting the sword beside her, the hilt ready to hand. Education was part and parcel of their charter, and besides, Blanca's tack hadn't looked this good since it was first made. Blanca, her great white head hooked over the stall, whickered agreement down the back of Crow's neck. Crow reached up to rub the velvety nose. "You know about the wars."

He nodded emphatically. "We all do. This is the first year in the last twenty that my father was able to sell all our wheat to the miller, and for a good price, too. 'Course the tithe to the king comes out of that, but it's half of what it was before." He scrubbed at a bit of stubborn tarnish. "It's why my father was able to apprentice me out when my Talent revealed itself. Father can afford to hire someone over the next few years."

She nodded. "King Loukas thinks that your father ought to be able to sell his grain without tithing to maintain an army. That's why he proposed the Treaty of the Nine."

"Yeah, but the king wasn't the one fighting the wars, that was the wizards." Zeno looked uncertain. "Wasn't it?"

"It was the wizards," Crow said. "Not all of them, but some. A few very great, very evil wizards, who were fighting each other for power and control."

"They wanted to be king?"

It was a lot more complicated than that, but close enough. "They did. So the king tithed the people to pay the army, then directed the army to fight the wizards."

"And they won."

"And we won," Crow agreed.

"'We' won?" Zeno said.

"I was a soldier in the king's army."

"Really?" he said, eyes wide. "Did you kill anybody?"

"Only enemies of the king," she said, and hoped it was true. "And yes, we won, but the problem still remained."

"The wizards."

"Yes. Two died in battle, and the third was tried, convicted, and executed in Hestia." She had been on duty at that execution and still remembered the curses with which Nyssa had fouled the air as she burned. The circle of wizards surrounding her pyre had been hard put to keep up with the counterspells. Even now Crow wondered if they'd managed to get them all.

"And then the king figured out a way to stop the wars."

"He hopes so. Everyone was tired of war, like you and your father. It was expensive, and destructive, and it killed too many of us. How much do you get paid to work here?"

He grinned. "A lot. Enough for me to send half home to my mother every week."

She smiled. "The king will be pleased to hear it. That was what he had in mind when he brought the Nine Provinces together to sign the Treaty, and when he worked with them to write the Charter."

"How does it work?"

She had repeated it so many times over the past three months that it rolled off her tongue like a monk's evening prayers. "In the Treaty, the Nine Provinces acknowledge the sovereign rule of Hestia. In exchange, the ruler in Hestia agrees to keep the peace."

"And you do that."

"And the Sword and Seer do that."

"How many Swords are there?"

"Nine Swords and nine Seers, one pair for each province."

His eyes slid to her sword.

"What?" she said, stifling a yawn. It was late, and Makarios's beer was finally catching up with her.

"How does it work, exactly? Is it permitted to say?"

She chuckled. "I am no wizard, young Zeno. I bear the Sword of Justice. It speaks through me. The Guild of the Magi has laid it under the most powerful of enchantments. Its power draws on theirs." And hers, and the Seer's.

"In Hestia? All that way away?"

"Yes."

"I didn't know magic could be made at such a distance."

"I don't think the wizards knew it, either, until the king wrote the Charter, and they had to find a way." She got to her feet. "And now, young Zeno, I'm for my bed, as you should be for yours."

"What's that?" he said, his head turning toward the stable door.

She heard it, too, a rising tide of sound with the unpleasant smell of riot about it. The hilt of the Sword slid into her hand.

A crowd was gathering, lit by torches held high. More people were emptying out of buildings, flooding down narrow streets to gather in the square, jerkins pulled hastily over nightgowns, confusion growing into an ugly, palpable anger. Crow saw Cornelius hurrying out of the inn and caught his elbow. "What is it? What's wrong?"

He halted, looking relieved to see her. "Someone has been killed, a girl, they say."

Behind him Crow saw Sharryn, staff in hand, Makarios at her heels. Both were dressed, barely. Sharryn heard Cornelius's words. "There's been a murder?"

Crowfoot climbed to the floor of a vendor's stand at the edge of the square and looked over the heads of the crowd.

The canvas roof over the dais from which the Kalliopean poet had been holding forth earlier in the day had been removed and a rope tossed over one of crosspieces. The noose at the end encircled the neck of a thin man with a bruised and bleeding face and both arms tied behind his back.

"Elias!" Zeno said, who had boosted himself up beside her, and disappeared into the crowd, heading in the direction of the man.

Crow swore. "Cornelius! Announce us!"

His eyes widened, and he stood up straight. Crow's request was in the nature of being appointed bailiff by royal command. "Make way for the Seer and Sword!" he called, and proved to have a bullfrog bellow that was admirably suited to the task. "Make way! Make way for the king's justice!"

Crow raised the Sword over her head, hand clasped around the scabbard, and followed him. Heads turned, eyes widened, people took involuntary steps back, and if a respectful silence did not fall, then at least a path was cleared to the focal point of the hubbub. Sharryn was at Crow's heels, and they both heard Blanca's urgent neigh and Pedro's whinnies. The crowd was surly and hostile, but they pushed through to stand in the small space created for them by Cornelius before the poet's dais, and the tableau waiting there.

The dead girl was blond and buxom. Her skirts were ruffled and dirtied, her bodice torn, and there were dark marks around her throat. The tip of her tongue protruded from her mouth in a manner that put Crowfoot forcibly in mind of the statues of the stone gargoyles lining the cornice of the roof of the Guild of the Magi back in Hestia. Those gargoyles, however, formed a ring of power designed to keep the forces of darkness from penetrating the sanctuary. This girl had had no such defense.

A man stood next to the body, tall, muscles going to fat. He had a heavy jaw and dark eyes set deep beneath a shelf of a brow. Collapsed against his side, tears sliding down her face, was a plump, blond woman, older than the girl but so similar in form and feature that the relationship was obvious.

Sharryn leaned down to close the girl's wide, staring blue eyes with a gentle hand. This small act of compassion had a soothing effect on the crowd, and Crow could feel a palpable easing of tension.

Sharryn stood up, leaning on her staff, and looked at the couple. "Your daughter?" she said gently.

He jerked his head at the blond woman. "Hers."

"I am so sorry," Sharryn told her.

The woman continued to weep with no reply.

Sharryn looked at the man. "Your name, goodman?"

His expression was not friendly, but he said civilly enough, "Nestor. This is my wife, Agathi."

"And this was . . ."

"Agathi's daughter, Nella."

"Not your daughter."

He shook his head. "From her first marriage."

"Ah." Sharryn looked around for her new bailiff. "Goodman, a blanket or a cloak, if you please."

Cornelius nodded, picked up the canvas that had been the roof of the dais, and spread it over Nella's body without waiting to be told.

"Now then," Sharryn said, looking at the young man with the noose around his neck. "I see you have determined who committed this foul deed."

"We have," Nestor growled.

"Good," Sharryn said. "You have proof, of course."

"He was found standing over the body."

"Ah. Who found him?"

"I did."

The crowd had crept closer again, the better to hear every word. "I see," Sharryn said.

He stuck out a truculent jaw. "It is our right, under the Charter, to exact justice."

"It is," Sharryn told him, "when it *is* justice."

Nestor's face darkened, and there was a corresponding mutter from the crowd.

The young man with the noose around his neck began

to struggle against it and received a cuff on one ear in response from one of the two men holding him. Crow recognized him, and then knew the man he was preparing to hang. These were the two who had fought over the girl in the square that afternoon. She looked down at the canvas-covered body. This girl.

Sharryn looked up at the young man in the noose. "Do you deny these charges, goodman?"

His mouth opened, and a kind of animal grunting came out, impassioned, forceful, but sounding more like a pig than a man. Sharryn looked at Nestor.

"A demon has him by the tongue," he said. There was a murmured chorus of agreement.

"Elias is possessed of no demon!" Zeno said hotly, forcing his way forward. "He is my friend, and a good man! He loved Nella! He would never have hurt her!" He looked around and found Crowfoot. "In the name of the Charter that binds the Nine Provinces, I call for justice! I call for the justice of the Seer and the Sword!" He ran to Crow's side. "You have to," he said in an urgent whisper. "Crowfoot, you must help him, he can't speak for himself!"

"Shut up, you little brat," someone growled, to a chorus of muttered approval.

"Hang him, then!" someone shouted, and others took up the cry. "Hang him!" "Hang the murdering bastard!"

"No!" Zeno cried.

Someone cuffed the boy across the face, and he flew backward into the crowd. Zeno was lost in a trample of feet.

Crow drew the Sword. She held it point up, hilt before her face, and cried, "Let the Sword sing!"

The moon, a new crescent, was well up in the sky, and its light danced along the blade. A single severe, sustained note sliced through the uproar like a sharp edge through flesh. The crowd melted back at Crow's approach, revealing Zeno prone on the ground. His mouth was bleeding, his cheek was bruised, and he winced and clasped his side when she nudged him to his feet, but he was ambulatory, and he followed her back to Sharryn. The Sword remained unsheathed, and Crow felt the link kick in solidly, with all the weight of Sharryn's considerable exasperation behind it.

Did you have to do that?

What did you expect, that I would let the child be trampled? Crowfoot kept her face impassive, but in truth she was as annoyed as the Seer was. Now the Sword could not be sheathed again until a verdict had been reached and a judgment rendered. She let the flat of the blade rest lightly against her left shoulder, both hands clasped on the hilt.

"We need no diviners here," Nestor said. "We can hang a murderer without your help. Yes, and bury our dead, too."

His wife sobbed out loud, but there was a growl of

agreement from the crowd. They had been cowed by the Sword's song, but there would have to be some resolution of the murder or, Crow had no doubt, there would be more murder done.

Sharryn kept her tone mild. "You live under the protection of the king, goodman. You are, as are we all, subject to the Treaty of the Nine and the Great Charter." She added distinctly, her eyes hard, "And you will address me as Seer."

He stared at her, his expression unpleasant. What he might have said next was drowned out by the crowd.

"To hell with this talk! Killer! Murderer! Hang him!" someone yelled, and there was another movement to press forward. Crowfoot stepped in front of Sharryn and raised the Sword. It sang again, the pure note descending into a clear baritone, a long, low pitch of warning that reverberated in the back teeth of everyone in the square. Many clapped their hands to their ears, a few were brought to their knees. A girl screamed, and babies wept.

It was a warning, as sharp as the edge of the Sword itself. It was the first time the Sword had been heard in Daean, but none who heard it could fail to understand it. The crowd fell back as one. The mob lust for blood had been broken with a single note.

"Sorcery," Nestor said, though he was as pale and shaken as the rest.

"Yes," said Sharryn. "Of the very strongest. Remember that, goodman." She turned to the dais. "Bring him down."

They brought Elias down forthwith and no arguing. Sharryn regarded the man who stood before her. He was looking at the canvas-covered body with tears tracing down his cheeks. She pulled the noose from his neck. There was another angry rumble from the crowd.

Crowfoot stepped forward. "Good people," she said. "You stand in the presence of the Seer of Truth and the Sword of Justice. By the pledge of the King, there will be order."

A translucent aura enveloped both women in a haze of light, casting their features in bold relief. Staff and Sword gleamed as if dipped in quicksilver. The illusion was gone in an instant, leaving only a tenuous memory of itself behind. Later, some would dismiss it as simple magic, a glamour conjured up to intimidate the ignorant and the foolish, yet another example of the wizarding sleight of hand that, out of control, had led to the last series of wars that had brought Mnemosynea to its knees. Others wouldn't be so sure. "I had my doubts about the Charter," old Pavlos said, wiping his mouth on the back of his hand after downing a tankard of Makarios's best. "But after watching those two witches at work the other night I'm thinking we've got a king we should keep."

"Bring a chair for the Seer," Crow said to Cornelius in a quiet voice. "Set it up on the dais. And cause torches to be lit, as many as may be found, and set them about the square."

It was done. Sharryn took the seat, staff in hand.

Crowfoot stood a little behind her on her right, Sword held in front of her. "I will hear witnesses in this matter," Sharryn said. It was all very irregular, lacking in the formality the king wanted to mark the dignity of the judicial process, and it was also night, a thing the Council would have abhorred. King and Council both wanted the Seer and the Sword to hold court in the full light of day, beneath the clear gaze of the full populace. But the Sword was out, and its appetite for justice, laid on by powerful geas, must be satisfied.

Cornelius's voice rang out. "All witnesses having knowledge in the matter of the foul murder of Nella, daughter of Agathi, stepdaughter of Nestor, come forward to be heard."

"When and where was the girl's body found, and who found it?" Sharryn said.

Nestor stepped forward. "I found it."

"Lay your hand upon my staff," Sharryn said.

He hesitated, and did as he was told. "State your name."

"I am Nestor, of the town of Daean, of the province of Kleonea." He looked at the staff as if afraid it might refute his words. It remained inert, a length of polished, knotted pine, gleaming coldly in the moonlight. He gained courage. "I own a bakery. Agathi is my wife. Nella was her daughter." Agathi sobbed into the shoulder of another woman, who patted her back.

"Tell us where and when you found Nella's body."

He looked at the staff, at his hand resting gingerly

upon it, and swallowed. “Seer, she was in the bakery when I went to close the shop. She was supposed to do it, but she was ever a flighty piece, more interested in flirting than she was in selling bread.” He pulled his hand free and pointed at Elias. “And I found him with her, crouched over her, interfering with her!”

The crowd erupted. “Pervert!” “Hang him!” “Filthy murderer!” “Killer!” “Hang him now!”

Sharryn waited with flinty composure until the cries died down. “Replace your hand upon the staff. Did you see him kill her, goodman?”

He hesitated, looked at Elias, back at the staff. “Seer. No. I did not see him kill her.”

“You said the girl liked to flirt. Was this man one of the men with whom she flirted?”

The baker scowled. “Seer, she flirted with them all. If she did not do more.”

“I see. Thank you, goodman. You may step back.”

The crowd shifted and stretched to see better. No one was yawning despite the late hour.

“I will speak to the accused next,” Sharryn said.

“Seer, he has not the ability to speak,” Cornelius said in a low voice.

“I understand that,” Sharryn said, and looked around for Zeno. He stepped forward, a little stiffly as the injuries inflicted by the crowd began to tell. “Can you understand him, Zeno?”

“Seer, I can!”

She beckoned to the accused. "Are you willing to have Zeno speak for you?"

The young man nodded once.

"Come forward, then," Sharryn said, "and place your hand upon my staff."

He did so without hesitation. His face showed more bruises than Zeno's, and he limped.

"Your name, goodman."

He looked at Zeno. "Seer, this is Elias, son of—"

"Your name first, goodman."

The boy looked startled. It was probably the first time anyone had called him goodman. He squared his shoulders. When he spoke next his voice had deepened and carried clearly to the edges of the crowd, silent now, and watchful. "Seer, I am Zeno, son of Nilos, son of Arete, of the village of Pierus—"

Ten leagues south of Daean, Crow thought.

Was it on the map?

No.

Typical.

"—of the province of Kleonea."

Sharryn gave a grave nod, and waited, somehow, rumpled and red-cheeked as she was, contriving to appear worthy to bear and exercise the will of King and Charter. The rule of law was so new to the Nine Provinces that no degree of authority could be lost to an apparent lack of dignity on the part of the Two. They were building a myth as much as they were an institution.

"Seer, this is Elias, son of Damara, of the town of Daean, of the province of Kleonea," Zeno said. His voice gathered force. "He is a smith, and my friend! He didn't kill Nella, he loved her!"

"He told you so?"

Zeno flushed. "Seer, he doesn't have to."

"In fact, he does," Sharryn said, not unkindly. "Please confine yourself to what the witness actually says. When did he come upon the body of Nella?"

Zeno conferred with Elias, who grunted and gestured. Zeno turned to Sharryn. "Seer, he says that they planned to meet at the bakery after work, to walk to the square and see who was performing for Festival. She was lying on the floor when he walked in." Zeno swallowed, his bruised face looking a bleached, blotchy purple in the torchlight. "He says her skirts were up over her head, and when he pulled them down he saw the marks on her neck."

"Was she cold to the touch?"

Elias shook his head violently and grunted at Zeno. "Seer, he says she was warm. He thinks her killer could not long have left her there."

Sharryn looked at Elias. He had not the build of the blacksmith, but you could not choose your Talent, it chose you. His shoulders and arms were well muscled, though, developed by his trade. His hand grasped her staff as if he needed the support.

"How did you lose your voice, goodman?" Sharryn said.

Elias looked at Zeno, who looked angrily at the crowd, and said hotly, "It's not because he labors under an evil curse, Seer, no matter what these people say."

Sharryn waited.

Zeno looked at Elias, who pressed his lips together and gave a curt nod. "His tongue was cut out, Seer."

"By whom?"

"By the army of Nyssa."

The crowd moved and muttered, and Crow knew Sharryn felt as she did the wave of almost tangible hatred. Nyssa had not wasted her occupation of Kleonea making friends, it seemed. Not that she'd had many friends in any of the Nine Provinces, judging from the cheer that had gone up as the wizard burned at the stake two years before.

"Why was your tongue cut out?" Sharryn said.

Zeno didn't have to ask Elias. "Seer, Elias was a spy for the king. He was betrayed to the wizard, who cut out his tongue in punishment."

The crowd gasped. "The smith spied for the king?"

"A likely story," growled the baker. His wife, collapsed in exhaustion in her friend's arms, had strained eyes fixed on the still form beneath the canvas shroud and was oblivious to everything else.

Crow was suspicious at this fortuitous turn of events. It's hard to hang a war hero. *Did you know?*

Such punishment for spies was common practice among Nyssa's troops. You should have paid more attention in history. By some trick of expression or movement Sharryn refocused attention on herself. To Elias, she said, "Why did you go to the bakery?"

Elias and Zeno put their heads together. There were more grunts, a few gestures, some wriggling of fingers. "Seer, Elias finished work early today, uh, yesterday now, I guess. He was anxious to see Nella. And—" He hesitated.

"And?" Sharryn said.

Zeno was reluctant, but Elias nudged him and grunted. Zeno flushed. "Seer, Elias was afraid that Nella had heard about the fight he had had with Deon."

By not a flicker of an eyebrow did Sharryn or Crow betray that they had been eyewitnesses.

"Seer, he was afraid Nella would be angry. He wanted to speak to her, to explain what happened."

Sharryn spoke directly to Elias. "Did you see anyone in the bakery besides Nella?"

The smith shook his head. "Seer, he did not," Zeno said. Elias grunted something. Zeno's eyes widened. "Seer, but he found something!"

"What did he find?"

Elias nodded at his tunic, and Zeno stuck a hand in the pocket. He pulled out a leather rectangle that curled naturally into a tube in his hand, straps and buckles dangling. He stared at it, puzzled.

"A fletcher's gauntlet!" someone cried.

They turned as one to the big, fair man standing behind Elias. "No," he cried. "No, not me, I didn't!"

"Step forward and show your left arm," Sharryn said.

"No, I—"

Rough hands were laid upon him, and he was thrust forward, his arm brought out by force. It was bare of anything but the sleeve of his dark green jerkin.

"He's the one!" "Guilty!" "Hang him!"

"Silence," Sharryn said mildly, but the force of the word rang like a tocsin, silencing the crowd. To Elias she said, "You found the gauntlet in the bakery with Nella?"

Elias grunted. "Seer," Zeno said, "Elias found it next to Nella's body. He put it in his pocket when Nestor refused to believe him and called down the mob."

"I see." Sharryn looked at the fletcher. "Step forward, goodman, and place your hand upon the staff."

The big man with the baby face did so, his eyes suspiciously bright.

"Your name."

His voice trembling in time with his knees, he said, "I am Deon, son of Andrew, son of Cyma, of the city of Daean in the province of Kleonea, and I did not kill Nella!" His voice caught on a sob. "I loved her, I would never hurt her!"

"How do you explain your gauntlet next to her body?"

Deon looked at his hand on the staff, the agonized fear on his face clear in the moonlight. He looked up at Sharryn, and said imploringly, "Seer, I—"

Sharryn was inexorable. "How do you explain your gauntlet being found next to her body?"

The fletcher was struck by sudden inspiration. "Elias must have stolen it and put it there to cast suspicion on me! I never went to the bakery, I—" He screamed, a high-pitched agonized sound that made everyone flinch. His legs went out from under him, and he remained upright only by virtue of the staff, gleaming in the moonlight, his hand clamped to it. "Make it stop, make it stop, ahhhhhhh, no!" He screamed again.

"How do you explain your gauntlet being found next to Nella's body?" Sharryn said pitilessly.

He screamed a third time, writhing like a fish on a hook, but he could not pull his hand from the staff. "I went to the bakery to see her, to ask her to spend Saturday at the festival with me, but she was already dead, I swear! I did not kill her, I did not! Make it stop, make it stop!"

Sharryn made no move, but his hand was suddenly free, and he crumpled into a boneless, sobbing heap before the dais.

"Raise him up," Sharryn said, her voice cold.

Elias and Zeno, their faces grim and awed, pulled Deon to his feet. Elias grunted at Zeno. "Seer," Zeno said, "Elias wishes to vouch for Deon. He has known

Deon since they were boys. He knew of Deon's love for Nella. He doesn't believe Deon would hurt her."

Deon looked steadfastly at the ground, shoulders shaking.

"It is certainly more than Deon was willing to do for him," Sharryn said tartly.

There was a brief silence.

Well?

She was strangled. Her killer knew she worked in the bakery, knew she would be there at closing time, and had strong hands.

And our choice is a smith or a fletcher. You're a lot of help. What does the Sword say?

Nothing. It won't until you identify the guilty and pronounce a verdict. You know that.

I live in hope. "Goodman," Sharryn said to Nestor. "Were there any signs of a struggle in the bakery?"

He shook his head. "Seer, there were not."

So she didn't fight. She knew him, and the attack came too suddenly for her to struggle.

"Who knew this girl?" Sharryn said. "Step forward and be heard."

There was a brief silence from the crowd, whose mood was by then more bewildered than hostile. They were still angry, but they were intent on every word spoken in the drama being enacted before them, determined to see the story through to its end.

"Excuse me," a strong voice said. The crowd parted to let two women through to the space before the dais. They were both delicate of feature and dark of hair and eye. Middle age had brought the elder laugh lines and gray hairs, and her waist was no longer as slender as her daughter's. Both were well dressed and bore the unmistakable stamp of the burgher. Both also bore the pincushion bracelet of the tailor.

"Seer," the older woman said, bending her head briefly. "I am Irene, daughter of Charis, daughter of Kiril, and a tailor in the city of Daean in the province of Kleonea. This is my daughter, Delphine. Nella was her friend."

Irene looked at Delphine, who didn't move. Irene placed a hand on her daughter's lower back and gave a firm nudge. Delphine was forced forward a step, and there she halted. Her brown eyes were wide and fearful, and she was obviously reluctant to speak. Her mother nudged her again.

"Seer," she said. "I—I am D—D—Delphine, d—d—daughter of Irene, d—d—daughter of Martin, of the city of Daean in the province of Kleonea." She clasped her hands before her tightly and looked imploringly at her mother. Her mother looked implacably back.

"Delphine, daughter of Irene, place your hand on my staff," Sharryn said. The girl looked desperately this way and that, found no help, and took three stumbling steps forward to place a shrinking palm against the wood. She looked surprised not to have her hand struck off at the wrist.

"You knew the dead girl?"

"Seer, I d—d—did."

Sharryn waited. Delphine knotted her free hand in her skirt.

"Come, goodwoman," Sharryn said. "There is nothing to fear here, so long as you tell the truth." Delphine cast a quick look at Deon. There was no blood or bruising on the hand that had lain upon the staff, but the fingers had yet to move, and he cradled it tenderly against his chest. "Did you see Nella yesterday?"

Delphine gave a quick nod. "Seer, I was at the bakery in the morning. Nella and I made plans to meet at the sweetshop and go round the square to see who was here for Festival."

Keeping a weather eye out for visiting poets, no doubt.

Quiet. "Did you see her again yesterday?" A shake of the head. "Did she speak of Elias or Deon to you?"

Delphine looked even more uncomfortable, if that was possible.

"Did Nella perhaps have many friends among the young men of the town?" Sharryn suggested.

Delphine's relief was immediate and immense. "Seer, she did. They were all in love with her. She was so beautiful, why shouldn't they be?"

"Did she favor any one above the rest?"

The girl's brow knit. "Seer, I believe she did not."

"Not Elias the smith? Not Deon the fletcher?"

"Seer, I believe not."

"It's not true," said Deon, "she loved me!" Elias said nothing, staring straight ahead with a face like stone.

"So you went to the sweetshop to wait for Nella," Sharryn said to Delphine.

"Seer, I did. But she did not come. So I went to the bakery."

"You went to the bakery?"

"Seer, I did, but the baker said she was gone."

There was a moment of silence. The hilt of the Sword began to vibrate in Crow's hands, and a faint, fine line of light limned the edge.

The kneading of all that dough also makes for strong hands.

"When was this, Delphine?"

"Seer, at a little before sunset. My mother let me leave our shop early."

Sharryn looked at Irene, who nodded.

"Did you go into the bakery?" Sharryn said.

"Seer, I did not. Nestor the baker came out the door as I came down the street."

"Did you speak to him?"

"Seer, I did. I asked him where Nella was, and he said she had left the shop before sunset to meet me."

"Step back from the staff," Sharryn said.

Delphine dropped her hand and scuttled behind her mother, standing on tiptoe to peer over Irene's shoulder.

"Nestor the baker, come forward," Sharryn said.

"I won't then," he said truculently. He raised his voice. "This is nothing but magic, and black magic at that! She has laid a geas upon us all!"

Irene looked at him. "Why?"

The simple question halted him for only a moment. "To make mischief, that's why! To bring the blackest of magic back to the Nine Provinces! To enslave us all again to the wishes of wizards! I found Elias kneeling over my daughter's body!"

Oh, so now she's his *daughter.*

"I will not come forward to lay my hand again upon that enchanted staff! Who knows what the wizard could make me say! It is the spirit of Nyssa come amongst us again! I will not!"

Sharryn raised neither the staff nor her voice. "Nestor the baker," she said, the words dropping oh so coldly into the torchlight, "come forward."

Nestor, his face contorted with anger and fear, was forced by an invisible hand to place one halting foot in front of the other, until he came before the dais.

"Place your hand upon my staff," Sharryn said, in that same cold, inflexible voice.

Inch by inexorable inch, his arm was forced up. He

cried out when his hand touched the wood, but it caught him fast.

"Nestor the baker of the city of Daean, father in law to Nella, now deceased, were you in your bakery yesterday afternoon?"

"Of course I was in my bakery!" he shouted. "It's my business, I own it."

"Was Nella also in your bakery yesterday afternoon?"

"She works there, she's my apprentice, of course she was there!"

"Were you both there when she was attacked?"

"No, I—aaaaaahhhhh!" Nestor screamed and writhed, tendons distended as he tried to pull free of the staff.

"Were you in the bakery when Nella was attacked?" Sharryn said.

"No, no, I tell you—" Nestor shrieked again. His feet were kicking, pushing at the dais. Tears were streaming from his eyes, mucus from his nose, and his mouth was pulled into a rictus of pain.

Agathi was staring at the scene before her, her eyes wide, her mouth a little open. "What is wrong with my husband? I don't understand. What is wrong?" Her friend put an arm around her and patted her wordlessly. Crow found a moment to pity her before Sharryn spoke again.

"I will not repeat my question a third time, Nestor the baker of Kleonea."

He broke, suddenly and absolutely and completely. "All right, all right, make it stop! Please, Seer, please, I beg you, just make it stop! I killed her! I killed Nella! Make it stop!"

And as simply as that his hand was free. He slumped against the dais, his face pressed into the sawdust at her feet, moaning and clasping his arm. Sharryn waited, looking in the moonlight like a statue. The crowd waited, too, silent, still; it seemed to Crow they had ceased even to breathe.

"On your feet," Sharryn said, and Nestor perforce was on his feet. "Place your hand again on the staff."

He cringed. "No, Seer, no, please, no, anything but that."

Sharryn's voice cracked like a whip. "Place your hand upon the staff!"

One hand, long-fingered, large-knuckled, heavy, roped with muscle, trembling, reached out and touched wood.

"Why did you kill Nella?" Sharryn said.

He hung his head, less in shame than in remembered pain. "I wanted her."

Agathi cried out. "No!" Her friend restrained her, but it wasn't easy. "No, it isn't true, it can't be true!"

"I wanted her, and she knew it, and she teased me with her knowledge. She raised her skirt for any young buck in town—"

"NO!" Agathi shrieked.

"Oh, it isn't true!" Delphine cried.

Elias shook his head violently. Even Deon left off nursing his hand to cry out a denial.

"—why not for me?" Nestor said. "Always in the house, parading around in her underdress, taunting me, tempting me."

Why does the staff not correct him?

It's the truth, as he sees it.

"I took her, I admit it. There was no bearing it any longer, she was off to gawk at the young men in the town square that evening. Why them and not me?"

"How did she die?" Sharryn said.

"She fought me," he said, and bared his chest, revealing a series of dark red scratches and one welt that looked inflicted by teeth. "Look here! She provoked me, she scratched me, she made me bleed! She screamed the whole time, I was afraid someone would hear! I just wanted her to be quiet!" He looked at his hand on the staff. "I just wanted her to be quiet," he repeated.

There was dead silence in the square.

Sharryn broke it by rising to her feet. She took a deep breath and shook Nestor free of the staff as if she were shaking off a fly. "In the matter before the sitting of this Assideres—"

The Sword began to hum.

"—in the city of Daean on the day of the solstice, this second New Year in the reign of King Loukas the Just, I, Sharryn the Seer, find Nestor the baker of Daean in the province of Kleonea guilty of the wanton rape and murder of his stepdaughter, Nella, by confession out of his own mouth, as attested to by the Staff of Truth." She stepped back. "Let the Sword of Justice come forth and render judgment."

Crow moved forward, holding the Sword before her like a banner, as indeed it was, the ensign of her command.

It began to hum.

Nestor scrabbled awkwardly backward on his hands and feet. "No! Keep it away from me! Stop it, stop it, I tell you! She made me do it! I shouldn't be punished, she made me!" A kick from the crowd sent him back into the circle.

Crow halted at the edge of the platform, the Sword brightening to a silver that seemed almost transparent, the blade reflecting the glitter of the stars and the glow of the torches, the stones on the hilt bright with right and rage. The hum rose to a cold, clear tone that went up and up in pitch and volume. People cried out and covered their eyes and ears. Nestor cowered on the ground, one arm raised in pitiful defense, afraid to look, afraid not to. Zeno and Elias crouched nearby, white-faced and staring. Sharryn and Crowfoot alone remained outwardly unmoved.

When Crowfoot spoke, her voice was as cold as Sharryn's and as clear as the song of the Sword. "In the name of the Great Charter of Mnemosynea, by the power vested in me by King and mage, let justice be done."

The glow of the blade increased to a blinding ray of light, spilling out over the heads of the crowd. The song increased in volume to the point of pain, reverberating in ears, teeth, bones, blood.

And then it was gone, and the light with it, and the blade returned to the sheath, a long slide of metal against metal, the hilt meeting the scabbard with a satisfied clank.

"The Sword has spoken," said Crow. Sharryn moved to stand beside her.

People stood erect again, shaken. They looked at Nestor, still sitting in the dirt. "Oh the gods," someone said, shock in his voice.

The Sword of Justice had taken Nestor's hands above the wrists. The stumps of his arms had been neatly sealed, no blood dripping, no bone showing, the skin healed cleanly across. The hands that had strangled the life from the young woman had been the price of their crime. The girl was dead, and her Talent with her. Nestor's Talent had been in his hands, and now it, too, was gone.

Magic destroyed was a debt owed. And debts to magic must always be paid. It was the First Law, and the most binding of them all.

Nestor stared at the stumps where his hands had been, unbelieving. He would be unable to practice his trade. Never to knead another batch of dough, never to slice fruit for a tart, never to ice cakes, none of it, ever again.

More, he would be unable to wash himself, to clothe

himself, to feed himself. Unless he could find someone to perform those tasks for him, banishment and slow starvation were his fate. And with the mark of the Sword burned into his forehead proclaiming his offense for all to see, there would be no succor for him anywhere.

In that moment Nestor himself seemed to realize the depth and breadth of his punishment, and turned mute, pleading eyes to his wife.

Agathi spat in his face, turned her back, and walked away.

So did everyone else.

The square emptied out in groups of five and six. Nestor hunched over his maimed arms and scrabbled away.

"We never do this in moonlight again," Sharryn said, descending from the platform.

"Agreed," Crowfoot said, following. "They did warn us."

"They did. Gods, I need a drink."

"I know where to find one," Crow replied.

There was a shy touch at her elbow, and she looked round to see Zeno, awe and gratitude warring for primacy on his young face. "Thank you, Sword. Thank you for saving my friend." Behind him, Elias bowed.

She managed a brief nod, a rough tousle of Zeno's hair, and turned for the inn and bed, and no one tried to stay their path.

At least not that night.

about the authors

Donna Andrews writes two mystery series. *You've Got Murder* (Berkley Prime Crime), featuring artificial intelligence personality Turing Hopper, won the Agatha for best mystery of 2002 and is followed by *Click Here for Murder*. *We'll Always Have Parrots* is the fifth in her multiple award–winning series from St. Martin's Press, featuring blacksmith Meg Langslow. Visit her website at www.donnaandrews.com.

Michael Armstrong is the author of three science fiction novels, *After the Zap*, *Agviq*, and *The Hidden War*. A staff writer for the *Homer News,* he has lived in Homer since 1994. When not writing, he hangs around on the beaches of Kachemak Bay. He lives with his wife, Jenny, on Diamond Ridge on the hills above Homer.

Anne Bishop is the award-winning author of the Black Jewels Trilogy, as well as *The Invisible Ring*, *The Pillars of the World*, *Shadows and Light*, and *The House of Gaian*. Her latest book is a four-story collection set in the Black Jewels world. Visit her website at www.annebishop.com.

Jay Caselberg is an Australian writer based in London whose short fiction has appeared in multiple venues around the world. His first novel, *Wyrmhole*, came out from Roc Books in October 2003, and the second, *Metal Sky*, in 2004. Visit his website at www.sff.net/people/jaycaselberg.

Mike Doogan is a columnist for the *Anchorage Daily News*. His first mystery story, which appeared in *The Mysterious North*, won the 2003 Robert L. Fish Award from the Mystery Writers of America.

Laura Anne Gilman has published more than twenty short stories, three media tie-in novels, and an original novel, *Staying Dead*, the first in the Retrievers series, featuring Wren and Sergei. She lives in New Jersey, where she runs d.y.m.k. productions, an editorial services company. Visit her website at www.sff.net/people/lauraanne.gilman.

Simon R. Green is the author of more than twenty-seven novels, including the best-selling Deathstalker series. "The Nightside, Needless to Say" is set in the world of his Nightside novels.

Charlaine Harris, who writes conventional mysteries as well as odder fare, lives in southern Arkansas with her three children, a husband, two dogs, one ferret, and a duck. The duck stays outside.

Anne Perry is the author of the Pitt and the Monk detective series, both set in Victorian England, a series set in World War I, two fantasy novels, and many short stories. Her first novel, *The Cater Street Hangman*, came out in 1979. She lives in Scotland.

Sharon Shinn is the author of *Archangel* and other books set in the Samaria world, as well as other science fiction/fantasy novels. She won the William C. Crawford Award for Outstanding New Fantasy Writer for her first book. A graduate of Northwestern University, she has lived in the Midwest most of her life.

Dana Stabenow writes the Kate Shugak series, the Liam Campbell series, the Star Svensdotter series, and the "Alaska Traveler" column in *Alaska* magazine. She lives in Anchorage, and can be reached through her website at www.stabenow.com.

John Straley is a novelist and former private investigator from Sitka, Alaska. He is the author of the Cecil Younger mysteries. "Lovely" is his first fantasy story. It was written as ravens walked across the tin roof of his writing studio.

COPYRIGHTS